HUNTERS OF THE DEAD

ALSO BY STEVE HOCKENSMITH

HUNTERS OF THE DEAD

HOLMES ON THE RANGE
BOOK 7

STEVE HOCKENSMITH

ROUGH EDGES PRESS

Hunters of the Dead
Paperback Edition
Copyright © 2023 Steve Hockensmith

Rough Edges Press
An Imprint of Wolfpack Publishing
9850 S. Maryland Parkway, Suite A-5 #323
Las Vegas, Nevada 89183

roughedgespress.com

Paperback ISBN 978-1-68549-345-5
eBook ISBN 978-1-68549-344-8
LCCN 2023945302

FOR MAR, H & F

HUNTERS OF THE DEAD

PRELUDE

OR, THE QUICK AND THE DEAD

IT WAS a dark and stormy morning.

Yes, *morning*. I know that's not how this sort of story is supposed to start, but what can you do? That's how it happened.

The night had been dark, too, of course. That's what generally happens when the sun goes down. But stormy, no. My brother and I made our rounds of the camp and the dig site and the scrubby hills around them perfectly dry. At least for a few hours. Then bursts of light flared behind the bluffs to the west just as the sky to the east began to purple with dawn, and a rumble of thunder rolled across the bleakly featureless southern Wyoming plains.

I sighed.

Night watch is boring. Night watch when wet and cold is miserable.

"Wait here," Old Red said. "I'll run back for our slickers."

"Thanks."

My brother disappeared into what was left of the nighttime gloom, leaving me alone beside a long trench that could have been either a halfhearted attempt at a ditch or a fresh-dug grave for a recently deceased giraffe. It was neither, I knew, being instead an abandoned dig site from some previous summer. The old bones extracted from it were probably back east now, still waiting to be measured and sketched and pieced together into some supposed expert's best guess at a monstrous body no human eyes had ever seen.

In another flash of lightning—this one brighter and closer now—I saw that one end of the pit had collapsed. In time, with enough gully washers like the one on the way, the whole hole would disappear without a trace. The earth reburying its dead.

I was attempting to turn this idle thought into something I could pretend was profound—I may be a former cowboy and a current detective, but I'm also a writer, after all—when Old Red returned to save me from myself.

"You awake?" he asked.

He was already in his slicker, and he tossed me mine.

"I'm standing here with my eyes open, so I'm guessing the answer's yes," I said.

My brother shrugged. "That ain't been no guarantee before."

And he walked right past me and dropped down into the pit.

He was also wearing, I now saw, a familiar knapsack, the leather strap over his left shoulder.

"Now that you mention it," I said as I shrugged into my coat, "either I'm dreaming or you are. 'Cuz it looks like you think you're a paleontologist. And a female one to boot."

Old Red carried on up the trench, making his way toward the end that had spilled down into a big pile of loose earth.

"The lady told me I could borrow her tools sometime," he said. "Well, this seems like the time."

"And why is that? Seems more like the time to be doing our job."

"Walkin' in circles in the dark? Feh."

My brother hadn't yet reconciled himself to the fact that detective work can be incredibly dull. More dull even than nighthawking a herd. At least then when a storm rolls in, there's a chance the steers will spook and stampede. Which isn't fun, I can tell you from experience, but the prospect of being trampled to death does tend to keep a man awake. Guarding the scattered shards of animals already long dead, on the other hand, doesn't give a fellow much reason to keep his eyes open. Especially when the lovely lady who helped dig them up isn't around.

Old Red went to a squat before the heap of dirt at the end of the pit. He picked up a big clod, examined it, then tossed it away and began rooting around in the knapsack.

"This'll be the best chance I get to do this for days," he said.

"How you figure that?"

"They ain't gonna let me try this back at the real dig. Not when I could mess up one of their precious fossils. And here I got me a hole already dug, with one end knocked loose. So no need for shovel work. Plus there's that."

He pointed up at the star-speckled sky with his left hand.

I looked up. "What? The Big Dipper?"

Lightning flashed again, followed a couple seconds later by another rumble of now not-so-distant thunder.

"Oh," I said. "That."

"Yeah. *That*. I reckon the rain'll bring the diggin' to a stop. They're scared enough of breakin' these old things when all they gotta do is brush some dirt off 'em. They won't wanna wrestle 'em outta the mud."

Old Red pulled a hammer out of the knapsack. He turned it this way and that as if he'd never seen one before, even pausing to stare in apparent wonderment at the butt end of the handle. Then he grunted and put it back.

"What exactly are you looking for?" I said.

"What a man should always be lookin' for." Old Red went back to poking around in the bag. "The right tool for the job."

"I meant down there in that hole."

"Ain't lookin' for nothin'. This is just for fun."

I gave that a snort.

As has been frequently noted, my brother's idea of fun and mine do not overlap.

He held up a brush—it looked very much like the kind you'd

use to whitewash a picket fence—then hunched over and started sweeping it across the biggest clumps of sod nearby.

"Hmm. Damn dew's already got everything moist," he muttered. "I'm just gunkin' up the lady's brush."

He set the brush aside and started digging through the pile of earth with his hands, clearing away the top layer so he could get back to his "fun" with dirt that was dry enough to sweep away with careful flicks of the wrist like a proper paleontologist.

"If you discover a new dinosaur, what do you think they'll call it?" I said. "'Oldus Redicus' or 'Grouchus Maximus'?"

"I like the sound of 'Shutus Upicus.'"

The world around us flashed brighter than day for a split second, and the thunder that followed came quick and loud.

A raindrop splatted on the brim of my Stetson.

"Sorry, brother—looks like Shutus Upicus will have to wait for another day." I held out a hand and felt another little splash of water on the palm. "Here it comes."

"I'll be damned," Old Red said.

But it wasn't the weather that had startled him.

He was staring down at something he'd uncovered, a big clump of dirt still clutched in each hand.

"You actually manage to find some fossils?" I said.

He dropped the clods he was holding and went back to digging.

"Not fossils," he said. "Boots."

"What?"

I'd learned a lot about dinosaurs the last day or so, but of course I was still far from an expert. I was reasonably certain, however, that your average Brontosaurus did *not* wear boots.

I felt a familiar tingling over my skin, and my ears began to ring. It says much about my life to this point that my first thought was, "Dear lord…not again!" But I allowed myself to cling to the not-very-calming thought that one finds all kinds of random things abandoned on the plains. So some passing would-be pioneer had discarded a pair of old boots and…and…and a coyote had buried them?

I told you the thought wasn't very calming.

I took a few quick steps along the edge of the trench, trying to look past my brother's stooped back. It was still too dark to see what he was unearthing until yet another flash of lightning lit up the world like fireworks.

Old Red was right. A pair of boots was sticking up out of the ground before him. And that wasn't all. Dammit.

As is so often the case with boots, legs protruded from them. Connected, one could only assume, to a pelvis, belly, neck, chest, and head.

A human body, in other words—buried under the mass of dark soil at the far end of the pit.

ONE
THE COLONEL AND THE CAPTAIN

OR, WE'RE ASKED A NUTTY QUESTION AND OLD RED HAS A BONE TO PICK WITH OUR LATEST ASSIGNMENT

MY BROTHER and I have had some mighty interesting experiences since taking up detective work two years ago. Riding a train off a cliff, for instance. Getting chased across San Francisco by hordes of men with hatchets. Watching a house burn down...*from the inside.*

That's never how things are supposed to go, though. No one sets us off on a case saying, "How'd you like to see a fellow smothered to death in cheese?" Yet almost inevitably that, or something equally disagreeable—such as random bodies in abandoned pits—is what we end up dealing with.

So I suppose I should have scoffed when our partner Colonel Crowe called us into the office recently to tell us he'd lined up a nice, boring yet lucrative job for the A.A. Western Detective Agency. He didn't say, "I'm sending you to Wyoming to stumble upon another murder" (something we seem to make a habit of). No—he started the conversation a very different way indeed.

"Are you familiar," he said, "with nut butter?"

"Are you asking us to pick up your groceries?" I said. "'Cuz I thought you said we had a new client."

The colonel scowled at me. Or perhaps I should say the

colonel *kept* scowling at me. He's always scowling at me. Let's leave it this way, in fact: Unless I tell you he's not scowling at me, he is.

"I am asking," he said slowly, "if you are familiar with nut butter."

"Well, we know it exists," I said. "Can't go into a general store anymore without seeing a whole shelf of the stuff. Seems to be quite the rage."

"Someone wants us to guard their nut butter?" Old Red said.

He was scowling, too. Also as usual.

Colonel Crowe leaned back in his chair and stroked the sleek brown curl that covered his lap. A few months before, Ira Hoop, one of the agency's other operatives, had returned from an assignment with a gift for the colonel and his daughter Diana: a dachshund they quickly dubbed "Captain Zimmer." (Apparently he reminded them of an old cavalry comrade. Me, I've never come across a soldier who struck me as particularly dachshund-like. They mostly seem like bulldogs and mutts in my mind.)

"No. You won't be guarding any nut butter," Colonel Crowe said. "You'll be guarding something *for* the biggest nut butter man in America."

"Professor Pertwee?" I said.

That whole shelf in the general store I'd mentioned to the colonel? It's three-quarters filled with Professor Pertwee's Health Miracle Nut Butter. There's a drawing of Professor Oliver Pertwee on every jar—portly, balding, bespectacled, grinning—and the man has reason to smile in it. He's cornered the market on ground nuts drowned in sugary oil. (Yes. I've tried it. And I actually kind of like it. I don't see how it could replace good old butter and jam when you're looking for something to spread on your bread, though.)

Colonel Crowe nodded. "Pertwee's using a considerable portion of his new fortune to fund a scientific expedition to Wyoming. You two will join the party as guards."

"A scientific expedition…to *Wyoming*?" my brother said.

"They're probably hunting old bones," I said. "The place is famous for all the big dead lizards they got just lying around."

Old Red switched from his standard scowl to his "That's not funny" glare. It's a look he uses on me often, but he quickly saw that this time it wasn't called for. I wasn't joking.

"That's right," Colonel Crowe said. "The expedition is searching for the *fossils* of ancient *dinosaurs*."

I think he was trying to tell us not to embarrass ourselves by talking about "old bones" and "big dead lizards" in front of any scientists.

"Well, why send me and Otto?" Old Red said. "If all they need is guards, send Hoop, Eskaminzim and Diehl."

"I already did," the colonel said. "But Pertwee wants more than three men, and I wasn't about to tell him the A.A. Western Detective Agency can't supply them."

"What about Burr?" I said.

Colonel Crowe shook his head. "This isn't his kind of work. And he's not available anyway."

Old Red threw a glance at the other desk in the office—the one the colonel's daughter usually sat at. She wasn't there now.

"You sent him off on a job with Diana?" he said.

"That's right."

My brother fumed about that for a moment. I did, too.

Whatever the colonel had Diana doing, it was surely a lot more interesting than guarding a pile of bones in Wyoming. Anything Diana does is interesting to me and Old Red. Heck, we find her fascinating when she's sitting around doing nothing. Which was probably why the colonel had someone else working with her.

"Gun work again," Old Red muttered. "Just like that job you sent us on in New Mexico. Feh."

"*Now look here*," Colonel Crowe said sharply enough to wake Captain Zimmer.

The dog's eyes popped wide, and he gazed up at the little man holding him (the colonel being about as big and burly as a china doll). Once Captain Zimmer realized his new master was annoyed with us, not him, he quickly went back to sleep.

"We agreed that the business side of the agency would be my

responsibility," Colonel Crowe said. "I would find the clients, and I would make the assignments. So I'm telling you: You are going to Wamsutter, Wyoming, where you, Diehl, Hoop, and Eskaminzim will serve as escorts to a party of paleontologists. I know you would prefer work that calls upon your skills as a 'deducifier,' but sitting around waiting to play Sherlock Holmes will not pay the bills. Pertwee is willing to pay good money to have guards for his pet scientists, and by god, we should be willing to take it."

"Feh," Old Red said again. And he slapped on his Stetson and stomped out.

Now, I've become quite the expert on my brother's Fehs over the years. So I knew this one wasn't the "You can stick that up the part of your body respectable folks don't mention" kind. It was of the "I think you're an idjit but dammit you win" variety.

"Don't worry," I assured Colonel Crowe. "He'll go."

"Good," the colonel said firmly.

Then—and remember I told you I'd let you know if this happened—he stopped scowling at me.

"I know it seems unworthy of your brother's talents," he said, "but you should both look at this job as an opportunity to hone new skills. There's a lot more to detective work than solving bizarre puzzles. Diehl, Hoop, and Eskaminzim have been at it a long time. Watch them. You'll learn a lot."

I just nodded, asked if arrangements had been made for train tickets (they had), got a few more details (what to do when we reached Wamsutter, whether Pertwee would cover expenses, etc.), then wished the colonel and the captain a good day and left. I usually try to needle Colonel Crowe on my way out the door— martinets bring out my mischievous side (which is most of me anyway)—but this day I didn't. Maybe I wanted to see how long I could keep that scowl off his face.

Old Red was waiting for me in the hallway.

"I suppose you told him I'm goin'," he said.

"I did. Because you are. I know you'd rather be bored on the job in Wyoming than bored waiting for something better here."

We headed for the stairwell. As usual, Old Red drew a few

looks from the folks we passed. Utah has plenty of cowboys, of course, but you don't often see them roaming the halls of the Ogden Chamber of Commerce Building.

I, on the other hand, have been happy to switch from drovering duds to business suits and bowlers when in town. So I can only assume any stares I got were out of sheer admiration for my panache.

"It make any sense to you?" Old Red asked me. "This 'Professor Pertwee' fussin' so much over whatchamacallits he'd bring in the Double-A?"

"Which whatchamacallits you mean? Fossils or dinosaurs?"

"What's the difference?"

"Depends on the fossils. They're not all giant lizards. They've found giant elephants, giant cats, giant sloths, giant rabbits."

My brother gave me a skeptical look.

"Really," I said. I rubbed my jaw. "Though come to think of it I might be wrong about the rabbits. Maybe it was giant rats...? And teeny little horses. Not much bigger than Captain Zimmer. Birds with teeth, too. It's crazy what all they've dug up."

Old Red's expression shifted, his doubt giving way to what looked like chagrin.

He's the brains of our outfit, and I never try to deny it. Yet here was a whole world of knowledge of which he was entirely ignorant. I only knew a little of it because of an advantage I've had on my brother for nearly two decades now.

I read. A lot, actually. Newspapers, magazines, books.

Old Red, on the other hand, hasn't been able to read much past D in the A-B-Cs. He's been working to change that the last few months with the help of a *McGuffey's Reader* Diana gave us. But even when he's got reading licked—and it's going to take him some time—there'll still be those big blank spots for him. Things he won't know of because he missed out on the chance to soak them up over the years.

It pained him, knowing that. And it pained me that it pained him.

On the other hand, it would keep me useful a little longer.

Once Old Red's reading for himself and a bit more worldly, I figure all I'll be good for is carrying his luggage and making jokes he won't laugh at. It was going to be interesting to see: a Gustav Amlingmeyer who doesn't need me. It was just a matter of time before I met him.

We both went silent for half a flight of steps. Then Old Red cleared his throat.

"Well, anyway," he said. "Crazy as some of those bones might be, I still don't see why anyone would pay a bunch of hired guns to stand around while they hunt for 'em."

"Find it mysterious, do you?" I snorted and shook my head. "You're just looking for a way to make this interesting."

"Maybe..." Old Red said in a "We'll see" sort of way.

Soon enough, of course, we did.

TWO
BAD EGGS
OR, WE ENCOUNTER WHAT SEEM TO BE READY-TO-HATCH DINOSAURS—AND SOME MEN HATCHING UP TROUBLE

THE NEXT DAY we got our first look at Wamsutter, Wyoming. It was a good thing our train was slowing to a stop at the time: If it had been going full steam we could have missed Wamsutter in a blink.

Not that there was much for Wamsutter to hide behind. The town's maybe thirty buildings spread out scattershot from the train station, with flat, scrubby expanse all around. The only terrain to speak of was some bluffs blurry with distance to the north.

The man waiting for us on the platform was as hard to miss as the town was easy: tall, broad-shouldered, dark-skinned, stony-faced, with a forty-five on his hip and a Winchester in his hands.

"Ira Hoop," I said with a smile as Old Red and I got off the train and walked over to him. I cocked an eyebrow at his rifle. "You here to greet us or shoot us?"

"Greet," Hoop said.

His flat tone seemed to imply that he was withholding judgment on the shooting. It might depend on how much I annoyed him.

We didn't know Hoop well, having only encountered him and his Apache compadre Eskaminzim briefly on a different job a few months before. He hadn't exactly been warm then, and apparently our absence since had not made the heart grow fonder.

"This way," he said.

He went striding away from the train. Old Red and I hustled to catch up, our carpetbags swinging.

"That Winchester really necessary when you're just walkin' around town?" Old Red asked.

"For show," Hoop said. "For them."

He nodded at a squat building about thirty yards ahead to the left. The windows had been covered over on the inside with butcher paper, but the front door was half ajar, offering a view of a big, gray oval sitting on the floor just beyond. I squinted at it, thinking it surely couldn't be what it looked like, until one of the men smoking near the doorway—the "them" Hoop had spoken of—glared at me.

"What are you lookin' at?" he said.

He and his friend were both wearing gun belts and sneers.

"Sorry to stare, fellas," I said cheerfully. "I'm new to town, and there's so much to see."

The men didn't point out that Wamsutter was far from a tourist attraction. They just went back to what they'd been doing before—drawing on their cigarettes and idly watching the train as we made our way past.

"Who are they and what was that?" Old Red asked Hoop.

"'They' are the competition. As for the 'that,' you gotta be more specific."

"That big whatever-it-was inside the building."

"That wasn't a dinosaur egg, was it?" I said.

That was exactly what it had looked like—an egg as big as a boulder—yet I was half-afraid Hoop would laugh at me. He's not much of a laugher, though. He's not even a smiler. I had yet to see any expression on him at all, in fact. If he hadn't been walking around talking, you might have thought he was carved out of marble.

"No—ain't an egg," he said. "The scientists call it a 'field jacket.' All plaster on the outside."

"And on the inside?" Old Red asked.

Hoop stuck out his chin. "Diehl'll explain."

Up ahead was another building—this one more ramshackle, with a rickety-looking corral beside it. Clearly a barn, once upon a time. A man was standing in the broad doorway watching us approach. In the shadowed gloom beyond him were large, lumpy, gray shapes just like the "field jacket" we'd spied a moment before.

"Don't tell me," the man said. He pointed at my brother. "Old Red." He swung the pointed finger toward me. "And Big Red."

"How ever did you guess?" I said, throwing my arms wide. Very wide. For they are very big arms. To fit the rest of me.

"I read the latest issue of *Smythe's Frontier Detective* on the way here," the man said. "'Cowboy Brothers Battle the New Mexico Death Baron!' Quite a tale. Quite a title."

"Quite a mouthful. I just wanted to call it 'The Double-A Western Detective Agency,' but..." I shrugged. "Publishers."

The man nodded as if complaints about the vagaries of publishing was old hat to him. He was tall-ish and slender-ish and forty-ish, with brown hair going gray and bright blue eyes alight with amusement. He was dressed like the rest of us—in simple, sturdy clothes befitting a working man of the West—yet there was an air to him that made you wonder why he was out here by a barn wearing a gun belt rather than behind a newspaperman's desk or writing the day's lesson on a schoolroom chalkboard.

"Oswin Diehl," he said, stepping forward with his arm outstretched.

"Nice to finally meet you, Mr. Diehl," I said as we shook. "Colonel Crowe's told us all about you."

He smirked at that as if he doubted the colonel would tell us *everything* that had passed between them. And he'd have been right to doubt: In reality, Colonel Crowe hadn't told us much about the man. All I really knew was that he'd been a cavalryman and a troubleshooter for the railroad, and now he worked for us.

"The pleasure's all mine," Diehl said, pivoting toward Old

Red. "I've been looking forward to seeing the famous 'Holmes of the Range' in action."

His tone had a sardonic note to it—not outright sarcastic, but not completely serious either—and my brother gave the man a wary look as they shook.

"Yeah, well…you're gonna have to wait a while for that," Old Red said. "The way the colonel tells it, there ain't gonna be any need for Holmesifyin' on this trip. We're just here to stand around with guns collectin' money from Professor Pertwee."

"That's the plan," Diehl said with a grin.

Standing around collecting money seemed a-okay with him.

"They were asking about the field jackets," Hoop said.

"Oh?" said Diehl. "What about them?"

Old Red moved closer to the barn and the large, gray ovals inside. "Well, what the hell are they?"

"Gift-wrapped dinosaurs," said Diehl.

I followed Old Red to the barn door. Inside were three rows of the "field jackets"—more than a dozen in all.

"There's dinosaurs in those things?" I said.

"Parts of them. And a whole lot of dirt," said Diehl. "It's a new system the paleontologists are using to get at the bones without breaking them. Rather than try to root them all out on the spot, they find a nice clump, dig around them, then cover it over with burlap and plaster. When they have enough—say, a train car full—they'll ship them back east, where they can take their sweet time separating the fossils from the dirt and rock."

I looked down at the nearest jacket. It was about the size of two troughs shoved side to side: four feet across, six long, two tall.

"They must weigh a ton," I said.

"Not a ton, but a lot," said Diehl. "Fortunately for the scientists, now they have rented muscle for moving them."

"Oh?"

I glanced back at Diehl. He was grinning at me.

"Oh," I groaned. "So, in addition to standing around with guns, we get to do manual labor."

"Idle hands…" Diehl said with a shrug.

I sighed. "This job just gets better and better."

"It has its upsides," Diehl said.

Before I could ask him what he meant, my brother jumped in with a question of his own.

"So if these bones belong to Professor Pertwee, how about the ones them other fellas are watchin'?"

"Ah. Our neighbors. Excellent question," said Diehl. "You know, I've been up against Kickapoos, Lipans, Chiricahuas, Mescaleros, revolutionaries, bandits, train robbers, strike breakers. And you want to know who stirs up the most vicious fighting I've ever seen?"

Hoop didn't exactly roll his eyes, but he did take a deep breath and stare off into the distance. The train was leaving town, and it didn't seem so much like he was watching it go as finding something—anything—to look at other than Diehl.

"Yeah?" I said.

"Academics," said Diehl.

"Who now?" said Old Red.

Hoop took another deep breath and kept his eyes on the horizon. He'd definitely heard this little spiel of Diehl's before.

"The intelligentsia," Diehl explained to my brother.

Not that the word actually explained anything to Old Red. Or to me, to be honest. I had to look it up later.

"Professors," said Hoop. "Scientists."

My brother held up a hand in a "Whoa now" way.

"You're tellin' me them rough-lookin' SOBs we walked past are *scientists*?" he said.

"No. Not them," Diehl laughed. "They're just some dumb thugs working *for* the scientists."

"Like us," Hoop said.

"Exactly," said Diehl.

He seemed perfectly happy to bask in his own self-amusement rather than get to the point.

Oh my god, I thought. *Is this what it's like talking to* me?

I forgave my brother for every time he's snapped at me.

"So there're other scientists around collecting fossils?" I said. "And they're feuding with Professor Pertwee?"

"Close," said Diehl. "There's another scientist around collecting fossils, and he's feuding with Professor *Durgin*. That's who we're taking orders from here. Pertwee's just the money. He's a thousand miles away."

"Got nuts to grind," said Hoop.

Diehl snorted. "Indeed he does. Apparently, dinosaurs are just a hobby to him. But Durgin—he's a real expert."

"So who's the other scientist then?" I asked. "The one this Professor Durgin's up against?"

"Ever hear of Hiram Loveland?" Diehl said.

My brother shook his head.

I nodded mine...though not with much confidence.

"Isn't he one of the big paleontalologists," I said. "Panelito-golists. Pajeontol...dammit!"

"Hard to say out loud till you've practiced it a bit," Diehl said, chuckling.

I licked my lips and tried again. "Paleontologists."

"Congratulations," said Diehl. "And yes—Loveland is 'one of the big ones.' Some say the biggest these days. Director of the New York Museum of Natural History. Our man Durgin used to work for him. Did all Loveland's fieldwork. Dug up bones for him all over the West. But Durgin quit last year. Got a new teaching job and a new patron."

"Pertwee," I said.

"Right. And now Durgin's back in Wyoming looking for fossils—"

"And this Loveland don't like his old hand strikin' out on his own," Old Red said.

"Well put. Loveland more than doesn't like it, though. He hates it. So much so he dragged his fat ass out of New York and came to Wyoming himself. Started his own dig barely a mile from Durgin's. And he hired riffraff like that"—Diehl jerked his thumb at the building the two gunmen had been loitering by—"to 'guard his finds.'"

"And scare off Durgin's workers," Hoop added. "Which they did."

"So Pertwee goes to the A.A. Western Detective Agency..." I said.

Diehl nodded. "And here we are."

"Speaking of 'we,' where's Eskaminzim?" I said.

I glanced around warily as if the man might spring out from under a rock and try to throttle me. Which I actually considered completely possible. When Old Red and I had encountered the Apache in New Mexico, he'd been entirely too enthusiastic about fighting me. Not that he'd taken any kind of dislike to me. That seemed beside the point. He just enjoys a good scrap, and me being a certain size I could provide one.

"He's out at Durgin's dig." Hoop pointed to the north. "About eight miles thataway."

"We've been keeping one man here and two out there," Diehl explained. "Hoop and I have been trading off the town duty. Leaving an Apache alone here...well, you can imagine how that would go over with the locals."

"And what would happen to them if they tried to do something about it," Hoop said.

I could imagine it. And it wasn't a pretty sight given what I'd seen of Eskaminzim and Hoop's abilities.

"So—that's the lay of the land," Diehl said. "We're spread a little thin at the dig site, so I figure you two should head out there. Make sure Durgin sees that Pertwee's getting his money's worth."

"And which of us will show them the way?" Hoop asked.

Colonel Crowe had told me I could learn a thing or two from Hoop and Diehl and Eskaminzim. So I was ready for my first lesson. What kind of strategy would they use when it came time to divide their forces? How would experienced operatives make decisions among themselves and carry them out?

Diehl reached into his pocket and pulled out a quarter.

"Call it," he said to Hoop.

He flipped the coin into the air with a flick of the thumb.

"Tails," Hoop said.

Diehl caught the quarter and slapped it onto the back of his left hand. When he lifted his right hand away, Hoop stepped in closer to look.

He wanted to see the coin himself. He wasn't just going to believe whatever Diehl told him.

"Tails it is," Diehl sighed. "You get to sleep here tonight." He looked over at me and Old Red. "And we get to enjoy the great outdoors…and night watch."

He stuffed the quarter back into his pocket and headed into the barn to collect his things.

"We got horses and saddles for you," Hoop told us.

He glanced down at our sides, then gave us a questioning look. *Is there something else we need to get for you?* his expression said.

My brother and I looked at each other, then opened our carpetbags and pulled out what Hoop had been searching for.

We'd stepped off the train without our gun belts on. But now it was time to go to work.

THREE
INTRODUCTIONS
OR, WE RIDE OUT TO MEET THE BONE HUNTERS AND DISCOVER SOMEONE'S HUNTING US

DIEHL LED us north on a strip through the prairie that was a shade more than a trail but not quite a road. I knew there had to be ranches or mines or *something* out there other than brush and rock and bones, but looking left to right, I couldn't see any sign of it.

Diehl noticed me scanning the horizon.

"God's country," he said, sweeping his left arm out grandly.

"Umm…yeah."

Diehl sucked in a deep breath as if savoring the fresh, cool spring air.

"A whole bunch of nothing," he said.

"Umm…yeah."

Diehl looked over at Old Red and me trotting along to his right.

"'We are told to look through Nature upward unto Nature's God,'" he said. He flipped his left arm around and pointed down at the ground. "'We are told there is a scripture written on the meanest sod. That the simplest flower created is a key to hidden things; but immortal over Nature, Mind, the lord of Nature, springs!'"

He smiled at us.

"Umm…yeah," I said.

My brother said nothing.

"Charles Swain," Diehl said, answering a question we hadn't asked. "The poet?"

"Oh," I said. "Nice."

Old Red still said nothing.

Diehl seemed to stifle a sigh, his smile fading. I think he was disappointed we aren't poetry lovers.

"So," he said, focusing on me, "you're a writer."

"I suppose I am," I said. "It's funny, though, now that you mention it. I never really think of myself that way. I'm just a fella who writes down things that happen. Then someone pays me for it and puts it in print."

"In *Smythe's Frontier Detective*," Diehl said.

"Generally." I shrugged. "Haven't shown up in *Ladies' Home Journal* yet."

Diehl smiled again. He leaned toward me and dropped his voice as if he didn't want to be overheard by all the people who weren't around us.

"So those 'things that happen.' Your stories, like 'Cowboy Brothers Battle the New Mexico Death Baron.' They're real?"

"Of course," I said. "'Things that happen' are things that happen."

Diehl cocked his head, still smiling. The look seemed to be inviting me to drop the hogwash.

"Really," I said. "Didn't you ask Hoop and Eskaminzim about it? They were there for 'Cowboy Brothers etc. etc.'"

"They were there for part of it. And they said the way you described what they saw was accurate…more or less."

"'More or less'?"

"But this 'deducifying' business," Diehl continued. "The Sherlock Holmes stuff. 'The Holmes of the Range'…?"

His gaze moved past me, to Old Red. His expression remained dubious.

"Perhaps that's where the 'less' comes into play more than the 'more'?" he said.

I furrowed my brow, trying to hash out what that meant.

As usual, Old Red worked it out quicker than me.

"If you want to tell us we're full of shit," he said, "just come out and say it, Mr. Diehl."

"Oh, my goodness—no!" Diehl exclaimed. "I've been rude. I apologize."

"It's all right. No offense taken," I said—though I felt I was being gracious in saying it.

"You was just curious. And skeptical," Old Red said. "No harm in that."

Diehl shook his head. "'Take the world as it is! If the surface be shining, never rake up the sediment hidden below,'" he recited. "'There's wisdom in this, but there's none in repining over things which can rarely be mended, we know.'"

My brother went silent again.

"More Swain," Diehl said. "Wisdom for all occasions."

"Umm...yeah," I said.

As we kept on riding, wordlessly now, toward the bluffs to the north, I turned Diehl's last quotation over in my mind.

"If the surface be shining, never rake up the sediment hidden below?"

In the very midst of a supposed apology, the SOB had worked in another hint that my stories about my brother are bull.

He continued to spare us more veiled insults and poetry, though, and after another half hour of quiet riding we rounded the biggest of the buttes visible from Wamsutter. The country stretching out beyond it was hillier but just as sparse, with brown ground speckled with tufts of green grass. Given that this was late May, there were dashes of red and yellow here and there thanks to patches of Indian paintbrush and mules-ears. But overall the landscape was muted, dry, almost dingy.

Two thin columns of smoke rose up into the cloudless pale blue sky, one close and straight ahead, the other further off and to our left.

My brother pointed at the first. "That Professor Durgin's camp?" He pivoted his finger to the left. "And Loveland's over there?"

"That's right," Diehl said. "How did you 'deducify' that?"

Old Red jerked his chin at the first column of smoke.

"'Cuz we're ridin' toward that one," he growled.

"Ahh."

Diehl nodded as if impressed by this amazing feat of Sherlockery. He himself was observant enough not to say more about it, though. The scowl on my brother's face was impossible to miss, even if half of it was hiding behind his walrus mustache.

Durgin's camp, we soon saw, consisted of half a dozen tents—two large, four smaller—in a circle on a low rise. Not far off was a rope corral with four horses. The fire was in the middle of the tents. A woman in a calico dress and tatty, oversized boots squatted beside it pushing coals up against a pair of Dutch ovens. She stood and put her hands on her hips as we rode up. She was a small, withered gal but not all that old—perhaps thirty, though weathered enough for fifty back east. The West seems to bake some folks dry, turning them to jerky, and she had that tough, stringy look to her.

There was nothing dry or dull about her eyes, though. They flashed with curious amusement as we approached, and when we reined up just beyond the tents, she stretched out an arm and pointed at me with her coal-poking stick.

"Send that one back," she said to Diehl. "He's too damn big. I'll never keep him fed!"

"I told you I was bringing a 'Big Red,' Cherry," Diehl said. "'Little Red' wasn't an option."

The woman—"Cherry," apparently—jabbed her stick at Old Red. "He qualifies."

"Yes, but I told you about him, too," Diehl said. "That's 'Old Red.'"

Cherry squinted at my brother, then grunted. "He ain't that old. He'll be 'Little Red' to me." She waved her stick at me again.

"And he can stay as long as he promises to leave some food for the others."

"You have my promise, ma'am," I said gravely. "Though I must say I'm getting a whiff of your stew, and if it tastes as good as it smells, I'll be hard-pressed to keep my word."

The woman threw back her head and laughed. "You've got competition, Diehl! You might not be the smoothest talker in camp anymore! So...aren't you gonna make introductions?"

"Sorry, Cherry. I wanted to see if you'd let them stay first." Diehl held out a hand toward me, then my brother. "Otto 'Big Red' Amlingmeyer, Gustav 'Old Red' Amlingmeyer...or 'Little Red.' Allow me to present Miss Cherry Dixon. Our cook."

"And just the cook!" Cherry said. "I am no one's wash-erwoman!"

"Heaven forbid I should ever be so presumptuous as to assume so," I said. I took off my Stetson and pressed it over my heart. "Miss Dixon, it is a pleasure to make your acquaintance."

Old Red just reached up and gave his hat brim a tug.

"Miss," he said. (It wasn't the first time he'd met someone who insisted on calling him "Little Red," and I'm sure it wasn't the first time it irritated him. But he wasn't the kind to contradict a woman when it came to something so trivial as his own name.)

"Oh," said Cherry. "Another of those men of few words, huh? Well, I like 'em chatty, like these two." She waggled her stick back and forth between me and Diehl. "But that's all right. I'll feed you anyway."

My brother—always shy around females in the vicinity of his own age—shifted uncomfortably in his saddle and said nothing.

"He thanks you," I told Cherry.

"Have you seen Eskaminzim?" Diehl asked her.

"If I did I'd throw rocks! You know how he's always stealing my bread. I don't even think he likes it that much. He just likes being sneaky."

"He does enjoy a challenge," Diehl said. "All right—we're off to the dig. If I see Eskaminzim, I'll tell him to leave your bread alone."

"You'd better. I've got pretty good aim."

Cherry gave us a nod—and a little smile that I think was just for me—and went back to her cooking.

"Quite a character," I said as we rode on into the hills.

Diehl nodded. "Every camp needs one."

"Back in town, you said Loveland's thugs scared off all of Durgin's workers," Old Red said. "Were you not countin' her? Or is she new, like us?"

"She's new. Replaced a man named Verardo...fortunately for us. Apparently the only edible thing Verardo could make was scrambled eggs. Everyone was turning yellow by the time he quit."

"So he and the guards—they let themselves get run off," Old Red mused. "And that little wisp of a woman is more brave than all of 'em?"

"I don't know if it's bravery so much as stubbornness," Diehl said. "And a lack of options. She mentioned once she came to Wyoming with a husband and two children, and the husband abandoned them."

"And the children?" my brother asked.

"Diphtheria."

"Ah," said Old Red. And he went quiet.

"Well, I for one am grateful this 'Verardo' turned out a coward," I said. "I like scrambled eggs fine, but stew and fresh-baked bread is YAAAHHH!"

I suddenly had company atop my mount: a man who'd sprung up behind me as we wound down into a gully. An arm wrapped around me, and cold steel pressed against my throat.

"Slice!" the man said as my spooked horse charged forward. "You're dead!"

The knife moved away, and I felt a pressure in my side.

"Or stab stab! There goes your liver!" the man said. "Dead again!"

I started to move my right hand to my gun—a "Bang! *You're* dead!" certainly seemed in order—but the man grabbed my wrist and smacked it three times with the spine of his blade.

"Hack hack hack," he said. "I cut off your hand, then I go back to stabbing or slicing. This was too easy!"

He let go of me and rolled off, and I was finally able to pull back the reins and stop my horse.

I looked back at my attacker—a square-jawed man with long black hair and a bandana across his forehead and high-shafted, boot-like moccasins on his feet—and cursed.

Eskaminzim laughed.

"Don't be mad at *me*!" he said. "Be mad at yourself! You must have known I'd want to fight you again. You should have been ready!"

I cursed again—though I knew he was right. Maybe *because* I knew he was right.

"Anytime you're headed down, like here, going below the horizon, you cut off your view all around you," Eskaminzim went on. "If you know someone might want to ambush you…someone who's not going to shoot you but jump you…" He shook his head slowly in mock disappointment. "Foolish."

"I was just following him," I said, flapping a hand at Diehl.

Eskaminzim kept shaking his head. "*Very* foolish."

Diehl rolled his eyes.

Eskaminzim glanced over at my brother. "Hello."

"Hello, Eskaminzim."

"How long have you been here waiting to scare the bejesus out of Big Red?" Diehl asked.

"Not long," Eskaminzim said. "I saw you coming ten minutes ago. I already had this spot picked out." He shifted his attention back to me. "You see how the ground keeps sloping away here but not so much over there? Leaving a ridge with a gully on the other side? That gave me a spot to leave my horse out of sight of the trail."

"Why do I feel like I ought to be taking notes?" I said.

Diehl got his horse moving again.

"Come on," he said. "We don't want Professor Durgin to start wondering where his guards are."

"Oh, he doesn't mind my being away while he plays in the dirt," Eskaminzim said. "I think I make him nervous."

"Now whyever would that be?" I said.

Eskaminzim shrugged. "I've never jumped *him*."

He grinned and trotted off around the ridge he'd pointed out to me. Nearby, I noted as I watched him go, was a pile of angular, dingy-gray shapes. Bones—big ones. They looked like they'd been built up into a small tower a couple feet high, then knocked over.

Old Red noticed them, too.

"Peculiar," he said.

"Maybe they're just rejects. Broken bones from dinosaurs no one cares about."

"Why leave 'em here piled up together?"

I shrugged. "Tidiness?"

My brother gave that a skeptical grunt, then started after Diehl. A minute later, as we made our way out of the gully, Eskaminzim caught up to us on a black and white appaloosa. There was another ravine after that, then another. As we topped the rise beyond this last we saw, on the long slope on the other side, a buckboard wagon, a horse tied to one wheel, and two trenches. There were people in the pits in pairs—a man and a woman in one, two men in the other—and they all popped up like gophers from their holes as we approached.

"As promised, Professor Durgin," Diehl said to the oldest of them—the man half in the earth beside a woman. He nodded at me and my brother as we stopped beside him. "Reinforcements."

Professor Durgin—tall, lean, and graying like Diehl, but with spectacles and a round face and thinning hair—looked me and Old Red over for all of a second, then nodded once and kneeled again. The two younger men in the other pit did the same, minus the nods. All of them held small tools in their hands—a brush, a pickax, a chisel. Almost immediately, they were using them again.

The woman, on the other hand, remained standing. For which I was grateful. Her appraisal of us was lasting far longer, which gave me ample chance to appraise her. And I liked what I saw.

Now, as I am a gentleman (or usually try to be), let me emphasize that it was the friendliness of her expression and the intelligence in her sky-blue eyes that warmed me to her immediately. She was slender but not bony like Cherry, with pleasing features and long, straight, blonde hair pulled back in a ponytail, and these details too, I didn't hold against her. For age, I pegged her at forty—an old maid or matron as some reckon it, but I'm not nearly so judgmental. She was going to liven up the scenery more than my brother or Durgin or the horses, that was for sure.

"Welcome to Camp Cashew," she said to us.

Old Red mumbled a shy, quiet reply the lady couldn't have heard had she been sitting in his lap.

I spoke up loud enough for both of us.

"Thank you, ma'am," I said. "But 'Camp Cashew'? I wonder if we're in the right place. I thought you were out here digging for dinosaurs."

The lady smiled, and immediately I liked her even more.

"We are," she said. "The name is for the nut that made our expedition possible."

"Shouldn't it be 'Camp Pertwee,' then?"

Durgin jerked his head up to glare at me, and Diehl shifted in his saddle and seemed to stifle another sigh.

But the lady laughed.

Still, my brother thought a little advice was in order.

"Can you wait at least a day," he said under his breath, "before you piss off the boss and get us fired?"

I could've pointed out that that's usually what *he* does. Instead I ignored him.

"No offense meant to Professor Pertwee. He makes a fine nut butter," I told the lady.

Like the men near her, she was holding a tool—a small, sharp-faced hammer—and she was dressed in work clothes, dirty at the knees. She wasn't there to bring the others tea.

"I'm sure he has fine taste in scientists, as well," I said.

One of the men in the other pit said something I couldn't catch. I did hear his trench-mate's reply, though.

"Oh, shut up, Wentworth."

Wentworth shot the other fellow a murderous glare. The two were about my age—the general vicinity of twenty—and from their sunburns and loosened neckties, I gathered they weren't strongback navvies hired from town. College boys, they looked like to me—not that I've run across many in person. But it was easy to see that digging under the Wyoming sun wasn't their usual occupation. They looked more like men with no occupation at all beyond book learning and beer swilling.

"All right, thank you, carry on," Durgin said.

He didn't seem to be speaking directly to Wentworth and his (non) friend or me and the lady or Diehl and Old Red and Eskaminzim. It was more a message to the entire world.

Whatever. Leave me alone. I have work to do.

He ducked down and went back to poking at dirt. The college boys followed suit, Wentworth with the frown still on his face.

"Well," the lady said, looking back and forth between me and Old Red, "it's nice meeting you."

"Likewise!" I said. I doffed my hat. "I'm Otto Amlingmeyer, by the way. And this is my brother Gustav."

"Ma'am," Old Red muttered, tugging on the brim of his Stetson as he had for Cherry.

The lady threw an expectant look down at Durgin, but he didn't get the hint. A bolt of lightning to his backsides wouldn't have been hint enough for him just then. Nothing was going to distract from his hunt for bones now that he was at it again.

I began to wonder if the lady might be Durgin's wife. He was certainly ignoring her thoroughly enough for that to be the case, and I was too far away to see her ring finger clearly.

Diehl jumped in to offer the formal introduction a gentleman was obligated to make (provided he was paying the slightest bit of attention).

"This is Miss Hayes," he said. "She's a student of paleontology, like Mr. Mead and Mr. Wentworth there."

The two college boys looked up. Wentworth said something under his breath again—all I could make out was a scornful "*student*"—and again Mead told him to shut up.

I acknowledged them with a nod.

They just went back to their work.

Quite the charming pair.

"Are we going to introduce the horses, too?" Eskaminzim said.

"You don't need to introduce them to me," said Miss Hayes, smiling. "I believe I'm acquainted with them all already. Gentlemen."

She hunkered down in the trench again and tapped at something with her little hammer. Old Red and I watched her, fascinated.

After a moment, Diehl cleared his throat.

"Boys," he said. "Don't get distracted."

"Who says I'm distracted?" Old Red grumbled.

"I do. Or you would've noticed *them*."

Diehl jerked his chin to the north.

"More introductions," said Eskaminzim.

Watching us from a ridge about a quarter mile away were two men on horseback. Each had a Winchester rifle propped upon his leg, the muzzle pointed at the sky…for now.

FOUR
THE DIPLO-WHATSIS

OR, OLD RED TRIES TO PICK UP PALEONTOLOGY, BUT IT'S ALL GREEK TO HIM

"BIG RED, OLD RED," said Diehl, holding a hand out toward the men in the distance. "Meet Gray Hat and the Indian."

"More of Loveland's gunhands," Old Red said.

Diehl nodded.

I squinted and *maybe* saw a gray hat on one of the men holding rifles. It was like trying to make out if a flea's giving you the finger. Too small for my eyes. But I took Diehl's word for it.

"So they've got their own Indian?" I said.

"Shoshone, I think, though he dresses half-white," said Eskaminzim. He shook his head in disgust. "Levi's and a Stetson. Ugh."

(Old Red and I were wearing Levi's and Stetsons.)

"They put in an appearance every so often to remind Durgin that they're around," said Diehl. "They generally don't get too close unless they can catch one of his people on their own. Speaking of which—"

"Cherry!" Old Red said. "Do you think they'd mess with her?"

"They've tried," said Eskaminzim. He grinned. "I mess with them first."

He looked at Diehl.

"Happy hunting," Diehl said.

Eskaminzim wheeled his horse around and went galloping back the way we'd come.

"I'm going to head that way," Diehl told us, pointing his chin to the north—and the men still watching us there. "You two stay here and make sure Durgin feels safe."

"How safe are *you* gonna be?" Old Red asked.

Diehl shrugged. "Probably pretty safe. They don't want any actual shooting. Probably. I can make sure they know these hills don't belong to them. Probably."

"That's a lot of 'Probably,'" I said.

"If we wanted to be certain about being safe, we wouldn't work for a detective agency, would we?"

"Good point." I rubbed my jaw thoughtfully. "Is it too late for me to quit?"

"As far as they're concerned?" Diehl said, nodding again at "Gray Hat and the Indian." "Absolutely."

And he went trotting off toward the north.

"He's a strange bird," Old Red said when Diehl was out of earshot. "I don't see why he does work for the Double-A."

"Maybe because no one will pay him to recite poetry." I looked up at the bright sun beating down on us and shifted my aching haunches on the hard leather of my saddle. "Or maybe it's because this is just so danged fun."

"Is everything all right?" Miss Hayes asked.

She was popping up out of her pit again to watch Diehl leave, and Durgin and the college boys straightened up and craned their necks for a look, too.

"Right as rain, ma'am," I said, flashing her and Durgin a reassuring smile. "Our colleagues Mr. Diehl and Mr. Eskaminzim are just off to patrol the perimeter. Gustav and I will remain here to continue acquainting ourselves with your procedures and needs."

Durgin nodded and dropped back down into his hole beside the lady, and Wentworth and Mead returned to their work as well.

Miss Hayes lingered, though, giving us a long—perhaps even skeptical?—look before getting back to her bones.

"Continue acquainting ourselves with their procedures and needs?" Old Red whispered. "Awful fancy way to say 'stand around doin' nothing.'"

"And the fancy way worked," I whispered back. "As for the standing—what a capital idea."

Cowboys, it is said, would eat, sleep and bathe in the saddle if they could. Walking around on your own two feet is thought by them to be something no dignified person does if they can remain atop a horse instead. But as I'm a cowboy no longer, I can admit it: My butt ached after the long ride out from town, not to mention the unexpected gallop with Eskaminzim attached to my back. So I was glad for a chance to put boots to the ground.

I swung down off my horse, led him to the old mare tied to the buckboard and—once I'd determined she wasn't the biting kind—left him hitched beside her. In the wagon bed, I noticed, were shovels and picks and heavy-looking sacks along with grain for the horse and a small barrel of water. And two new shotguns.

Now, my brother clings to cowboy ways with a tighter grip than I, so he didn't follow my lead and unsaddle himself straight off. He kept watching Loveland's men in the distance, ready to dig in his heels if they gave Diehl any trouble. But when he saw them turn and disappear over the far ridge as Diehl got within two hundred yards, he reluctantly did as I had, and soon there were three horses tied to the buckboard.

Old Red wasn't just afoot to give his butt a break, I soon saw. Though we started off moseying in a big oval around the two pits, swaggering with our hands near our guns, trying to look imposing, my brother's route kept shrinking and shrinking. Soon he was circling just one trench—the one Durgin and Miss Hayes were working in. Not just circling it but eyeing it. It was maybe twelve feet long, ten across, and four-and-a-half deep, with a raised pedestal of unshoveled soil in the middle jutting up like a huge, yellow-brown mushroom. It was this big earthen table in the center that Durgin and Miss Hayes were focused on, brushing and picking at gray shapes visible in its dull sides.

The professor remained absorbed in his work, only glancing

back at us when my brother's shadow fell across the spot he was poking at. Old Red hopped out of the way, and the professor immediately got back to his poking. But Miss Hayes swiveled around and looked up at my brother and, seeing his obvious curiosity, smiled.

"It's a diplodocus," she said. "The biggest and most complete ever found, perhaps."

"A diplo-whatsis? I…I thought you was lookin' for dinosaurs," Old Red said reluctantly.

Clearly he was afraid of saying the wrong thing. And he had. But the lady kept smiling—and not in a condescending way.

"A diplodocus is a kind of dinosaur," she explained.

"Order Dinosaura, sub-order Saurupoda," Wentworth pontificated from the other trench. "Jurassic herbivorous quadruped. Named 'diplodocus' for the rafter-like shape of the chevrons attached to the caudal vertebrae. 'Diplo' from the Greek 'diplóos,' meaning 'double-sided.'"

"'Docus' meaning 'beam,'" Mead threw in begrudgingly, just to show that Wentworth wasn't the only student around who'd done his homework.

"Originally named 'diplodocus longus' by Othniel Charles Marsh," Wentworth went on. "'Longus' meaning—"

"Long," I said before Wentworth could.

He glared at me from his big gopher hole.

"Just a guess," I said.

He didn't correct me, so I assumed it was a good one.

Old Red swung his gaze from one pit to the other. They were about fifty feet apart.

"The same animal?" he said.

"It seems to be," said Miss Hayes. "We think diplodocus could grow as long as eighty feet, and the bones could be spread out far further than that. Scattered by predators, scavengers, weather, then eventually movements in the earth itself over millions of years. So what we find is often widely dispersed, incomplete, mixed in with the remains of other animals. It makes for quite a puzzle."

My brother grunted, still looking from one trench to the other. He had that faraway look in his eyes that he gets when he's chewing on a mystery. It was as if this diplodocus was a new case for him.

"I don't think you're gonna catch the killer," I said to him. "Looks like he got away with it."

Old Red grunted again, this time in that way of his that says, "This ain't a laugh cuz that ain't funny."

"Thank you, Miss," he said.

He started to turn away from her...then quickly pivoted back on his heel.

"What'd this thing look like, anyway?"

"Well..."

Miss Hayes threw a glance at Durgin, perhaps to see if he—the real expert—preferred to answer. Or perhaps to see if he was going to get cranky about distractions and chatting with the help and the need to get back to work. But the professor just kept chipping away at the sod before him with cautious little taps of his pickax.

"Small head, long neck, whip-like tail," said Wentworth, jumping in to show who the expert was as far as he was concerned. "Thick body, four trunk-like legs. Typical sauropod."

My brother furrowed his brow at that.

"Sort of like a fat lizard with a stretched-out neck," Miss Hayes told him. "The size of a whale."

Wentworth whispered something sneering to Mead, who muttered back what felt like another "Shut up." I was tempted to add my own, much more clear "Shut up," as it was obvious Wentworth couldn't stop talking over and sniping at the lady.

She ignored him, but her smile took on a tight, long-suffering look.

Old Red kneeled near her and lowered his voice.

"So these big, fat lizards used to be all over the place here?"

"They did," Miss Hayes said, keeping her voice down, as well. Wentworth couldn't interrupt or criticize what he couldn't hear. "This is my first expedition, but I've heard the fossils used to be so plentiful in this part of Wyoming—just lying strewn about on the ground—ranchers could use them to build fences. There's a whole hut made from them just a quarter of a mile away."

"Kinda like that pile we saw," I said to Old Red. "Like someone started on a hut and quit after their first blister."

For some reason, that seemed to be the remark that finally crossed the line for Durgin. He lowered his pickax and jerked up his head.

"Your interest is appreciated," he said sharply, "but Miss Hayes and I are occupied, and I do believe you have a job to do, too."

Old Red straightened up and stepped back. "Yes, sir."

"If you have more questions about dinosaurs, we'll be happy to answer them tonight," Durgin said, his tone softening. "After we've lost the light. But for now…you understand."

"Of course. Miss—I'm sorry to have taken you from your work."

Miss Hayes gave my brother a nod and another smile, then turned back to the pedestal of earth in the middle of the pit.

Old Red swung around to face me—and froze. Something behind me had slapped a grave look on his face that I did not care for at all.

I turned to see what it was. There was no mirror handy, but I can only assume my expression wasn't any more cheerful than Old Red's.

While we'd been gabbing away about dinosaurs, Diehl had begun racing back to the dig—with half a dozen riders on his tail.

FIVE
RABBITS AND WOLVES
OR, WE AND OUR RIVALS COME FACE TO FACE, AND SOME OF US ARE TEMPTED TO TURN TAIL

"ARE we really about to get into a shootout over dead lizards?" I said under my breath as we watched the riders approach.

"We've been in shootouts over dumber things," Old Red whispered back.

I thought that over a moment.

"Have we?" I said.

Diehl was only about three hundred yards away now. The men following him, on the other hand, were twice that distance off and weren't rushing to close the gap. They were approaching at an easy canter as opposed to Diehl's gallop.

Maybe they weren't really chasing him. Or maybe they were so confident they'd get away with whatever they had planned they didn't feel the need to hurry.

"Gray Hat's in with 'em," said Old Red. "And the Indian."

I squinted at the riders as they loped over a hill in the distance. One in particular—half of a pair leading the group—caught my attention.

"And someone's grandma?" I said. I squinted harder. "Wait... make that a tubby fella in a dress...? Carrying a parasol...?"

"Yeah, I see him," said Old Red. "I just ain't decided yet whether to believe my eyes."

"Is something going on?" Durgin asked, rising up from his trench.

When he followed our gazes to the north, his jaw dropped.

"Who is that?" he said, scrambling up to join us. "Who's coming? Loveland's ruffians?"

"Looks like," said Old Red. "And maybe someone else…?"

"Someone with…a unique sense of style?" I added.

Miss Hayes started to push herself up out of the pit, as well.

"Hold on, Miss," Old Red said. "You might want to stay down there till we've seen what this is all about."

"Don't be ridiculous, Mr. Amlingmeyer," the lady said, carrying on her climbing. "I'm not going to hide in a hole in the ground."

She stood and stepped toward us, dusting off her hands.

Wentworth and Mead, on the other hand, not only seemed inclined to stay in their trench, they looked like they were thinking of tunneling into it even deeper.

"Peter, Andrew," Durgin said to them. "Get the shotguns."

From the stricken looks on their faces, I could see that this was *exactly* what they didn't want to hear.

"Hurry!" Durgin snapped when they didn't move.

They began slithering up out of their pit. But I assure you they were *not* hurrying.

Diehl was almost upon us by then, and just as he rode in Eskaminzim topped the rise behind us on his appaloosa.

"Ah! Good!" he said, taking in the approaching party of riders. "I saw dust and was hoping it was this!"

Before I could ask what exactly he was hoping for—a nice, cozy little bloodbath?—Diehl reined up near us and pointed at Wentworth and Mead, who were ever so slowly trudging toward the buckboard.

"What are they doing?"

"Getting our shotguns," said Durgin.

Diehl shook his head. "Oh, no. Not those two. No offense, fellas."

The college boys looked profoundly unoffended. Relieved would've been more like it.

"I don't know what this little visit is all about," Diehl said, "but it's not just the guns that are coming. It's Loveland and Glaze. We need to hear them out without any twitchy fingers near any triggers."

Durgin adjusted his glasses and peered at the approaching riders. They were less than a quarter mile off now.

"Damn," Durgin said. He'd been keyed up for a confrontation, but now he sagged, some of the fight seeming to go out of him. "It is Loveland, isn't it?"

"Pretty unmistakable," said Diehl. He looked over and gave me and my brother a long, appraising look. "Why don't you two go ahead and grab those scatterguns? Then position yourselves on opposite ends of the dig site. One east, one west. A few steps to the north of the rest of us. Everyone else just stay calm and act casual."

Old Red and I glanced at each other, then headed for the wagon.

"Guess we should feel honored," I muttered. "*Our* fingers aren't too twitchy."

Old Red looked over his shoulder at Diehl and Durgin and Miss Hayes.

"Is Loveland the fella in the evenin' gown?" he said.

Diehl nodded, a grim smile creasing his lean face. "It's more of a dressing gown, to be fair."

"He doesn't like the sun," said Durgin. He didn't bother with a smile and just stuck to grim.

"Who's this 'Glaze' then?" my brother asked.

"Loveland's chief bone hunter," said Miss Hayes.

"So he's Professor Durgin's replacement?"

Durgin grimaced. "No. He's worked for Loveland for years."

"Ah."

Old Red let it drop after that. I guess he felt like he knew enough for the moment.

Durgin's old boss was coming to call along with a former colleague who was (judging by the grimace) less than a friend. With them were four other less-than-friends with guns on their hips and Winchesters in their saddle scabbards.

It promised to be quite a reunion.

My brother and I retrieved the shotguns and some extra shells from the wagon bed, gave each other a nod, and set off toward opposite ends of the dig. Eskaminzim rode around to my right, on the east side of the site, while Diehl positioned himself to Old Red's left on the west side.

"They'll stop about there," Eskaminzim said to me, pointing at a spot thirty feet before Durgin and Miss Hayes. "Then we'll have a crossfire. If they try to spread out too far, we spread out further, too. We don't want them on our left *and* right. Just to your left, and your brother's right. Makes them easier to watch—and easier to shoot. Both barrels to start, then reload fast. If you're lucky, you won't even need another shot. They'll all be on the ground after the first."

I looked over at my brother and saw that Diehl was speaking to him in low tones, pointing ahead at the same spot Eskaminzim had picked out.

I turned back to the Apache.

"Thanks for the lesson, Professor," I said. "What do you call this class anyway?"

"Staying alive," Eskaminzim said.

"Ah. Well. I'll hope to be the teacher's pet."

Loveland and his men were less than a hundred yards off now, heading up the long, grassy slope that led to the pits.

Moving slowly, deliberately, Diehl and Eskaminzim pulled out their rifles. Diehl settled his across his lap. Eskaminzim propped his on his right thigh.

"Miss Hayes," Diehl said, "are you sure you wouldn't rather stand back by the wagon? It'd be nice if someone would keep the animals calm."

"They're fine," the lady said without looking back at the hitched horses. Or moving at all, except to face Diehl.

"Oh—" Durgin said to her softly. He stopped himself and started again. "Lydia, I think it's a good suggestion."

Yet still she didn't leave his side.

"John, you know I've never met Professor Loveland," she said. "How am I supposed to ask for his autograph from way back there?"

That got another sneering whisper out of Wentworth. It sounded like a mincing "Oh, Lydia...ooo, John." The kind of thing a smirking schoolboy would say.

I'd known the man less than half an hour, and already I'd had my fill of his sourness—and him in general.

"Stop it," Mead told him.

"Well, if no one else is going to see to the horses, I will," Wentworth huffed.

He hustled over to the wagon...and proceeded to go around to the far side, nowhere near the horses. He didn't try to climb inside the water barrel or simply scamper off over the hill, but neither would have surprised me.

"Hey," Eskaminzim said to me. "Don't watch the rabbit. Watch the wolves."

"Right."

I'd been looking back at Wentworth.

I kept my eyes on our visitors as they covered the final fifty yards between us.

Loveland and his "bone hunter," Glaze, were still in front, but the men behind them—Gray Hat and the Indian and two others with rough clothes and hard eyes—began to fan out.

The one we'd been calling "the Indian" was actually dressed more like a cowboy, with a Stetson on his head and a neckerchief round his throat and his Levi's stuffed into his boots. Those boots were deerskin adorned with bright floral patterns, though, and he wore his hair in long, dark braids. His handkerchief was knotted through a big silver concho most drovers would've considered too close to jewelry for comfort, and the sheath at his side for his Bowie knife was beaded and embroidered like his boots.

He drifted to Loveland and Glaze's left, as if about to line up directly across from Eskaminzim. He kept going, though, flanking us. Eskaminzim sent his horse ambling to our right to match him. For a moment, they rode slowly in parallel, neither willing to stop until the other did.

"We keep going this way we'll end up in Pittsburgh," Eskaminzim said. He shook his head. "I hate Pittsburgh."

I was surprised to learn he had strong feelings about anything east of the Mississippi, but the Indian just glared at him and said nothing.

"Joe," said Gray Hat, who'd stopped across from me.

The Indian turned his horse to face Eskaminzim and reined up.

Eskaminzim stopped, too—after getting in three extra steps to ensure that he was flanking "Joe."

"Shoshone?" Eskaminzim asked him.

Joe grunted in a way that seemed to say yes.

"Apache?" he asked Eskaminzim.

"Mescalero," said Eskaminzim.

Joe grunted again—though this time in a way that seemed to say something I wouldn't be allowed to set in print.

Our other callers had stopped by now, as well, Loveland and Glaze side by side in exactly the spot Eskaminzim had predicted: facing Durgin and Miss Hayes, close but not too close. Loveland looked ungainly in the saddle, like Humpty Dumpty perched upon his wall and just as likely to fall. It didn't help, perhaps, that he had to keep one hand on the parasol he was holding over his head or that his clothes—jowl-crowded collar and necktie sticking up from a housecoat of quilted emerald satin—was more fitting for lounging around the boudoir than riding the high plains.

Glaze was a different story altogether. He looked so comfortable atop a horse he almost seemed a part of it—like one of the centaurs the Greeks (or was it the Romans?) used to believe in. (Have they found fossils for those yet?) His clothes—brown fedora, suit jacket, flaring breeches, high, shiny boots—gave him the look of a railroad construction boss or the like. Someone with a little authority who's used to wielding it in the wild.

"John," Loveland said to Durgin.

"Hiram," Durgin said. "Glaze."

Glaze said nothing. He had a hard, inexpressive face. The only part of it that didn't look like it had been baked in a kiln was his mustache.

"I heard your ranks were swelling, so I came to see who'd joined you," Loveland said. "I thought perhaps they might be colleagues of ours. Or perhaps journalists." He swung his gaze from right to left—from Old Red to me. "But I see that's not the case. Just more of your brutes."

"You're one to talk," said Miss Hayes. "Riding in here trying to intimidate us with your gang of mercenaries."

Loveland glowered at her with a mixture of surprise and dismissive contempt.

She'd never get that autograph now.

"Madam, I don't know you, so I don't know if you'll care," Loveland said. "But you are keeping bad company. I suggest you separate yourself from it." His gaze moved past Miss Hayes to Wentworth half-crouched behind the buckboard. "I offer the same advice to you, young man." He looked over at Mead. "And you. A scientist's reputation is important. You wouldn't want to destroy yours before your careers have even begun."

I gave Mead credit for the air of firm resolve he managed to project as he met Loveland's haughty glaze. I didn't glance back to see how Wentworth was holding up, but I assumed he was either packing his bags to go or waving a white flag.

"How would any of us be harming our reputations by being here," Miss Hayes said, "with the greatest paleontologist of our time?"

Loveland let out an explosive snort that startled his horse so much it nickered and took a step to the side. He had to grab his saddle horn with one hand to keep from toppling off. Somehow, though, he managed to keep his parasol up and himself in the shade the whole time.

"I assume, madam," he said once he was steady again, "that you refer to *me*?"

Miss Hayes just snorted back at him.

Durgin couldn't match the lady's grit. In fact, he looked more embarrassed than defiant.

"If you've just come here to offer insults and threats—" he began.

"Looks like quite a find," Glaze said. His voice was as cold and flat as a frozen pond. "And you're already, what? Over four feet down? This early in the season? You sure got digging fast."

Loveland tried to push himself up in his stirrups for a better look at the pits, but it seemed to me he only got an extra eighth of an inch in elevation out of it.

"And goodness me—is that my friend diplodocus, I see? You just be patient, dear! I'll soon have you in New York where you belong!"

The diplodocus chose not to respond.

"In case you've forgotten, Professor Durgin doesn't work for you anymore," Miss Hayes said. "The closest you'll get to *this* diplodocus is reading about it in a journal. And there will be a journal article about it. Under Professor Durgin's name this time, not yours."

Loveland shot something back—I think it was about getting Durgin blackballed by the top journals—but I lost track of the talk. A little blur of movement had pulled my attention away.

Across from me, Gray Hat had cocked his head to the side, and I saw when I focused on him that he was rolling his eyes to boot.

He was bored. So bored he forgot to hide it for a second.

I guess your average desperado isn't all that interested in who writes what in which science journal. Surprise surprise.

When he saw me watching him he straightened in his saddle and put on a scowl. It was a good scowl, too. He had the right kind of face for it. Deeply lined, arcing scar under one eye, unshaven. I thought about scowling back, but I knew he had me beat. My face is altogether too pleasing to be any good for buffaloing folks. So I smiled instead.

"What are you doing?" Eskaminzim said to me.

I shrugged. "Just standing here."

"Well, don't be so friendly about it." Eskaminzim jerked his head at Gray Hat and Joe. "They need to know how much you would enjoy killing them if they give you a reason." He looked over at the men. "You know that about *me*, right?"

Joe scoffed.

"Believe me, Indian," Gray Hat said to Eskaminzim. "The feeling's mutual."

"Vollmer? If you don't mind…?" Loveland said. "We are having a conversation here."

"Right." Gray Hat—a.k.a. Vollmer, I now knew—glanced over at Joe. "Be quiet."

Of course, Joe hadn't been doing the talking, but you know how it goes.

"Where was I?" Loveland said.

"Lawyers," said Glaze.

"Ah! Yes!" Loveland cleared his throat. "If you find these hired guns of mine intimidating, just wait until you see my lawyers at work."

He smiled smugly at Durgin and Miss Hayes.

I got the distinct impression he'd been waiting to say that for a long time.

"What have your lawyers got to do with it?" Miss Hayes said.

"Well, to be more precise, they're the museum's lawyers," Loveland said. "The ones who'll be working tirelessly to invalidate John's claim to this site." His saddle creaked as he leaned forward to glower down at Durgin. "One way or another, John, that diplodocus will be mine. Why don't you do the right thing and withdraw? Now, before it's too late. It's one thing to throw your career away. That's done. But to put so much more at risk…? So many others…?"

Loveland's round, white moon of a face had actually jutted

out into the sunshine, and when he noticed, he jerked back under his parasol.

"It won't end well," he said.

"Hiram…" Durgin said.

His voice was quiet, his expression sheepish. So much so that Miss Hayes was eyeing him with trepidation, clearly fearful he was about to give in right there and then.

"Go to hell," Durgin said. He looked over at Glaze. "And you go with him."

Loveland harrumphed, eyes blazing. But Glaze didn't react at all beyond a steely "Suit yourself, Durgin."

"You can't say I didn't warn you," Loveland said. He looked around at the whole bunch of us, from Diehl and Old Red at one end of the dig site to Eskaminzim and me at the other. "All of you. Whatever happens now is on your own heads."

He tried to make a dramatic exit, jerking his reins to the side and giving his mount his heels. But he almost lost his balance as the horse turned, and again he had to grab hold of the saddle horn lest his Humpty Dumpty imitation come to its natural conclusion. Which actually would have been pretty dramatic, though not in the way he was shooting for.

Rather than follow Loveland down the slope, Glaze actually urged his horse forward at a slow walk—straight toward Durgin and Miss Hayes.

Out of the corner of my eye, I saw Eskaminzim bring down his rifle so that the barrel was in his left hand. Pointed at Glaze.

Vollmer and Joe tensed, and I moved my (rather twitchy, to be honest) index finger inside the shotgun's trigger guard.

When Loveland had said whatever happened now would be on our heads, I didn't think he meant *now* now. Like the second he managed to move out of the firing line. That's the way it was starting to look, though.

Glaze kept moving toward Durgin and Miss Hayes. The two of them were forced back a step—then to the side, separated, as the horse came between them.

Glaze finally reined up. He leaned down to his left, toward

Durgin, and spoke in a low croak barely above a whisper yet also somehow clear as a bell.

"I know you've always looked down on me, *Professor*. But you need me. You think you learned enough of my tricks to beat me at my own game, and you are very wrong. You're going to see how wrong. Soon. And then you won't be in a position to look down on anybody."

He got his horse moving again after that, off at a trot between the two trenches before swinging around to head after Loveland.

The gunmen facing Old Red and Diehl went with him, but Vollmer and Joe lingered.

"I'll see you around," Joe said Eskaminzim.

"Only when I want you to," Eskaminzim replied.

Vollmer's eyes were locked on me.

"I'll see you around, too," he growled.

"Lovely," I said. "We'll have coffee."

When Vollmer and Joe were out of earshot, well down the slope with the others trailing Loveland and Glaze, Eskaminzim looked over at me and shook his head.

"You have a lot to learn about earning respect," he said.

"Is that what you fellas were doing? It seemed like it was just everybody hinting around about killing each other."

Eskaminzim nodded approvingly. "Now you're catching on."

Diehl slid his Winchester back into its scabbard.

"Well, they wanted a close look at us and the dig, and they got it," he said.

"They wanted more than a look," Miss Hayes said. "They wanted to run us off."

"Yeah. Lotta threats," Old Red said. "Lotta…"

He paused, searching for the right word.

When he thought of it, he said it to Professor Durgin.

"Insinuations."

Durgin met his gaze—then turned away.

"Yes, well…they won't work," he said. "Wentworth, you can come out from behind there now. They won't come back, and there's still a couple hours of daylight left. The best way to defy

Loveland is to remain focused on this find. His bluster isn't going to stop us from unearthing the biggest, most complete diplodocus yet!"

It was meant to be rousing. I saw no sign anyone was roused, however.

Wentworth stayed frozen behind the wagon, and Mead also made no move. Durgin went striding to his pit and dropped in again, but though Miss Hayes went with him, she did it slowly, thoughtfully. It looked like she was now chewing on something along with Old Red.

"What now?" my brother asked Diehl.

"Eskaminzim and I will keep an eye on them," he said, nodding at the departing riders. "You and your brother stay here. With the shotguns handy. Just in case the professor's wrong and there is another unexpected visit today."

He gave Eskaminzim a nod, and the two rode off side by side.

"You know," I said, glancing down at the shotgun that now weighed so heavy in my hands, "if I'd had any idea science was this exciting, I would've paid more attention to it in school."

"Yeah, well," my brother muttered. "Let's just hope this is as excitin' as it gets."

He had a pensive, brooding air about him, though. Almost as if he already knew that hope was in vain.

SIX
SHOTS IN THE DARK
OR, NIGHT FALLS, AND SO DO I

DURGIN and his team got back to their work, but a pall had fallen over the camp, and the scientists spoke low and moved slow. Old Red and I circled them with the shotguns, my brother asking the occasional question about dinosaurs or fossils or Loveland and Glaze. But the answers he got were distant and clipped now, even from Miss Hayes, and after a while, he set his questions aside and kept his eyes on the horizon.

Eventually Durgin took a look at the sky himself and declared that it was time to pack up and go. Old Red and I helped move the equipment to the wagon and hitch up the horse for the short ride back to camp. When everything was ready, Durgin gave the reins a snap and off they rolled, Miss Hayes beside him on the spring seat and Mead and Wentworth trudging along behind. My brother and I rode on either side of the buckboard, and as we crested the hill Old Red swiveled in his saddle for a look back at the dig site.

"So you just leave them bones of yours when you call it a day?" Old Red asked.

"Well, we can't very well take the *fossils* with us every night," Durgin said, reminding my brother of something Miss Hayes had explained to him earlier: that the fossils aren't technically bones at all. They started as bones but are now rock, having been transformed through the eons by…I'm not even going to pretend to understand it.

"We can't make camp on top of them either," Miss Hayes added. "Not without disturbing the find a thousand different ways."

"But ain't y'all worried Glaze'll sneak back in and make off with 'em?"

"No, actually," said Durgin. "You've seen yourself how painstaking our work is. How many hours of probing and digging are needed to free the smallest fossil from the matrix. It takes hours more to make a field jacket and let it dry and hoist it into something like this to haul it."

He patted the side of the wagon.

"I see," Old Red said. "Mostly. What's this 'matrix' stuff you say the fossils are in? Just looked like plain ol' Wyoming dirt to me."

"That *is* the matrix," said Miss Hayes. "It's just a fancy word scientists use to describe whatever's around the fossils. The material we have to clear away to get at what's important."

My brother mused on that a moment.

"'The matrix.' The stuff you gotta brush away to get at what's important…" He gave a single, firm nod. "I like that."

Miss Hayes cocked her head and smiled, surprised and amused by the curiosity of this odd and uneducated but clearly not unintelligent man.

"So Glaze couldn't steal the fossils for Loveland. Not in one night," he said. "But would he mess with them some other way? If Loveland decides he ain't gonna get 'em by bullyin'?"

"How do you 'mess with'?" Miss Hayes said.

"Bust 'em up. Destroy 'em out of spite."

"No," said Miss Hayes. "No paleontologist would ever—"

"Yes," Durgin said to Old Red. "He might."

He looked over at Miss Hayes. Her eyes widened in dismay.

"I've seen him do it," Durgin said. "When he knew we were

going to lose the claim to a good find. Rather than just walk away, he dynamited the site."

"Why didn't you stop him?" the lady asked, horrified.

Durgin turned away from her and gave the reins a halfhearted snap. "I tried, but…he knew Loveland would back him over me. It's not just important to Loveland to get the glory of a great discovery, even if he's nowhere around. It's that no one else gets any glory at all. Ever. So…Glaze denies others the glory whenever he can. However he can."

Miss Hayes went silent, her expression troubled, reproachful. She wasn't just aghast at what Glaze had done on Loveland's behalf. It was the way Durgin talked about it.

Maybe Durgin tried to stop Glaze when he destroyed fossils rather than see them go to someone else. But it felt like it had happened more than once—and that Durgin hadn't fought all that hard against it.

Old Red turned for another long look past the back of the wagon, and Mead and Wentworth marched along behind. The college boys were keeping a dozen feet between them as if the idea of walking side by side was altogether too much after putting up with each other in a hole all day.

It was hard to read Mead. He had a handsome but taciturn face, the edges of his mouth ever pulled downward in what could have been disapproval or determination or simply the grim realization that he'd just swallowed a bug.

Wentworth I would've called "nondescript" if not for the one feature that leaps out when trying to describe him: his spite. He was glaring ahead at Miss Hayes, lips curled with contempt. When he noticed my brother and I glancing back, he jerked his head to the side and pretended he was sneering at the vast, gently rolling nothingness to the west.

Old Red hadn't even been looking at him, though. He was gazing past him at the rise we'd just crested. On the other side now were the twin pits of the dig site.

He obviously couldn't believe we'd really leave them

unguarded till morning. Someone—most likely us—had a long, cold, boring night ahead.

It was something to ask Diehl and Eskaminzim about whenever they decided to show up again. Until then, all we could do was try to earn our fee by riding along looking attentive and tough. My brother's better at both than me, despite my advantage size-wise, but I tried to help him out by staying awake and resisting the urge to whistle.

After we made it back to Camp Cashew, Old Red and I occupied ourselves seeing to the horses and taking a quick tour of the tent Cherry had put up for us. "A quick tour" was actually the only kind one could make of the thing. It was a pup tent—and the runt of the litter to boot. I'd have to decide if it was my scalp or my toes I wanted to freeze that night, for if I stretched out flat on my back, one or the other was going to poke out past the canvas.

"No dreams tonight," I told Old Red as we took it in. "There's no room for 'em in there."

"Who says we'd have time for dreamin' anyway?"

"Now there's a consolation. They got us bunking in a tamale, but we'll probably hardly be in it long enough to saw half a log. Thanks, brother. You've really cheered me up with your silver lining."

"Oh, go—"

Before my brother could finish his thought (and what a very cheerful one it promised to be) three shots rang out in quick succession. They were thin, high-pitched pops, not the deeper blasts of a big rifle or even a handgun. Still—when you've got men like Vollmer and his Shoshone friend Joe skulking around, gunfire is gunfire…and if it's aimed at you or your friends, that's not good.

Old Red and I whipped out our forty-fives—we'd left the shotguns in the wagon, parked near the rope horse corral—and ran toward the sound. It seemed to be coming from the shallow gullies to the east. We hurried down the slope a bit (knowing enough not to make outlines of ourselves at the top of the bluff we were camped upon) and peered into the growing gloom below.

"Don't shoot back, boys!" Cherry called out. "It's probably just Mead missing another jackrabbit! He couldn't hit the broad side of a barn if he was inside it with one of the shotguns!"

"Mead went out hunting?" I called back. "After what happened today?"

"No! He went out guarding! But he likes to pretend he can hunt! Borrowed my twenty-two again so he could shoot more hills and rocks!"

"What's he guardin'?" Old Red said.

"Wentworth!"

And Cherry cut loose with a cackle far louder than her twenty-two. Neither Professor Durgin nor Miss Hayes deigned to shine any more light on the matter from wherever they were, so that seemed to be all the explanation we were going to get.

"Guess we'd best check it out," Old Red said.

I sighed. I was far more interested in checking out Cherry's stew. But a job's a job.

"Should I run back for the scatterguns?" I said.

"Nah. Not dark as it's gettin'. I'd already be worried about shootin' the wrong fella. No use sprayin' buckshot into the whole countryside."

I wasn't entirely convinced by this reasoning. If you spray buckshot into the whole countryside you're at least improving the odds that the whole countryside won't shoot you first. But Old Red didn't give me time to argue. He set off down the hill again, angling to our left. There was a hump of earth that way—the foot of the next hill over—that could easily hide a man or two or six. So it made sense for him to start the search there. Which didn't necessarily mean I wanted to start it with him. Yet I did. I'm loyal like that. Or stupid, take your pick.

We wound around the foot of the hill and—having remained, for the moment, unshot—continued on as it snaked its way into a deeper, darker gully beyond.

"Shit," I said, freezing in place.

"You hear somethin'?" my brother asked, stopping a couple steps ahead.

"No. I just thought of Eskaminzim…and how much he'd love to catch me out here."

I looked to my left, then to my right. There was nowhere a man could hide—just grass and a few tufts of sagebrush hardly big enough to conceal a weasel. But that was little comfort when it came to Eskaminzim. He could be hiding under my hat for all I knew. I was almost tempted to take it off and look.

"Don't worry about Eskaminzim," Old Red said. "He's got better things to do than skulk around tryin' to scare the bejesus outta you."

"I know that. But does he?"

"Oh, come on."

Old Red turned to go…then *he* froze.

"Do *you* hear something?" I asked him.

He shushed me. Which meant yes.

I tightened my grip on my gun and listened. After a couple seconds of—to my ears—silence, I heard it, too. Footsteps up ahead. Coming closer.

I looked around again but of course nothing had changed in the last twenty seconds, except perhaps to become ever so slightly darker. There was still no place to hide.

"Do we just let 'em walk up on us or what?" I whispered.

Old Red opted for "or what."

"Who goes there?" he called out.

"It's just us," someone replied.

I still couldn't see him, but I recognized the surly whine right off.

Wentworth.

"Mead—you speak up, too, if you're there," my brother said.

"I'm here," Mead replied. "Everything's fine."

I gave my brother a quizzical look.

"Sounds like two men, but one of 'em coulda been Vollmer or one of them other boys with a gun to Wentworth's back," he explained.

"What a vivid imagination you have."

I was grateful for it, though. Many's the time we'd have ended up dead without it.

Wentworth and Mead emerged from the darkness ahead. Mead had Cherry's rifle in his hands—and nothing else.

"No rabbits for the stew?" I said.

"I missed," Mead grumbled.

"And it was a deer," Wentworth added smugly. "A big one. A nice easy target."

"Better to have missed," Old Red said. "To bring down a full-grown deer with a twenty-two you'd have to hit it smack between the eyes. Otherwise you're just sendin' it runnin' off to die slow miles away."

Mead just grunted. How deer die didn't seem to be something he concerned himself with.

Old Red and I holstered our guns, and the four of us started trudging back toward camp.

"Nice of you to escort Wentworth around," I said to Mead. "That's what us fellas from the detective agency are here for, though."

Mead gave Wentworth a sidelong glower. "He was too embarrassed to ask you."

Wentworth glared back at him hatefully.

"Embarrassed about what?" Old Red asked.

"I'm not used to roughing it," Wentworth said. "And the food... it's appalling. It was actually better when that grubby little Italian Verardo was doing the cooking. How bad can you make scrambled eggs? But the swill Cherry serves us...what it does to me..."

He shuddered and put a hand to his stomach.

"Ah," I said.

That was enough conversation on *that* topic as far as I was concerned. But Old Red felt different.

"If Cherry's grub don't sit well with you, maybe you should see what Miss Hayes could whip up," he said. "Long as we gotta put up with two women out here, we may as well make the most of it, right? Or does the lady not pitch in with the chores?"

Now, my brother's not the type to make the usual assumptions about what women should or shouldn't do. If he had been, our tough old Mutter would've cured him of it with a thorough tongue lashing, and if that hadn't done the trick, one of our dearly departed sisters or our friend Diana Crowe would've finished the job. So I knew he was laying out bait. And Wentworth took it.

"Her?" he snorted. "She's not here to 'pitch in.' Not in any way that's useful. Not to us."

"Wentworth," Mead growled.

It didn't stop him.

"She's here to 'assist' Durgin. With the field labels. The grid mapping. The cataloging. Never mind that she has no experience to speak of. Or that she's doing half the things Mead and I thought we'd be doing."

"*Wentworth,*" Mead said again.

Still he went on.

"We're here to learn. She's just here to play scientist...and play house."

"Dammit, Wentworth—shut up!" Mead snapped.

Wentworth reached over and gave him a shove that sent him stumbling to the side.

"Stop telling me to shut up! I've had to put up with it all day, and I'm sick of it!"

Mead hustled around in front of Wentworth, blocking him, and the two young men practically bumped chests.

"*You're* sick of it?" Mead said. "I'm sick of *you* and your constant whining about Miss Hayes!"

"Why are you always sticking up for her? Are you hoping to get some of what Durgin is?"

"Oh, sh—" I groaned.

I knew what was coming then, and it came fast. Before the "—it" even reached my lips, Mead hauled off and slugged Wentworth across the jaw. Which was rather merciful, really, considering he still had the twenty-two in his other hand.

Wentworth's head snapped to the side, and he staggered back a couple steps but managed to stay upright.

"You arrogant, priggish son of a bitch," Wentworth snarled, rubbing his jaw with his left hand.

He clenched his right hand into a fist and moved toward Mead.

This time, Old Red and I had enough warning to do something. He jerked Mead back while I grabbed hold of Wentworth.

"Whoa there!" my brother said. "Settle down!"

"He started it!" Wentworth said, leaning around me and pointing at Mead.

I pushed him back a step.

"It doesn't matter who started it," I said. "It's finished now."

"But—!"

"It's finished," I said firmly. I drew myself up to my full height —which is not inconsiderable—and looked over my shoulder at Mead. "Right?"

Mead glared back at me a moment…then nodded.

I looked at Wentworth again, leaning in a little to emphasize the five or six inches of extra altitude I had on him.

"Right?"

Wentworth took a deep breath, then he nodded, too.

I let him go.

"Good," I said. "We got enough to watch out for around here without fighting each other."

That's when someone jumped me.

The blood-curdling cry the man let out as he sprang from the blackness told me who it was even as I fell, stunned and helpless, to the ground. He landed on top of me and pressed in hard with a knee, making it impossible to get back the breath he'd just knocked out of me.

I heard Wentworth shrieking as he ran away up the gully.

"For god's sake…" Old Red began.

"Slice. I cut your throat," Eskaminzim said into my ear. "Or stab hack cut. There goes your liver again."

"How many times are you gonna kill me today?" I wheezed.

"I don't know. It depends on how many chances you give me. And you keep giving me chances. You were so busy stopping those fools from fighting you forgot about the people who want to fight *you*."

"Noted. Now seeing as you're done killing me for the moment, could you maybe let me breathe?"

"All right. If you really want to."

The weight lifted from my back, and I rolled over, sucked in a deep breath, and let out a moan.

"Is this some kind of…game you're playing?" Mead said.

He was standing a little ways off, clutching the twenty-two uncertainly.

I pointed up at Eskaminzim looming over me with a grin on his face.

"He's the one playing it," I said. "I keep hoping he'll let me quit."

"Nah," said Eskaminzim. "It's too much fun."

"You best hurry back to camp before Wentworth gets everyone worked up about an Indian attack," Old Red told Mead.

Mead nodded reluctantly and walked off the way Wentworth had gone. When Eskaminzim followed him, Mead started walking a lot faster.

"How come you never jump my brother?" I called after Eskaminzim. "He can fight all right, too. Be a nice change of pace for you."

"Thanks," Old Red muttered.

"He's too little," Eskaminzim said without looking back. "No challenge."

"Thanks," Old Red muttered again.

"Plus, Colonel Crowe didn't tell me to," Eskaminzim added.

"Wait," I said. "What?"

But Eskaminzim just laughed and disappeared into the darkness.

SEVEN
FOOD FOR THOUGHT

OR, DINNER WITH THE SCIENTISTS GIVES US A LOT TO CHEW ON BESIDES CHERRY'S STEW

"YOU THINK Eskaminzim really keeps jumping me cuz Colonel Crowe told him to?" I asked Old Red as we plodded back up the hill toward camp.

"Yup."

"Well, why? I'd have thought if the colonel wanted anyone bushwhacked for giggles, it'd be you, given what a burr under the saddle you are to him."

"I reckon it ain't for giggles. Not for the colonel, anyhow. It's business."

"How is that? I don't see the business sense in making one of your partners fight off an Apache every time he...oh."

Suddenly I did see the business sense in it. And the business sense in having Eskaminzim and Diehl over explain their every little move to us, too. All you had to do was remember the reason he was *Colonel* Crowe to us rather than Mr. Crowe. He was a big noise in the Southern Pacific Railroad Police when we met him, but for decades before that, he'd been an Army man.

"We ain't just here for guard duty, are we?" I said. "We're here for training."

"I suspect that's the idea. To know for sure, we'll have to ask Eskaminzim and Diehl."

We didn't get a chance for that when we reached Camp Cashew, though. Diehl was still out in the dark somewhere. Eskaminzim, meanwhile, was sitting by the fire with the rest of the party, a plate of food in his lap. I didn't feel like asking why he kept handing me my ass when there were so many spare ears around to hear his answer. So I set my questions aside for another time and grabbed a plate of my own from a little folding table set out nearby.

"Sorry, boys—you shoulda got back quicker," Cherry said. "The others already polished off the champagne and caviar."

She cut loose with a cackle, then hopped up and snatched the plate away from me.

"Just kidding about the champagne," she said as she covered the plate with a hunk of bread from her Dutch oven and a ladleful of stew from the pot. "Professor Durgin runs a dry camp…so be sure to sip your whiskey where he can't see ya."

She straightened up, gave me a big wink, and thrust the plate back at me. When I took it she grabbed another and started filling it up the same way.

"Now don't tell me that's too much," she said as she forced the second plate into Old Red's hands. "You're gonna eat it all and ask for seconds. And I'll give 'em to ya. We gotta put some meat on you, Little Red. Why, you're hardly any bigger than me, and I'm more scrawny than an Arizona prairie chicken!"

She cackled again and set herself down in her spot by the fire.

My brother looked profoundly embarrassed by the attention.

"Where's *your* plate?" he said to Cherry. "We can't very well ask for seconds when someone's goin' without."

Indeed, there was no plate on the ground where the cook sat down. She stretched out her legs, her clunky old boots practically plunging into the glowing embers, and swiped a hand at Old Red.

"I been nibblin' all day. Heck, half the meat in that stew's probably got my tooth marks on it."

She brayed out another big laugh. If the woman could cook as good as she could amuse herself, I was in for quite a meal.

Old Red and I got spoons off the little table—Cherry allowed us to do this for ourselves—and sat on the ground near Eskaminzim. The scientists were spread around the fire on little folding chairs, Durgin and Miss Hayes side by side across from us, Wentworth and Mead sulking to our left and our right respectively, the flames between them.

"Howzabout Diehl?" my brother said as I tucked in. "He already get his nibbles in, too?"

"No. He's scouting near their holes," Eskaminzim said, lifting his chin at Durgin and Miss Hayes. "I'll bring him something when I'm done, and we'll stay on watch the first half of the night. You and your brother eat, sleep. I'll come for you when it's your turn."

I stopped chewing.

Eskaminzim grinned at me.

"Something wrong?" he asked innocently.

I was wondering if I'd be able to sleep at all knowing how I'd probably be awakened: with a knife at my throat and a whispered "Slice…you're dead."

"Just give us a time, and we can wake ourselves," my brother said. "We're used to it from our droverin'."

"Fine. Be ready when the moon is…" Eskaminzim scanned the sky, then jabbed his spoon at a spot past Durgin's shoulder. "…*there*."

Old Red nodded. "We'll be ready."

I got back to chewing, but I'd lost a lot of my appetite. Despite my brother's confidence, I wasn't so sure I trusted us to be up at moon-over-there o'clock…and I *really* didn't want Eskaminzim to literally catch me napping.

"This feels like the first time you've done this sort of work together," Miss Hayes said. "Is that so?"

Up to now, she and Durgin and the college boys had been eating silently, shoulders slumped, expressions pensive. But the lady's curiosity about us seemed to have perked her up a bit.

"We worked together once before," Eskaminzim said, the grin

still on his face. He jerked his head at me and Old Red. "Not that they knew it at the time."

Miss Hayes furrowed her brow.

"It's a long story," my brother muttered.

"One with a name, too," I was about to add.

This was my opportunity to do a little advertising for my sideline as a writer—one could also call it "bragging," I suppose—but Old Red went on before I could tell the lady about my regular appearances in *Smythe's Frontier Detective* (or offer to autograph the latest issue for her).

"Seems like we could say the same of you all. That it looks like the first time you worked together. That right?"

"It is," Miss Hayes said. "In fact, this is the first field expedition at all for Peter and Andrew and I."

"So how is it you three got picked for this one?"

"That's a good question," Wentworth said.

He didn't quite sneer it, but he came close.

"Wentworth and I are students of the professor's at Gulf Coast University in Galveston," Mead said quickly. He threw Wentworth a glare across the fire, warning against any more near-sneers. "And Miss Hayes is…uh…a friend of the professor's."

"An amateur enthusiast," Durgin amended awkwardly. "A very talented one. And a great supporter of the university."

Miss Hayes actually looked pained by the praise—or perhaps the resentful look Wentworth was giving her.

"Yes, well…I'm no Professor Pertwee, but I do what I can," she said. "It's been an honor to assist Professor Durgin with such a momentous discovery."

"You mean the diplo-duckius?" Old Red said.

Wentworth snorted.

"*Diplodocus,*" he said.

"Well, whatever you call it," my brother said with admirable restraint (meaning he didn't throw his stew at the little toad), "I'm curious. Why's findin' one so 'momentous'? I mean, there's so many fossils just lyin' around here we seen 'em left piled up like firewood."

"Any fossils you see like that are meaningless. Worthless," Professor Durgin said. "They tell us next to nothing on their own, removed from context. But a nearly complete specimen in one place…something we can piece together to approximate the whole. *That* is momentous."

My brother nodded slowly. "Yeah, I heard that a couple times today. That this here…" He glanced over at Wentworth. "…*diplodocus* is just about 'complete.' And I understand why that would mean somethin', tell you more. But it also felt like it's special just because it's a diplodocus. Sure seemed to mean a lot to Loveland that it is."

Durgin grimaced at the mention of Loveland.

"Yes, well…you're right," he said. "Diplodocus is much sought after."

"Yeah, but why? That's what I'm askin'."

"Diplodocus is the largest sauropod yet discovered," said Mead.

"The largest dinosaur of any kind," Wentworth threw in.

"Ahh!" Eskaminzim aimed his spoon at Durgin. "So you want it, and *he* wants it…" He waved his spoon at the north, toward Loveland's group out there in the dark somewhere. "…just because it is *big!*"

"I suppose you could put it like that," Durgin said defensively. "Pieced together and displayed for the public, it could—"

"'Displayed for the public'?" Eskaminzim repeated with a look of gleeful incredulity. "You mean you not only hunt things that are already dead so you can pull them from the earth, you want to put them back together and invite people to come stare at them?"

"Yes," Miss Hayes said. "Exactly that."

Durgin was sitting up straight on his little stool looking flushed and agitated, but the lady wasn't letting Eskaminzim's needling get to her.

"All the major natural history museums are exploring the idea," she went on calmly. "The amount of interest it could excite in the general public, the groundswell of support it could create for more research...it would be a tremendous boon to pale-ontology."

"Sounds like a great idea to me," I said. "It's one thing to read about dinosaurs. But seeing a full skeleton of one with your own two eyes—that'd give you a real sense of the thing. Be pretty amazing, really."

Eskaminzim jabbed his spoon at me now.

"You're crazy!" He laughed. He swirled the spoon in the air, waving it at everyone around the fire. "You're all crazy!" He stopped when the spoon was pointed at Cherry. "Except you. I like your stew."

Somehow he managed to get back to eating despite the huge grin stretching his lips.

"I've heard the Shoshone don't approve of digging up fossils," Miss Hayes said, still unoffended. "They think the dead should be left alone. Is that how the Apache feel, too?"

Eskaminzim shrugged.

"Depends on the Apache," he said without slowing his chewing.

"How about you, then?" Miss Hayes persisted. "You said we're crazy. Do you think what we're doing is wrong?"

"Well, I'll tell you this..."

Eskaminzim took another slurp from his spoon, then began mopping the plate with his bread. He didn't speak again until he'd popped the soggy bread into his mouth.

"My people think it is very rude to ask a direct question."

He swallowed, set down his plate and spoon, picked up the rifle lying at his side, and hopped to his feet.

"Diehl and I will be moving back and forth between the holes and the camp," he said to me and Old Red. "You should do the same when it's your turn. There is an old hole over there." He jerked his head to the Northwest. "Left over from some other dead thing that was stolen from its resting place. Watch out for it. Once a hole is a grave, it doesn't like to be empty."

And he turned and went striding away, his moccasin boots making not a sound as he disappeared into the night.

EIGHT
WHEN IT RAINS, IT POURS
OR, A STORM BLOWS IN, AND A LIFE IS SNUFFED OUT

"'ONCE A HOLE IS a grave it doesn't like to be empty'?" Wentworth said, repeating Eskaminzim's warning. "Is that some kind of threat?"

He said it quietly, lest Eskaminzim hear him from wherever he was in the dark.

"Just a little friendly advice," said Old Red.

"Doesn't sound very 'friendly' to me," said Mead.

I shrugged. "Eskaminzim has a funny idea of friendly."

Threat or not, the Apache's parting words put a damper on things for most of the folks around the fire, and Durgin, Wentworth and Mead finished their eating quickly and quietly. That left it to Miss Hayes to answer the questions about fossil hunting my brother kept throwing out. She did so cheerfully, unfazed by the gloomy mood that had once again descended upon the camp. She even told him he could borrow her tools if he wanted to give digging a try sometime—they were in a leather knapsack in the back of the wagon.

Soon after that, the party broke up, with the scientists heading off to their tents for the night. I was surprised to learn that Wentworth and Mead, like Old Red and me, were sharing a pup tent.

That one of the college boys hadn't already smothered the other in his sleep seemed a miracle.

We offered to help Cherry with the clean-up—"Just go make sure that Indian of yours doesn't scalp someone," she said, shooing us away—and checked on the horses. Then it was time to squeeze ourselves under the little canvas handkerchief that was our new home.

Not so long before, we'd end most days with a reading from the good book…meaning *The Adventures of Sherlock Holmes*. ("The *great* book" my brother would probably insist it be called.) I'd have done all the reading—out loud—for despite his overabundance of brains Old Red has a near-total lack of schooling. He's finally started catching up on his A-B-Cs thanks to the *McGuffey's Reader* our friend Diana gifted us with for Christmas. But I guess our wee patch of fabric didn't feel much like a schoolhouse, and he left his primer buried in his carpetbag this particular night. Instead he just laid back, settled his hat over his face, and took a deep breath that told me the catching of winks was about to commence.

"Brother?" I said.

Old Red took another deep breath. This one a sigh.

"Yeah?"

"Do you really think Durgin and Loveland would let things get shootin'-bad over a bunch of fossils?"

"Yup."

"Really?"

"I said 'Yup.'"

"Bu….*really*?"

"You saw them gunmen today. Vollmer and Joe and the rest of that bunch. They look like the types to shy away from shootin'?"

"No. But I'm asking about Durgin and Loveland. A couple professors. Men of science."

"Ol' Moriarity was a professor, and look what he done," Old Red said, slow and somber.

It had been nearly six months since we'd got our hands on "The Final Problem"—Dr. Watson's account of the death of

Sherlock Holmes—and my brother still couldn't speak of it without going glum.

"True," I said. "But whatever they may be, Durgin and Loveland aren't 'Napoleons of crime' like Moriarity."

"No, but they are men, and there's pride and power and position at stake. And money, too. You heard Miss Hayes. Museums wanna turn these bones into some kinda show. And the bigger the bones, the bigger the crowds, the bigger the profits, they're probably thinkin'. You mix all that together with the pure hate between Durgin and Loveland and that Glaze fella, and it almost seems like we'd be lucky if there *wasn't* any shootin'."

"Cheery thought. Thanks."

"You asked. And offerin' cheery thoughts ain't my job."

"True. If it was, we'd have starved a long time ago."

Old Red gave that a grunt—I was pretty sure under his hat he was rolling his eyes—and squirmed in deeper beneath his blanket.

"Brother?" I said.

Old Red sighed again.

"What?"

"Why are you so interested in dinosaurs? Mr. Holmes didn't care a lot for stuff like that. Remember in 'A Study in Scarlet' how he didn't even know the earth goes around the sun?"

"And he didn't care 'cuz it don't have nothin' to do with crime," my brother said. "'Course I remember."

"Well? Why all the questions about old lizards then?"

"You think I'm only interested in things Mr. Holmes was?"

"Pretty much."

"Well, maybe I'm broadenin' my horizons."

"Nah, that ain't it. Is it 'cuz you like the lady?"

"What? No! It's got nothin' to do with her. Shut up and go to sleep, will ya?"

I turned on my side and closed my eyes and said nothing. For a few seconds.

"Brother?"

Old Red didn't sigh this time. He growled.

"*What?*"

"Please don't snore."

My brother turned on his side, too—so that he was facing away from me.

"I ain't makin' no promises."

It was a good thing he didn't, too. It's a promise he would've broken, for within a minute, he was sawing logs. From giant redwoods, it seemed like. Still, I somehow managed to nod off despite the racket. It was a deep sleep, too—for a while. Then I became aware of a sound other than the steady *honk-chew* from the other side of the tent.

A low moan was building to a whistle outside—the wind picking up as it blew through the hills. Gusts began to push and pull on the canvas of the tent as if the world itself was taking deep breaths, working up to some exertion to come.

"Get up," Old Red said.

"Five more minutes," I mumbled.

"It's time, brother."

"Make that five more hours."

"All right. You stay cozy." I heard Old Red start to crawl out of the tent. "I'll let Eskaminzim get you up."

"I'm awake! I'm awake!"

Soon we were both outside, a chilly wind tugging on the brims of our hats like it wanted to snatch them away and try them on itself. Old Red had his moon timing just right, apparently, for we'd hardly been up two minutes when we heard movement in the grass, and Diehl called out softly, "Patrol coming in."

A moment later, he and Eskaminzim emerged from the darkness to join us at the edge of the camp.

"Your turn," Diehl said. "Keep your eyes and ears open—especially just east of here. Some of Loveland's men were out there again."

"'Again'?" Old Red said.

Diehl nodded. "Every once in a while they like to skulk around out there in the middle of the night. Always to the east. There's nothing there but another one of those old bone piles. We figure they're just trying to keep us jittery."

"It's not working," said Eskaminzim.

"Speak for yourself," I said.

Diehl gave me a long look as if trying to work out if he was joking or not.

"They've been gone a couple hours, so it's probably not anything you have to worry about," he said. "Just keep going back and forth between here and the dig, nice and easy. Don't get too predictable, though. Mix it up now and then in case they're back and you're being watched."

"Go around a hill instead of over it," Eskaminzim said. "Zigzag. Walk backward for a while. That kind of thing."

"We know what 'mix it up' means," Old Red said.

Eskaminzim shrugged. "I wasn't sure."

Diehl shuffled off toward one of the pup tents. "Good night."

We looked at Eskaminzim.

He just stood there staring at us.

"Aren't you going to bed?" I asked.

The Apache shrugged again. "Eventually."

"Why not now?" I said. "You must be tired."

"Not particularly."

"Oh, go on. You've earned it."

"Maybe. In a while. If I don't think of something else to do."

Eskaminzim smiled.

I didn't.

"Well...all right, then," I said. "See you later."

Old Red and I walked around him, headed north toward the dig. He turned to keep his gaze on us as we left.

After a minute, my brother glanced back at the top of the hill.

"He still just standing there staring at my back?" I asked.

"Yup." Old Red narrowed his eyes. "Although now I think he's sharpenin' his knife, too."

I groaned and put a hand to my forehead. "When will it end?"

"He's just tryin' to give you another reason to stay awake. I betcha he's fast asleep five seconds after we round the first ridge."

"Well, come on then. Let's get our asses around that ridge."

I doubled my pace into the darkness—and quickly stubbed my

toe on some invisible rock or fossil or cement block in the low brush at the bottom of the hill.

"Ow!"

"That's another way to keep yourself awake," Old Red said.

"I hear a kick in the pants can help, too. You want one?"

My brother didn't bother answering, which I took as a no. So we just carried on (me limping for a bit) around the ridge and over the next hill and so on to the dig site. Then we turned around and came back. Then we did it all over again. It made watching paint dry seem like a day at the races, but at least I didn't stub my toe again.

"Let's swing around that way this time," Old Red said, nodding to the Northwest. "You know—to mix it up."

"Sure. It'll be exciting to not-quite-see something different than the same hills we've been not-quite-seeing the past damn hour."

We ended up not-quite-seeing a *lot* of new ground, for Old Red kept pushing us so far from the established path I started thinking we were "mixing it up" with a detour to Oregon.

And I was half-right, actually. It was a detour. Just not to Portland.

"Ah!" Old Red said.

"Oh," said I.

Stretched before us was a long strip of nothingness even blacker than the rest of the night. The hole Eskaminzim had warned us about.

My brother began walking slowly along the edge, peering down into what could've been a bottomless pit for all I could tell. Then suddenly I could see it had a bottom after all—for a flash of lightning lit everything up like the flare from a photographer's flash powder.

Thunder rumbled in the west, and the nippy wind I'd been trying to ignore bore down harder on the grass and brush. And me.

I sighed.

A gullywasher was on its way, and we were going to get a washing, too.

"Wait here," Old Red said. "I'll run back for our slickers."

"Thanks."

I didn't bother keeping the sarcasm out of my voice. I was cold and tired and bored, and slicker or not, I was about to add "wet" to the list. I wanted Old Red to know who I thanked for that.

I wasn't surprised when my brother returned not just with my slicker but with a leather satchel—Miss Hayes's bag of tools. I wasn't even surprised when he dropped down into the pit and started poking around at the heap of loose dirt at the far end. No —I was just surprised I didn't shoot him.

I'd learned to tolerate—even embrace—my brother's notions about playing detective. But now he wanted to play paleontologist while I just stood around waiting to get soaked? He was lucky I have so much practice being long-suffering.

He didn't get a lot of time to work on his bone collecting, as it turned out. He tried out a hammer (giving it a surprised look as if he'd pulled a muskrat out of the bag instead of a tool) then a brush before resorting to sifting through the soil with his bare hands. But soon after that, the first raindrop splatted on the brim of my hat.

I stretched out a hand and felt another drop moisten my palm.

"Here it comes," I said.

"I'll be damned," said Old Red.

He wasn't paying any attention to the rain, though. He was looking at something he'd uncovered in the pit.

"You actually managed to find some fossils?" I asked him.

The end of the hole he was hunkered in had collapsed sometime before, leaving a slope of loose sod and rock, and he went back to burrowing into it.

"Not fossils," he said. "Boots."

"*What?*"

I hustled up the side of the trench to get a look around my brother. Despite the dim glow of dawn that was starting to light up the horizon, I couldn't see anything down in the ground until there was another flare of lightning—not so distant now to judge by the quick, loud growl of thunder that followed.

There they were, just like my brother said. Two boots, the toes pointed up toward the fading stars.

"Sweet Jesus," I said. "From the way them things are lying there, I'm pretty sure they ain't filled with dirt."

Old Red stopped digging and reached down to give the boots a tentative squeeze.

"There's somebody in 'em, all right," he said. "And I think I know who."

"Yeah?"

"Yup. They're black leather, tall, in good shape, recently polished. Pretty sure we saw 'em yesterday."

A heavy, steady rain began to fall as Old Red clawed away more clods and rock.

"Tan pants…cotton twill flared out along the thighs. Yeah. It's him. Or someone who borrowed his boots and pants, but that don't seem very damn likely."

I thought of all the people we'd seen since arriving in Wamsutter. I could recall only one in high, black boots and jodhpurs.

"The bone hunter?" I said. "Loveland's man? The fella Durgin used to work with?"

"That's the one," said Old Red. "Glaze."

The rain grew even heavier, dumping down on us like a water-fall, and the pit started turning into a pond.

"Any way to tell how he got down there?" I shouted over the roar of the downpour.

"Not from the waist down! He sure as hell didn't just fall in, though!" Old Red shouted back. "Looks like we've dug us up a murder!"

His words struck me like lightning. In fact, I almost wished it *had* been lightning. At least that would be over quick. Instead I was still alive—and, thanks to my brother, in a hell of a mess.

"'*We've* dug us up a murder'?" I roared. "'We'? 'Us'? No. It's you! Way out here in the middle of nowhere, and you manage to find a corpse? It's unbelievable! Dammit, brother—sometimes I don't think I should let you out of the house!"

"Don't get all huffy with *me*! I didn't kill him!"

"Well, who did, then?"

I took a step back from the edge of the pit and looked this way and that, as if the killer might be lounging nearby enjoying my reaction to his handiwork. But there was nothing to see but bleak, barren countryside getting doused with a downpour in the dim light of dawn.

"How should I know who did it?" Old Red said. "If there are any clues, they're under a hundred pounds of mud. And it's gettin' worse by the second."

I looked back down into the trench and saw that he was right. Just as quickly as he'd dug up a murder, Mother Nature was burying it again.

The rain had quickly turned the dirt in the pit into sludge, and the little landslide my brother had been digging through was now an oozing blob that was reswallowing the legs and boots he'd uncovered.

Old Red grabbed the body by the booted ankles and began tugging. It didn't budge.

"Get your ass down here and help me pull him out!" my brother shouted.

"Why?" I shouted back. "There's no rush—the man's dead! We can get him out with a rope when we've got a horse to put him on! Hell, you and me probably couldn't get all that dead weight out of that hole *without* a horse! I'm not even sure you'll be able to get out yourself if you don't do it quick!"

Old Red let go of the boots and took in the state of the trench. Not only were the sides going gloppy, there was now more than an inch of standing water.

Old Red shook his head and muttered something that looked like "Damn." (It was impossible to hear it with the rain pounding down on my Stetson like hail on a tin roof.)

He had to face it. The impossible had happened.

I was right.

He pulled Miss Hayes's knapsack from the muck—it came free with a moist, sucking *gloop*—and lifted it up to me. Then he raised his right hand.

I set aside the bag, grabbed hold of my brother and—with help from a little scrambling and clawing at the mud on my brother's part—managed to drag him out of the hole. He stood up with a long smear of muck down the front of his slicker, but the stain wouldn't last long the way the rain was beating on it.

He picked up the knapsack and began tramping back toward camp.

"We better hope we find Professor Durgin snuggled up snoozing in his tent," I said as I tramped after him. "Be just our luck if he's not. He's what? Our seventh client? Eighth? And we work for him one day before we dig up a man he murdered?"

"We don't know Durgin killed him," Old Red said.

"I bet he didn't! But that ain't gonna matter, is it? You know folks'll assume he did."

"Or they'll think—"

"I know, I know! Don't even say it! I'm too pissed we're in this position…again! You and your goddamn detectiving…"

My brother wisely remained silent after that. That grave behind us was plenty big enough for more bodies. I could always turn around and toss him back in with Glaze.

Yes, a lot of people were going to assume Durgin had killed the man. But why should he when he had hired guns to do his dirty work for him?

Which was why some people were surely going to think *we'd* done it.

NINE
RAW DIEHL

OR, WE BREAK THE NEWS TO OUR NEW COLLEAGUE, AND HIS REACTION NEARLY BREAKS MY BROTHER

THE DELUGE EASED up within a few minutes, and by the time we reached Camp Cashew it no longer felt like someone was upending a bucket over my head every second. The sun was barely over the horizon, but to my surprise, the wagon was already gone. The scientists were gone, too, as were Eskaminzim and Diehl. Only Cherry was still there—trying to go back to sleep to judge by her groggy expression when she poked her from her tent in answer to my "Anyone here?"

"Nobody who counts," she said, her words sleepy-slurred.

"Where are the others?" Old Red asked. "They ain't actually trying to dig in this weather, are they?"

"No. They're trying to *protect* the dig. When the rain started, Durgin came flying out of his tent like a bat out of hell, yelling for Mead and Wentworth. They loaded up the wagon with tarps and a pump and went charging off. Well…as much as that old nag they use can 'charge.'"

"They were gonna cover up the holes they been workin' on?" Old Red guessed. "So the rain don't flood 'em or wash away the matrix?"

Cherry woke up enough to grunt out a chuckle.

"You're starting to sound like a professor yourself, Little Red," she said. "Yeah—that was the general idea."

"All right. We'll head that way in a minute. You seen anyone from Loveland's—?"

Before Old Red could finish his question, Cherry's head withdrew back into her tent like the woman was a big, canvas-backed turtle shrinking into its shell.

"Uhh…Cherry?" my brother said.

"I'll make coffee in a minute," she said sleepily. "Once it stops running."

Old Red and I looked at each other.

It had stopped raining two minutes before.

"When you do come out," Old Red said to the tent, "you oughta keep your twenty-two handy. We…think somethin' odd's goin' on."

We heard a muffled mutter in return—perhaps "Always something odd with this bunch" mumbled into a pillow. And that was the end of the conversation.

Old Red jerked his head toward the west end of camp, where the horses were kept, and off we went.

"I don't think she's seen any of Loveland's men, if that's what you was gonna ask," I said. "I don't think she's seen much this morning other than the insides of her eyelids. Can't blame her either. If I could've stayed under a blanket today, I sure as hell would've."

Apparently my brother didn't think that worthy of a reply, for he made none.

"Why didn't you tell Cherry about Glaze?" I went on. Then I threw out a notion that had occurred to me on our long slog back to Camp Cashew. "You thinking maybe we should just sit on that? He's buried again by now, and there's no reason anyone else would go to that pit. If we was to keep our mouths shut—"

Old Red tried to come to a sudden stop. It didn't quite work in all that fresh mud, and he skidded a bit as he spun around to shoot me a glare.

"You sayin' we should ignore a murder?"

"What? I am shocked and appalled that you would think me so low."

And so stupid, I didn't add.

Yes, I'd considered—for about two seconds—the advantages of letting someone else discover Glaze's body. Perhaps some lucky paleontologist a billion years from now. An intact human still in his boots would be quite the find. And we'd be long dead and past blaming for putting him in the ground to be found. But—

"The murderer's probably in among us," I said, lowering my voice even though Cherry wasn't in a condition to listen to anything but her own snores. "And who's to say he's done murdering? I'm not gonna stand around whistling Dixie waiting for you or me to end up in a pit next. Plus—assuming and *praying* Durgin's not the killer—it's our job to figure out what happened. We're here to protect the expedition, and now we got more to protect it from. Namely our employer getting strung up for murder."

"Oh. All right, then."

That was all Old Red said before continuing on toward the horses.

I guess on top of digging up a body, he was finding me being right so often in one morning a tad overwhelming.

"What I was going to say before I was so rudely interrupted," I said, "was *if* we don't say anything about Glaze now we could snoop around for the killer without him knowing we was onto him."

My brother just grunted.

"Then again," I went on, "*if* someone finds the body in the meantime and can place us out in that direction this morning, it's gonna look all the worse for us."

My brother gave me another grunt.

"But then again," I said, "even *if* someone was to look down in that pit all they'd see the next couple days would be a nice new swimming hole. So we've probably got us a little time."

Old Red threw me a sidelong glance. "You always got so many ifs bouncin' around your skull?"

I shrugged. "I try to consider all the angles."

My brother grunted yet again. This time skeptically.

"Well," he said, "I reckon when we get out to the dig, the first thing Durgin and Diehl both are gonna say is 'Where the hell have you been?' And it won't do to play games with our answer when there's a killer skulkin' around, and some folks might think it's us."

We'd reached the rope corral for the horses by then, and Old Red paused before picking out his mount.

"Interestin' thought, though," he said. "Maybe we'll try it the next time we find a body."

I suppose that was pretty generous of him, approving of my idea and all, but it didn't lift my spirits much. I was too busy thinking *The next time...?*

We spent the next quarter hour revisiting fond memories of cattle drives with a rousing round of Catch and Saddle the Horse in the Mud. (That's all sarcasm, by the way. The only thing I miss about cattle drives is...is...I'll have to get back to you on that.) As we rode away from Camp Cashew, I couldn't help but notice Cherry wasn't out by the fire making coffee. If we were lucky, maybe she'd wake up and get around to it before bedtime.

Even with the hills still mucky-slick it didn't take us long to get out to the dig site on horseback. We found the wagon parked in the same spot it had been in the day before, but the scientists weren't down in their trenches again. Instead the pits had been covered with tarps, with a hose run down into one. Wentworth was working the hand pump the hose was attached to, and muddy water was spewing out in nasty brown coughs. Mead stood near him, waiting for his turn at the pump with obvious distaste. He was going to have it easy compared to some, though: Durgin and Miss Hayes were kneeling by the other hole with buckets at their sides, and it sure looked like they were getting set to slide in and start bailing.

Eskaminzim was off a little ways atop his horse, watching the already mud-caked scientists with a sort of bewildered amusement.

"Where have you been?" he asked as we rode up.

So my brother had been right about the inevitable question. Just not who'd ask it first.

"We got sidetracked," Old Red said. "Where's Diehl?"

"Out looking for you." Eskaminzim leaned toward us and lowered his voice—though it was still plenty loud enough for Durgin and the others to hear. "Or so he says. You're all just trying to stay away so you don't get asked to help slop out mud, right?"

"There's a bit more to it than that," my brother said.

"Though that's not a bad idea," I added. "How come no one's asked you to help?"

Eskaminzim laughed at the very thought of him bailing out a hole in the ground. Or anyone having enough nerve to ask him to do it.

"So there it is," Miss Hayes said. She was looking at the knapsack Old Red had slung from his saddle horn—the tool bag he'd borrowed in the night. "I noticed it wasn't in the wagon this morning."

"What were you doing with that?" Durgin asked.

My brother steered his horse over to the buckboard and leaned down to put the bag back in the bed.

"Diggin'. Found somethin', too," he said. "Pardon me."

He pulled his forty-five from its holster, pointed it skyward, and fired off two rounds.

The horses whinnied and flinched. Some of the scientists, too.

"What the hell—?" Mead blurted.

Wentworth slapped his hands over his ears.

"What are you doing?" said Durgin.

"Callin' in Diehl. There's something we all need to discuss."

"What is it?" said Miss Hayes.

"You'll have to pardon me, Miss, but I'd rather wait till Diehl gets here to say."

"Really, Mr. Amling...uh...major. We're very busy here, as you can see," Durgin said. "Is this melodrama necessary?"

"Well, I don't know about the melodrama...cuz I got no idea what that is," Old Red said. "But yes. This is necessary."

The scientists looked at each other, Durgin and Mead clearly annoyed, Miss Hayes intrigued, Wentworth (as usual) miserable.

Eskaminzim, meanwhile, turned his appaloosa so he was facing Old Red. He seemed to be anticipating something that would shock and upset the others—which amused him no end.

He didn't have to wait long for the show. Diehl crested the hill due east of us, and soon he was trotting up on the dun mare he favored. Eskaminzim only had a Winchester, not a handgun, so Diehl knew it wasn't the Apache who'd done the shooting. He looked back and forth between me and Old Red a moment, finally settling on my brother, who was obviously (for once) more eager to talk than me.

"Where the hell have you been?" Diehl said.

If Old Red ever loses interest in detecting he could earn a living as a sideshow fortune teller. He wouldn't even need a crystal ball.

"Otto and me took Eskaminzim's advice last night," he said. "Didn't stick to the trail back and forth from here to camp. Paid a call on that old hole he warned us about, in fact."

"With my tools?" Miss Hayes asked.

Old Red looked over at her and tugged at the brim of his hat. "Indeed, Miss—and I thank you for the loan. I found myself quite taken with y'all's methods yesterday and thought I'd steal a minute to try 'em when you could best spare your hammers and brushes and what all."

Diehl cocked his head and peered at Old Red as if he suspected my brother was some kind of strange mirage. "You 'stole a minute' in the middle of the night—with rounds to make and Loveland's guns sneaking around and a storm blowing in—so you could practice digging for fossils?"

"Well, dawn was coming on by then, but yeah. That's pretty much it. I wasn't really looking for fossils, though. I wasn't looking for anything in particular. I was just…tryin' it on for size. But the thing is—I did find something in that pit."

Old Red paused, perhaps giving the killer a chance to say, "The body I tried to hide?"

The killer did not oblige.

"There's a dead fella over there," Old Red went on. "And I'm pretty sure it's Loveland's man Glaze."

"*What?*" said Diehl.

"*What?*" said Durgin.

"*What?*" said Miss Hayes.

"*What?*" said Mead.

"Oh my god oh my god oh my god!" said Wentworth.

"I told you to stay away from that hole!" said Eskaminzim. Laughing.

"Anybody got any ideas as to how he got there?" Old Red said over the hubbub.

Diehl held up a hand. "Hold on. What do you mean you're 'pretty sure' it's Glaze?"

"All I got uncovered of him 'fore the rain kicked in was his boots and trousers. We'll have to dig him out all the way to be certain."

"So he was buried in the pit?" Miss Hayes asked. "Not just... lying there?"

"That's right."

The lady turned to Durgin. "The side of the trench must've collapsed on him. But what would he have been looking for? You said that site was played out. A bust. And why try to work it alone in the middle of the night?"

Durgin shook his head. "I don't know. I don't understand it."

"Y'all ain't got the right picture here," Old Red said. "This don't look like no accident."

"Oh my god, oh my god, oh my god," Wentworth said again. "It was Indians, wasn't it?"

It was my brother's turn to blurt out a "*What?*" Which he followed with a firm "No."

"Oh, I don't know," said Eskaminzim, grinning. "I like that idea."

Diehl shot the Apache a *That's not helping* glower, then looked at Old Red again.

"You could tell Glaze was murdered from his boots and pants?" he said.

"I could tell it was likely, yeah."

"So you saw wounds? He was shot? Stabbed?"

My brother shook his head. "Naw, I didn't see nothin' like that."

Diehl clamped his mouth tight. Teeth-gritting tight.

"Mr. Amlingmajor, there's something you need to understand before you make any rash claims," Durgin said. He pointed at the nearest of the canvas-covered trenches. "The sides of these pits do collapse. It's something we have to be very careful about. I've never heard of anyone getting buried and suffocated, but I've had close calls myself. So has Glaze, for that matter. Several times. The safest assumption is that his luck ran out, and there was no one there to help him."

"Ain't no such thing as a safe assumption," Old Red said.

"It seems to me," Diehl said slowly, "that *you're* the one making an assumption, Amlingmeyer."

Perhaps he threw in the name just to let Durgin know he was getting it wrong. Or maybe it was to show he wasn't on a first-name basis with my brother—and didn't care to be.

"The professor's right," Diehl went on. "We're probably looking at a simple, tragic mishap. There's no need to turn it into a murder." He steered a little of his scorn my way. "Even if that would make for a more exciting story."

I've seen Old Red fume, of course. I've seen smolder. I've seen him simmer and seethe. A lot. But outright explosions—those are more rare. Thank god. They're not pretty. But it sure looked like we were about to get one from the way my brother's fists clenched and face darkened.

"The toes of his boots were pointed up," he grated out. "And they weren't at the wall of the pit. His head was."

All went quiet for a moment as what he'd said sank in. I could see everyone trying to picture it and work out what it meant—other than that, my brother was crazy, perhaps.

Miss Hayes saw what he was saying quickest.

"If he was digging when the pit fell in on him," she said, "why would he have been lying there on his back?"

Old Red was still fuming, smoldering, simmering, and seething, but he gave the lady a grateful nod.

"Exactly," he said. "Even if all that dirt comin' down had knocked him back on his a—onto his hindquarters, his head would've ended up toward the middle of the pit, not flush with the side. Him lyin' where he was, face up...well...I'm *not* makin' any assumptions, but I sure as heck call that suspicious."

The more my brother spoke, the more Diehl's shoulders and head slumped. Eskaminzim noticed—and seemed to love it.

"You know what you need to do. Go do it," the Apache said. He gave Diehl a smug smile. "I'll stay on guard here."

Diehl shot him a glare, then heaved one of the deepest sighs I've ever seen—one loaded not just with regret for the choices that had brought him there but dread for what lay ahead.

"All right," he said, turning to Old Red. "Let's haul out that body and see who's right."

TEN
HOUSE OF BONES (PART ONE)
OR, WE ENCOUNTER A MACABRE SIGHT ON OUR WAY BACK TO THE MACABRE SITE

IT WAS DECIDED that we would take the wagon with us—the body had to go *somewhere* after we dug it out—but Durgin declined when Old Red asked if we could have the pump as well. The pit was probably going to be knee-deep with water and clearing that out first would make the nasty job ahead of us a wee bit easier. The zillion-year-old dead took priority over the new, though: The professor wanted *his* pits emptied out first. Maybe later, if we still really, really, really needed it, we could come back and ask for it again.

I noticed Miss Hayes giving Durgin a dubious look as he told us this, but she didn't try to change his mind.

I was voted driver by Old Red and Diehl—I think they both wanted the freedom to ride this way or that to point out something the other had overlooked or misconstrued—so I hitched my horse to the back of the buckboard and climbed up in front. With a snap of the reins, we were off...very, very slowly. The water-logged soil sucked away any momentum I could've built up (which wouldn't have been much anyway), and I had to steer clear of the deepest bogs and steepest hills.

As we rounded one of these last, we came upon an eerie sight.

Off to our left, nestled in a dip in the foothills, was what looked at first like a shack made out of sun-bleached driftwood. A longer look, however, revealed the "wood" to be long, cracked bones.

It was the hut made of fossils Miss Hayes had told us about the day before. Appropriately enough for a building made from the dead, it was the size and shape of your average mausoleum. It looked like a cozy place to settle in...if you were a witch or a ghost.

"Anyone actually live in that thing?" Old Red asked Diehl.

"Not anymore. I think some shepherds threw it together ten, fifteen years ago. Or maybe it was supposed to be a ranch line shack for an outfit that's long gone. Cowboys will do some pretty strange things when they're bored."

Diehl gave my brother a blank, bland look, waiting to see if he'd notice the needling.

Old Red let the dig slide on by like the little house of bones—though I could tell from the way his mustache puckered that he was biting back a reply in kind.

Not long after that, the three of us were lined up side by side looking down into the ground. As we'd feared, there was standing water at the bottom of the pit—about a foot of it, it looked like. Nothing was visible of the body but two little black bumps poking up from the dark brown water: the toes of the dead man's boots.

"There's someone down there, all right," Diehl sighed.

"You thought maybe we made it all up?" Old Red said.

"No," said Diehl. "Not all of it."

He started toward the end of the trench, and my brother went with him.

"Well, damn," Diehl said, staring first at the big heap of soaked dirt where the pit had collapsed, then at the ground all around us.

"Rain washed away any sign there'd be to find," Old Red said, announcing to Diehl that he saw exactly what the other man did. "No footprints and no way to tell what brought all that dirt down on top of the body."

"Yeah. Whatever there is to learn here, we're gonna learn it from him."

Diehl nodded at the bottom of the pit.

He and Old Red looked at each other, then they both turned to look at me.

I said something I won't bother recording here, as the publisher would just take it out anyway, indecency laws being what they are. Suffice it to say there can be a price to pay for being the tallest and most strapping man around. Especially when someone has to slide into a five-foot-deep slime hole and wrench a dead fellow's legs up out of the sludge.

It was also up to me to tie the rope around the ankles and, once Diehl's horse was pulling, oversee to make sure we didn't yank the man in half. When the first ten seconds of tugging didn't do the trick, I grabbed hold and helped with more muscle of my own. There was an inch or two of slow movement, then with a mighty *shlorp* the suction broke, and the whole body busted free. It came shooting out fast after that—so fast that the man's right arm caught me across the shins and swept me off my feet. The only silver lining as I splatted flat into the gloop was that at least I didn't fall on the corpse since it was already shooting away to the other end of the trench.

"Stop!" Old Red shouted to Diehl, who was leading the horse. "Stop!"

I expected his next words to be "You all right?" called down to me.

Instead he said, "We gotta take this next part slow so we don't bang up the body any more than it already is. Otto—get over here and grab the head and shoulders when the feet start comin' up the side."

The glamorous life of a detective. I'd have more fun sweeping up after the elephants in a circus parade.

A moment later, I was bent over cradling a dead man's head. As soon as it came out of the water, I could see that—surprisingly, given my brother's extremely limited wardrobe—Old Red's eye for fashion was sharp indeed. Those were Glaze's boots and jodhpurs, for here was Glaze in them. His eyes were half-lidded in that sleepy look some of the dead wear, and as the body went up the side of the pit mud and dirty water flowed from his open mouth. I couldn't see the back of his head yet, but it was clear that's where the wounds were that had killed him, for the scalp hung free in ragged flaps in two spots. (See the previous paragraph for my feelings upon witnessing all this.)

Once the body was fully free of the pit, I started to haul myself out as well.

"Hold on," Old Red said. "You ain't done yet."

"What do you mean?"

"Somebody needs to search where Glaze was layin'. Gotta see if whatever killed him got buried with him. Or if anything came outta his pockets. And...well..."

I looked down at my mud-covered hands—and, beyond them, the mud-covered rest of me.

"It may as well be me?" I said.

"No need for all of us to get mucked up."

Diehl was kneeling by Glaze now, and he rolled him over to get a look at the gashes on the back of his head. Old Red turned away from me and leaned in over the corpse, too.

This was something I wouldn't mind missing, even if it did mean I was going to be rooting around in mud like a pig after truffles.

I started slogging my way back to the other end of the trench.

"Well, that's obvious enough," Diehl said. "He was whacked in the back of the head. Several times."

"My gosh, Diehl...how do you think a thing like that coulda happened *by accident*?" Old Red said with sarcasm so thick it would put a feather bed to shame. "Or do you think maybe he whacked himself in the back of the head?"

"'Oh, govern your temper,'" Diehl said. "'For music the sweetest was never so sweet, nor half so divine...'"

He was either reciting poetry again or having a stroke. I looked back to see if he was frothing at the mouth or having a conniption, but he was still just kneeling there beside my brother and the body.

"'…as a heart kept in tune,'" he went on, "'which the moment thou greetest breathes harmony dearer than notes can combine.'"

He went quiet in a way that told us the performance was finished. Neither of us applauded.

"And that means?" Old Red said.

"Don't be pissy. I concede it: You were right," he said. "It's Glaze, and he was murdered."

"Ah," I said. "And you think telling Gustav Amlingmeyer 'Don't be pissy' isn't going to make him even pissier?"

But Old Red flapped a hand at me. "I can govern my temper and keep my heart in tune or whatever. What's important is figurin' out what happened here." He turned to Diehl and nodded down at the body. "Shall we get back to it?"

"Let's."

Diehl and my brother began examining Glaze's wounds again. Which was my cue to turn and get going in the opposite direction again.

When I reached the spot we'd hauled Glaze from, I bent down and plunged my hands into the water—and the gunk beneath it. There was really only one way I could figure to search such stuff, so that's what I commenced to doing: squeezing the gloppy sod in big handfuls and, feeling nothing but muck, moving on to repeat the process a few inches off.

"You see them bits there?" my brother asked Diehl. "That from his skull, you think?"

"Maybe. You can see the skull's cracked there and there. It's not shattered, though. Not pulverized, like whatever that is."

There was a pause, then Diehl spoke again.

"They are hard like bone."

"More like pebbles, I'd say."

Apparently Old Red and Diehl were actually touching the mysterious bits they'd discovered in Glaze's lacerations. It made me grateful to be plunging my hands into something as relatively wholesome as mud.

"Don't quite smell right, does he?" I heard my brother say.

"He's dead. He's not going to smell like lilacs," said Diehl.

"It ain't that. It's…"

There was the sound of a deep breath being sucked in through a big nose.

"Aw, he was down in that slime too long," Old Red said. "But I'd swear there was *something* off about him."

"Well, he'll get a nice bath from the undertaker soon enough."

A pause followed of the sort I knew well: My brother was glaring at Diehl in irritation and disappointment.

He'd found one more person in the world who wasn't as brilliant as him. He was in for a lifetime of disappointment.

"You findin' anything over there?" Old Red called to me.

"Absolutely," I said. "A renewed bewilderment that you and I could possibly be blood kin. I'm knee-deep in it, in fact."

"That's *his* fancy-ass way of sayin' no," Old Red explained to Diehl.

"So I assumed."

They went back to pawing at the body for a while, pointing out rips and abrasions on Glaze's collar and coat that indicated he'd been hit across the back of the neck and shoulders, as well.

He'd been beaten to death. Struck from behind and pummeled with half a dozen more blows to ensure the job was done.

"Well, that's a relief," I heard Diehl say.

"Yeah?" said Old Red.

"If Eskaminzim had killed him, there'd just be a slash across the neck."

"Or the liver would be ripped out," I added, wrist-deep in goo again. "Eskaminzim mentioned that approach when he was practicing on me."

"Hold on," my brother said. "You ain't just jokin'? You and Eskaminzim weren't together all night?"

"We were rarely together at all. We can cover a lot more ground split up. Plus Eskaminzim would rather work without me around anyway. I cramp his style."

"It his style to kill a man and not tell you about it?"

"Possibly, depending on the circumstances. He wouldn't have any reason to kill Glaze, though. Not unprovoked."

"Threats ain't provokin' enough?"

"No. You get used to being threatened in this line of work."

"I have so much to look forward to," I said.

I squeezed two more handfuls of squishy nothing.

"You spot anyone leaving camp last night?" Old Red asked Diehl.

"No. But there were plenty of long stretches where I didn't have the camp in sight. I didn't really think they'd mess with Durgin and his group at night. I was more concerned with the dig."

"The college boys went off together for a while," I pointed out.

My left hand closed around something solid in the slop, and I pulled out a vital clue: a rock. A boring, smooth, unstained, cookie-sized one of exactly the sort one would expect to find when digging around in the Wyoming soil. It wasn't big enough to brain a chipmunk. I tossed it over my shoulder and plunged my hands back into the sludge.

"Wentworth and Mead wasn't gone near long enough to walk all the way over here, beat Glaze to death, bury him, and walk back," Old Red said. "And you're gonna tell me they was so terrified by bein' threatened they'd work up the nerve to sneak away and kill a man? And how would they have known Glaze would be out here to kill? Speakin' of which, why was Glaze away from his own camp in the first place? If he was lookin' for something in the pit, why wait till now and why do it at night? If he was comin' over to fool with Durgin, why didn't he have Vollmer or Joe or one of them other gunmen with him?"

"You ask good questions, brother. And this much I can tell you for sure." I straightened up and turned to face Old Red and Diehl again. "There ain't no answers down here. So can I please get out of this damn dirty hole now?"

Old Red rolled his eyes—but waved for me to climb out.

"Well, I must admit," said Diehl. "It's another relief hearing you two talking like this."

"How do you mean?" I asked.

I put my hands on the side of the trench, hopped up, and started squirming my way back to solid ground. Which wasn't very solid, of course. So immediately, much of it was smearing itself across the front of my coat.

"Thanks...for...the...help...brother," I said as I struggled to kick up a leg and smear that, as well.

Old Red started toward me reluctantly. "You ain't gonna pull me in, are ya?"

"Not...on purpose...though...I should."

My brother grabbed hold of my right arm and hauled me up enough for me to get some purchase. With a little more wriggling, I managed to swing both legs up over the side, and a moment later I was back on my feet again.

"And thank you for *your* help," I said to Diehl as I caught my breath.

He hadn't moved from the other end of the trench. He was still bent over Glaze—going through his pockets now.

"You didn't answer Otto's question...though I know what you meant," Old Red said to him. He glanced over at me. "He'd been wonderin' if *we* done it."

"Killed Glaze...and then went and told everyone exactly where the body was?" I said.

My brother shrugged. "Tryin' to throw suspicion elsewheres maybe...?"

"Heck of a stupid plan."

"Yup." Old Red turned back to Diehl. "Glad you decided it was too stupid, even for us."

Diehl pulled a small wad of money from an inside pocket in Glaze's filth-covered coat, counted it, then stuffed it back where he'd found it. "Did Sherlock Holmes ever have anything to say about coincidences?"

"Nothing we come across," said Old Red. "I can guess what he would've thought of 'em...though I *know* he hated guessin'."

"'A 'coincidence' is just an explanation waiting to happen,'" Diehl said as if reciting another line from his favorite poet. He gave us a tight smile. "That's what Holmes would've said. Or something like it. I've read a few of Dr. Watson's stories, too, you know."

"The coincidence here being Gustav hopping into a random hole in the plains and finding a dead man who'd threatened us the day before?" I said.

Diehl held a hand out toward me. "Very good. You're ready to be a state's attorney. It's a good thing I *do* believe in coincidences. They don't."

"It wasn't no random hole," Old Red grumbled. "It means somethin'." He cocked his head and gave Diehl an approving nod. "'A coincidence is just an explanation waitin' to happen,' huh? That *does* sound like Mr. Holmes. I like it."

"I can have *you* say it in *my* next story," I told him. "Assuming I'm still alive to write it after the trial."

My brother swiped a hand at me. "Ain't gonna be us on trial. We'll figure it out."

Diehl buttoned Glaze's coat and stood up.

"How?" he said.

"'There is nothin' more deceptive than an obvious fact,'" Old Red said. "*That* Mr. Holmes did say. And the 'obvious fact' here—the one we'll get stuck on if we think like state's attorneys—is that someone from our camp killed Glaze cuz of the feud with Professor Durgin. But what if that ain't true at all? There's a whole other bunch of people out here who've been havin' more dealin's with Glaze than us. How do we know none of them had a reason to kill him?"

Diehl nodded slowly. "That is an excellent point. Now *you're* thinking like a defense attorney. Spread the doubt around, and there'll be less certainty to stick to any of us."

My brother frowned. "I ain't tryin' to spread doubt around. I don't want any doubt at all. I want data. And it's obvious where we need to go to get it."

"You want us to go see Loveland?" I said. "And those nasty

SOBs he's got working for him?"

"Gotta go where the data is," Old Red said. "And we got a damn good excuse to go there, don't we?"

"Oh?" said Diehl.

My brother just pointed at Diehl's feet—and the body lying beside them.

"Oh," said Diehl.

We had a corpse to deliver to Loveland's camp.

We just had to hope Loveland's men wouldn't make three more when we got there.

ELEVEN
THE DELIVERY

OR, WE PAY A CALL ON LOVELAND, AND CALLS FOR US TO PAY (DEARLY)

SOON WE LEARNED that it would actually be *four* new corpses we had to worry about Loveland's men making: Once we managed to get Glaze's slimy body loaded onto the buckboard, Diehl announced that he was off to collect Eskaminzim to join us for the ride into Loveland's camp.

"They're not going to believe a word we say," Diehl said. "But at least with four of us there to say it they'll be a little less inclined to act on it."

"Why don't you go back to town to get Hoop, too, then?" I said. "And maybe the Tenth Cavalry while you're at it. I don't mind waiting a week or two for them to get here."

Needless to say, Diehl did not take my suggestion. When he returned with Eskaminzim, though, it *was* with news of reinforcements. Of a sort. Durgin and Miss Hayes were insisting on coming along as well—Durgin because he felt it was his responsibility, Miss Hayes because (in her words, apparently) "someone's got to keep the conversation rational."

"We shouldn't put the lady in danger like that," Old Red said.

"I think the lady assumes that with a woman present, there *is* less danger," said Diehl. "And I'm inclined to agree in this case. Plus, Durgin's the boss, and she talked him into it somehow."

"You didn't hear what she said to him?"

Diehl shook his head. "They whispered about it a bit. Then it was settled."

"Feh," said Old Red.

It didn't look settled with *him*. He went along with it, though.

So soon—once we swung back to the dig to pick up the professor and the lady—we were up to *six* potential corpses. Not surprisingly, Mead and Wentworth didn't volunteer to get the tally up to eight. They just kept on pumping water and averting their eyes from the wagon bed. Durgin did take a look in—and immediately called for a tarp to spare Miss Hayes the same sight.

Once Glaze was under his canvas shroud, we started off. Durgin and Miss Hayes were side by side in the driver's seat while Diehl rode to the left, my brother and I to the right, and Eskaminzim behind. Befitting a makeshift funeral procession, there was a respectful silence for a time (minus the customary soft weeping of the bereaved). But after we'd been moving ten minutes or so, down one muddy slope and up another, Old Red could rein himself in no further.

"This Glaze," he said with a nod back at the wagon bed. "What kinda man was he?"

"I know you didn't see much of him yesterday, but you got the flavor," Durgin said. "He was always a hard man. And bitter."

"What he have to be bitter about?"

"Me, mostly. Or so it often seemed. He knew dinosaurs well enough, and he was an excellent fossil hunter. But that was the result of reading and listening and natural skill. He had no degree. No pedigree, as it were. He resented that Professor Loveland put me in charge. Trusted me more. And then—when we clashed over his unscrupulous methods—I think his resentment turned to hatred."

"Uneducated, huh? A talented amateur the supposed professionals are reluctant to trust. Well, he may have been an unpleasant, 'unscrupulous' cuss…" Old Red leaned forward in his saddle to look past the wagon at Diehl. "But maybe I can sympathize a little."

Diehl pretended to be extremely interested in something very far away.

"Any idea why he might've been pokin' around in that hole? Or anywhere nearby? At night?" Old Red asked Durgin.

The professor shook his head. "None. We came across the pit when we were working in the area last year. He had all summer to look it over. It wouldn't make any sense for him to sneak back there now. It was empty. Played out."

"You know who dug it?"

"No. I'd call it an inelegant excavation, though. And the fact that it was left unfilled afterward for anyone to fall into...? I'd guess it was one of the less-experienced expeditions of the sort you'll see stumbling around out here soon enough. This part of Wyoming's considered prime fossil-hunting territory—"

"Thanks to you," Miss Hayes threw in.

Durgin thanked her with a little nod, but his expression was rueful.

"And Glaze," he said. He looked back over at my brother and me. "By mid-June, there'll probably be half a dozen active digs in this county alone."

"Oh? You spot any of them others yet?" Old Red asked. "Close enough maybe to bump up against Glaze?"

It was Diehl who provided the answer this time.

"I know what you're thinking, but no. It's just Professor Durgin's group and Loveland's out here right now. No other pale-ontologists."

"No one else to blame," Eskaminzim added from his spot riding drag.

"So no jumpy ranchers or homesteaders?" my brother pressed. "No rustlers or robbers? Wyoming's known for 'em. They say the Hole-in-the-Wall's so jam-packed with gangs they have to stack 'em up like cordwood."

Diehl swept an arm out before him, palm up. "You see any ranches or homesteads or rustlers or robbers?"

At first Old Red seemed set to ignore Diehl's rhetorical question. But then he glanced ahead and sat up straight in his saddle.

There *was* something to see out there: a gray-white smudge in the midst of a sea of green grass. As we drew closer, I could make out a jumble of individual shapes within the dull, blobby mass. It was a pile of something.

Bones.

"It's like that knocked-over heap we spotted yesterday when we were first coming to Camp Cashew," I said to my brother.

Old Red looked over his shoulder. The other bone pile was back there, perhaps a mile due south, with Durgin's dig and camp in between.

"Cairns of that sort aren't uncommon in this area," said Durgin. "We think they were put up by the Shoshone."

"Nope!" said Eskaminzim.

Durgin stiffened, startled.

"Well...or Basque sheepherders, perhaps," he said. "That's another theory. That they're some kind of territory markers."

Old Red nodded slowly. "That'd make sense."

He started to face forward again but froze halfway through his turn.

"Aha," he said.

"All the better to have our arrival announced," said Diehl. "We don't want to surprise anybody."

I looked back and forth between them in confusion.

"We been spotted," my brother explained. "Rider over thataway."

I followed his gaze to the west but saw only hills and a cloudy sky.

"He's gone now," Old Red said. "Took off fast."

"If you're not going to use your eyes, can I have them?" Eskaminzim asked me. "They'd look good on a string of beads."

"I like 'em where they are," I said.

"Was it one of Loveland's thugs?" Miss Hayes asked Old Red. He nodded.

"It was the Shoshone!" said Eskaminzim. "I wish we *did* want to surprise them."

He smiled wistfully, apparently imagining what he'd do to the Shoshone to maintain the element of surprise.

He wouldn't have had much time to do it, for a couple minutes later Joe the Shoshone returned to watch us from another ridge, this time with a man in a gray hat—Vollmer—beside him. Vollmer didn't stick around long, wheeling his horse and galloping off to the north. The Shoshone stayed behind, observing our passing with an utter stillness that seemed to be a perverse dare.

You don't like me sitting here staring at you? Make me stop.

Eskaminzim and Diehl studiously ignored him as we rode by the bluff he'd affixed himself to, but the rest of us couldn't help peeping up at him every so often to see if he'd pulled the rifle from the scabbard by his right leg. As that would require actual movement, he refrained.

A moment later, we rounded the hill and found ourselves facing a collection of blocky yellow shapes—tents—on another rise two hundred yards ahead. We had Loveland's camp in sight at last. Though there were more (and more comfortable-looking) tents than at Camp Cashew, only four residents were out in plain view. One was Loveland himself, resplendent again in his big, billowing dressing gown (although with the sky still as murky as it was, he'd elected to leave his parasol elsewhere). Near him were Vollmer and two of the other gunmen, one thin and pale, one pot-bellied and slovenly, all on horseback.

As we closed the gap between us, I looked back and saw what I expected. Shoshone Joe was still atop his bluff, but he'd moved now. He'd turned his horse to face us—and finally pulled out his rifle.

If you were simply counting guns, it was four against four. But the Shoshones would be pointing at our backs.

"What's going on, John?" Loveland called out when we were within fifty yards. "Why are you here?"

There was trepidation in his voice. Somehow I didn't get the feeling it was fear of what we might do, though. He was afraid of what we were there to *say*.

Then Durgin said it.

"We're bringing back Walter's body, Hiram. We found him not far from our camp."

You wouldn't think the sound of a gasp would carry that far, but Loveland's did.

"You *found* him?" he said. "What does that mean—you 'found' him?"

"He was in an abandoned excavation," Durgin said. "Dead. Buried. We dug him out."

Vollmer leaned down toward Loveland and said something under his breath.

Loveland gave his head a jowl-flapping shake in response.

"I don't know. Perhaps," he moaned. "It doesn't make any sense!"

Vollmer straightened up and focused on the approaching wagon.

"You say he was buried," he said to us. "In what way? On purpose-like? Or could it have been some kinda cave-in?"

Old Red and I looked at each other. His eyes were wide with surprise. Mine probably were, too.

It was very understanding of Vollmer to even suggest that Glaze's death could have been an accident. Shockingly understanding. Perplexingly understanding.

"It was on purpose," Diehl told him. "Glaze was beaten to death."

Loveland gasped again.

Vollmer sat back in his saddle, a grimace on his scar-carved face. It wasn't the type of scowl I'd been expecting from him, though. Not the "You lyin' sons of bitches" kind. More like the "This can't be happening" variety. Dismay rather than blame.

"Indians?" he said to us.

"Nope!" said Eskaminzim.

"It seems like Indians to beat a man to death then *bury* him?" Diehl said. He jerked his head back at Joe on the bluff behind us.

"And are there even any around here anymore other than yours?"

Loveland raised a trembling hand to point at Eskaminzim. "And yours!"

Eskaminzim scoffed. "I'm not his Indian."

We were just twenty yards from Loveland and his men now, and Durgin finally pulled back on the reins and brought the wagon to a halt. Diehl, Old Red, and I stopped, as well, but Eskaminzim kept on until he'd rounded the back of the buckboard and drawn up to my right.

Loveland stepped forward and jabbed a finger up at Diehl. "How do I know *you* didn't murder Walter?" He zigzagged the finger to Diehl on one side of the wagon, then Old Red and me and Eskaminzim on the other. "Or one of you?"

"Professor Loveland..." Miss Hayes began calmly.

A cooler head was going to attempt to prevail. Just not the one we expected.

"Professor," Vollmer cut in, leaning toward his employer and dropping his voice again. "I'm still not so sure it wasn't Indians. And there's all kinds of riffraff out here. Tramps, bandits. Why don't you let me and the boys poke around a bit before this gets out of hand?"

Loveland gawked at the man in astonishment.

"But it beggars belief," he said, flapping a hand at us in a way that made the droopy sleeve of his silk gown flap like a flag in the wind. "Some random maniac *just happens* to come across Walter and kill him and they *just happen* to find his body after he..."

He cleared his throat before finishing his sentence.

"...went off on his own?"

"It'd be real helpful to know what Mr. Glaze was up to out there in the middle of the night," said Old Red.

It was the first time he'd spoken in Loveland's presence...and Loveland didn't like it. His face turned sunburn red as he looked my brother up and down, bulbous body trembling with rage beneath his flowing robe.

"Oh, I just bet that would be 'helpful'! I just bet!" he bellowed.

"First you steal my diplodocus, then you kill Walter Glaze, then you want my help to shift the blame! The nerve!"

"It's a fair question, Hiram," Durgin said. "If we knew what Walter was doing when he was killed, we might be able to—"

Loveland didn't let him get any further.

"Do you recall your last words to me yesterday? The last thing you said to Walter, so far as I know? I certainly remember! 'Go…to…hell'—that's what you said. Well, I say that to you now, John! You won't get away with this. I'm going to see to that."

"I'm not trying to get away with anything, Hiram."

"Ha! That's all you've been doing for the past year! And now you've gone too far!"

Loveland turned to Vollmer and the other gunmen on horseback beside him.

"Get rid of them," he said.

To my far left, on the other side of the buckboard, Diehl put his hand to his gun belt. To my right, Eskaminzim wrapped his fingers around the grip of his Winchester.

In between them was me (and probably Old Red, too) thinking, "Ohhhh, shit."

"Uh…what?" Vollmer said.

"Show them out!" Loveland snapped.

He raised a hand toward the south. I guess he was used to kicking folks out of his home or office or classroom or museum or whatever, but out here, it looked like he wanted us thrown out of all of Wyoming.

"Oh. Right," said Vollmer.

For a second, he appeared relieved—as was I to learn that "get rid of them" didn't mean *permanently*. But he quickly affixed an expression of contemptuous resolve to his scarred, stubble-covered face. Seeing that it was time again to earn their pay, his two compadres toughened themselves up the same way.

"All right, you…" Vollmer growled at us.

"You're forgetting something, Professor Loveland," said Miss Hayes, ignoring Vollmer. "As Mr. Glaze's employer, it's your responsibility to inform the family...and make the proper arrangements with them."

Loveland glowered at her a moment before it sank in.

We hadn't just come to share bad news. We were making a delivery.

His gaze slid past her to the back of the wagon.

"Of course, you're right," he said, voice softer. "If you would just have your men...unload there where you are, we'll bring our own wagon around."

His gaze flicked over to Vollmer, who gave him a nod—and immediately passed the buck.

"Benji—get to the dig and fetch the wagon," he said to the tub-gutted gunman beside him.

Without a word, "Benji" wheeled his mount around and rode off.

Vollmer and the remaining gunhand—the one so skinny he was almost skeletal—went back to glowering at us.

"Gustav, Otto—if you wouldn't mind?" Diehl said, without looking our way. He was too busy returning the other men's glares.

When I realized what he wanted us to do, I *did* mind. Then again, someone had to do it—while someone else had to keep an eye on Vollmer and his friend. I didn't love the division of labor— me and Old Red for the first job, Diehl and Eskaminzim for the second—but I couldn't say it didn't make sense.

My brother and I got down from our horses and started unloading Glaze's body.

"Leave him under the tarp," Durgin said as I climbed into the back of the buckboard. "We can spare it."

"Right."

It had only been a couple hours since we'd fished Glaze out of the mire, but already I noticed a difference in him. He'd been on the rigid side before, but full rigor mortis had set in now. We may as well have been unloading a cigar store Indian—one that weighed north of a hundred sixty pounds.

After some grunting and quiet cursing and tricky maneuvering my brother and I got Glaze laid out in the grass. I started to turn away, back toward Vollmer and his skin-and-bones pal, but Old Red lingered a moment over the body. There was no clue to be had from looking down at it—it was still under canvas. Yet my brother stayed frozen there, a grim, determined look on his face. I got the feeling he was making a promise.

"Professor Loveland," he said when he finally looked away. "Why were some of your men sneakin' around to the east of our camp last night?"

I guess he figured we'd dropped off our package so he had to grab his chance for data before we were run off. But the only data he got was what *not* to say to Loveland just then.

"You impertinent worm!" the man roared. "You bring me the body of a man you probably murdered and then have the gall to ask *me* insinuating questions! How dare you? Get out of here! Go! Now! Go, or so help me, I will have you shot!"

"Professor—" Miss Hayes said.

Loveland jabbed a pointed finger at her. "You are not exempt, Miss Hayes! Lie down with dogs, and this is what happens!"

Durgin jumped in with a "Hiram, please" that just enraged Loveland even more (despite that seeming impossible).

"I swear some of you will hang for this!" the old man raged, waving his wagging finger at the rest of us now. "Maybe all of you! I will not rest until I have seen justice done!"

"We need to go," Diehl said to Durgin and Miss Hayes. He looked over at me and Old Red. "Immediately."

"I agree," said Durgin. "There's nothing else to be accomplished here."

My brother and I remounted our horses, and Durgin set the wagon rolling. It seemed to take years for him to turn it southward and build up some speed, which gave Loveland plenty of time for more tongue lashing.

"The full weight of the law is about to be brought crashing down upon you! Crushing you for what you have done! A good man is dead, and there will be retribution for those responsible! Walter Glaze shall be avenged! That is a promise!"

"How long do you think he can keep that up?" I asked Old Red as we rode off.

"The county sheriff will hear of this!" Loveland raved. "The federal marshal for this district! The governor! The president, if need be!"

"We'll see," my brother said. "I don't know which he's gonna run out of first: breath or threats."

"All the world shall know of your shame!" Loveland howled.

Silence finally fell—for about three seconds. Then Loveland started in again louder than ever. Which I guess answered Old Red's question.

"Before Walter Glaze is in his grave, you will be in jail! And then *your* graves won't be far off for you! Filthy murderers! Thieves! Philistines!"

"What's that last thing he called us?" my brother asked me.

"'Philistines.'"

"What's that mean?"

"Ignorant folks. Dumb. Crude."

"Oh. Well, now I am insulted."

"That's enough repartee," Diehl said. "Everyone—move faster without looking like you're moving faster."

I half-expected my brother to say, "What's repartee?" But the urgency in Diehl's voice got the idea across. This wasn't the time to joke around.

Old Red and I looked back at Loveland and Vollmer and the skinny gunhand, sixty yards behind us now. Loveland was shaking his fist. The other men just sat atop their horses, staring back at us.

"Don't look like they're gonna do anything," my brother said. "Not just now anyway."

"Maybe not them," Eskaminzim said. "But what about the Shoshone?"

"*Don't stare*," Diehl warned us even as our heads whipped to the right toward the bluff Shoshone Joe had been watching us from.

It only took a glance to see there was no one there now. Joe was gone.

Old Red and I locked our gazes on the rolling plains ahead—and got our horses up to a trot.

"Where do you think he went?" Miss Hayes said.

"Somewhere to make trouble," said Eskaminzim.

"The only question," Diehl added, "is if he's there already."

TWELVE
THE STAMPEDE
OR, SHOSHONE JOE DOES SOME HORSING AROUND, AND WE GET ROPED INTO A CHASE

AS SOON AS we rounded the nearest hill and were sure we weren't being followed, Diehl turned to me and my brother.

"Stay with the wagon," he told us.

"What if—?" Old Red began.

But Diehl and Eskaminzim were already galloping off.

"Dammit!" my brother spat. He shot a glare after Diehl and Eskaminzim as they sped southward, toward Durgin's dig and camp, then peeked over at Miss Hayes in the buckboard. "Beggin' your pardon for the language."

"It's quite all right," she said. "Given the circumstances, I sympathize with sentiment."

"Are we sure we're not all overreacting?" Durgin said. "We don't know what this Indian fellow is up to. And how much trouble could one man cause?"

"Ask your friend Glaze that," said Old Red.

Durgin clamped his mouth shut. He looked like he wanted to say something a lot stronger than "Dammit" but was restraining himself. Barely.

"Loveland, let us ride away just now," I said to my brother. "I don't think he'd change his mind all of a sudden and send

Vollmer and them others after the professor and Miss Hayes here."

Old Red grunted and rubbed his chin, obviously thinking the same thing I was: The trouble was going to be elsewhere, not back with the wagon and passengers we'd been left to nursemaid. Were we really going to stay behind just because Diehl told us to?

"Feh," my brother said—but he kept his horse to a trot beside the buckboard.

We were going to follow Diehl's orders. For now.

Old Red took a long look back at the hill we'd just come around. When no riders raced round it, guns blazing, he turned to Durgin and Miss Hayes.

"Tell me, Professor…" he said. "Is Loveland good at his job?"

Durgin blinked at him. He was still vexed, but now—unaccustomed to the sudden, seemingly random questions my brother's prone to throw out when he's puzzling on something—he was confused, too.

"With bones, I mean," Old Red continued. "He as good as you at recognizin' this or that dinosaur from just a glance? Or as good as I assume Glaze was? Or is he just lucky or rich or got important friends or something?"

Durgin blinked again.

"You've said he's competent enough, John…" Miss Hayes prompted him.

"Yes. That's true," Durgin said slowly. "Hiram's a passable anatomist, though he's been known to make mistakes. Walter was the same way. His special skill was finding fossils, not identifying them. As theorists, I'd call them both…undistinguished. That's why Hiram's had to rely on others for the insight and imagination he lacks."

"You mean rely on you," Miss Hayes said.

Durgin didn't deny it.

"The thing that really made Hiram is timing," he went on. "He was one of the first American scientists to pursue fossil collecting with any real vigor. Now he's a grand old man of the field."

"Even though he hasn't actually been *in* the field in fifteen years," Miss Hayes added.

"Ah," said Old Red. "I been wonderin' about that. When does he actually get to see the bones if he ain't out here scoopin' 'em out?"

"It's usually several weeks or even months after they were excavated," said Durgin, warming up to the topic at hand now that it was the workings of paleontology. You wouldn't have been able to tell that he'd been fuming at my brother a minute earlier or dropping off a body to howled threats ten minutes before that. "To save on shipping, they're not sent back piecemeal. They sit until there's a full load, then they go to New York where they wait for the preparators. Hiram doesn't see anything but field notes and sketches until they've done their work."

"Wait...until who's done their work? 'The prep-ara-tors'?"

Durgin nodded. "They're museum assistants who specialize in removing the plaster and matrix. Their work is painstaking. It can take them months to finish one field jacket. It leads to quite a backlog, especially for the less exciting finds. I think Hiram's still got jackets in storage from three years ago."

Old Red gave that a "Hmm" and let Durgin take a breather rather than request another lecture.

I took the opportunity to lean toward my brother and ask a quiet question of my own.

"Is any of this important or are you just passing the time while we sit on our asses back here drying to adobe?"

I gave the front of my slicker an irritated tap. It sounded like I was rapping on a two-by-four. The mud still smearing me from the pit had stiffened as the sun came out and the air warmed, and my coat was starting to feel less like cotton muslin than a suit of armor.

Old Red scowled at me.

"'It is a—'" he began.

Just those three words and the sanctimonious way he said them told me what was to follow. He was going to unload his favorite Holmes quote on me: *It is a capital mistake to theorize before one has data.*

I wasn't having it.

"Oh, for god's sake—I ain't asking you to theorize," I snapped.

"Yes, you are," Old Red snapped back. "How am I to know what's 'important' and what's not till I got more to work with? 'I cannot—'"

I knew where that was going, too. More Holmes.

"Yeah, yeah. Can't make bricks without clay," I said. "Usually, that's all well and good. But right now, while you're here trying to scrape up clay, Eskaminzim and Diehl might be out there riding into bullets."

"And you're anxious to ride into one yourself? That ain't like you."

My first reply got caught behind gritted teeth, and I swallowed it. We'd been trying to keep our voices down, but we were so close to the wagon there was no way Durgin and Miss Hayes hadn't heard nearly every word. And the two I almost said to my brother would've been a *lot* worse than an innocent "Dammit."

"No, I don't particularly enjoy getting shot at...or digging up corpses, for that matter," I said. "But I also don't like getting treated like a tenderfoot kid when there might be trouble to deal with. And I know you don't like it either."

"Maybe I don't. But if that Shoshone Joe is makin' trouble, Eskaminzim and Diehl can handle it," Old Red said firmly... before adding a far-from-firm "Probably."

I leaned even closer to him—so far, the dried mud on my slicker cracked like a twig—and lowered my voice to a wisp of a whisper.

"Has it occurred to you that maybe Diehl wasn't keeping us out of danger by making us stay back here? That maybe there's something he doesn't want us to see or know?"

My brother glared at me in a way that somehow managed to say both "What a shameful thing to think of a partner" and "Of course, it occurred to me. *Everything* occurs to me."

I was about to give up my arguing when a sound from up ahead made the case for leaving much better than I could.

Gunfire. A single shot echoed out from somewhere beyond the rolling hills to the south.

"There's no 'if' about trouble now. Someone's making some," I said to Old Red.

He looked over at Durgin and Miss Hayes.

"Go," the lady said. "We'll be all right."

Durgin didn't seem so sure. He glanced back the way we'd come.

We still weren't being followed.

"Yes…I suppose…" he said uncertainly.

"*Go*," Miss Hayes told us again.

It had the certain firmness of an order. And my brother and I took it like one, digging in our heels and galloping off.

Old Red quickly steered us toward the nearest, highest rise southward, and when we reached the top, we reined up again and scanned the horizon. There was a lot to see: Horses seemed to be spreading out in all directions. Four—the most distant—were each racing away on their own, riderless. Another—this one with a man in the saddle who, though a speck to us, had to be Shoshone Joe—was headed northwest at an angle that would take it past us about a quarter mile to our left. The final two horses we knew well, as we did the riders. It was Eskaminzim and Diehl, hot on the Shoshone's trail.

A puff of smoke drifted away behind Joe's horse, and a half second later the sound of a gunshot reached us. He was taking shots at his pursuers—which hopefully meant he was too busy to have noticed us.

Old Red and I sent our mounts back down the north side of the hill, getting ourselves out of sight again.

"Looks like Joe stampeded Durgin's remuda," my brother said. "Probably figured we was too distracted by Loveland's tantrum to notice him slipping back to Camp Cashew."

"He figured right, too. I just hope the horses is all he messed with."

Old Red gave that a grim nod. If a man bent on mischief had caught Cherry napping—and indeed napping seemed like all she was interested in when we'd seen her a couple hours before—who could say what might happen?

Whatever *had* happened at the camp, it was too late to stop it. All we could do now was try to catch the man who'd done it.

My brother pointed at another hill a few hundred yards to the east. "He keeps goin' straight—and I think he will, speed bein' foremost on his mind right now—he's gonna pass by on the other side of that right there."

"And we can cut him off?"

Old Red nodded.

"And do what to stop him?" I asked.

Meaning, were we going to shoot the son of a bitch.

Running off your horses isn't nice, but it hardly rates a death sentence. And anything else Joe might've done was still pure worry on our part, not established fact.

On the other hand, I didn't think the man would stop to clear things up with a friendly chat just because we popped out in front of him to ask politely. More likely he'd stop shooting at Eskaminzim and Diehl and start shooting at us.

My brother chewed on all that a moment, then reached down to pat the rope strapped in a coil to his saddle. I had one, as well: We'd brought along extra lengths in case one wasn't enough to get Glaze out of his muddy grave.

"Maybe we oughta see how rusty we are with these," he said.

"Interesting idea, brother. I like it better than shooting a man in the back." I held a hand out toward the hill Joe was headed toward. "Shall we?"

Joe fired off yet another shot as we rode over and got set up—Old Red on one side of the little dale beyond the hill, me on the other. Depending on how the Shoshone preferred to load his pistol, he either had three shots left or two. Enough for both of us…with bullets to spare if he carried a second handgun on him or was a good enough rider to pull and use his rifle while in the saddle. Either of which seemed entirely possible.

With every second we waited I became more convinced my brother's idea was less "interesting" than it was "suicidal." Fortunately (or perhaps it would turn out to be *unfortunately*), we didn't have long to wait.

The sound of hooves pounding soppy sod rose up from the south, and a moment later I heard words, as well.

"Come and get me, Apache bastard! I'm saving some lead just for you!"

My brother and I locked eyes as we listened to the hoofbeats grow louder. We couldn't wait for Joe to ride past us: By the time we built up momentum and matched his speed, he'd be fifty yards ahead and out of reach. No—we'd have to charge out before he made it to us…and hope he was still watching over his shoulder for his chance to put that lead in Eskaminzim.

There was no signal from Old Red when the moment came. Just action. He sent his horse charging out into the dale, and I did the same. Almost immediately, he was whirling his loop over his head, and I got to doing that, too.

Joe was still thirty yards off, about to race between us. He was indeed looking back, and he'd lost his Stetson somewhere, but he was still easy to recognize with his red neckerchief and embroidered boots and long, dark braided hair bouncing up and down as he rode. I don't know if he heard us or saw something out of the corner of his eye or just decided it was time to look where he was going again, but he faced forward just in time to catch sight of me angling in from his right.

He swung his forty-five toward his right, too. Toward *me.*

Old Red let loose with his lasso before the Shoshone could get off a shot. It was also before my brother was really ready to make his throw, apparently, for the big noose didn't settle over top of Joe. Instead it whipped into his left shoulder, fell, and slid limp off his mount's haunch.

That didn't slow Joe, but it did startle him. He cried out in surprise and squeezed off a shot so high over my head it probably plugged a hole in a cloud. Before he could try again, I made my throw.

Like my brother, I'd built out my loop extra-large—what some of the cow hands used to call a Blocker or a Mother Hubbard—so as not to behead Joe if the rope went around his neck. So when my aim proved perfect (for once, Old Red usually being twice the roper I am) it drooped down over him clear to his middle. I pulled on the rope hard and quickly dallied it twice around my saddle horn.

For all of two seconds, it might have looked like Joe could just keep riding off into the hills wearing the extra-large belt I'd just given him. But then the lariat went taut, and Joe, belly-roped, was suddenly defying gravity. There he was suspended in mid-air while his horse went galloping on toward the horizon.

Of course, gravity wouldn't be defied for long. Joe dropped straight down to the ground with a moist *sploosh* and a mighty "Oof!" His pistol, meanwhile, had tried its best to carry on with the horse, flying from Joe's hand when he was jerked to a sudden stop. It only made it a few yards, though, tumbling into the mud out of his reach. Just to be safe, though, I slowed my horse and dragged Joe back a bit. He retched and wheezed for a moment, but with surprising speed, he was cursing and kicking and flailing at the rope.

"Oh, knock it off, or I'll take you for a *real* sleigh ride," I told him.

The cursing, kicking and flailing didn't stop.

Old Red reined up nearby and began drawing up his lariat.

"Got some questions for you, Joe," he said.

Joe told him what he could do with his questions. It sounded painful.

Before my brother could decline to oblige, Eskaminzim and Diehl came trotting up, their mounts breathing hard.

"Nicely done, Otto," Diehl said. "I guess you really were a cowboy, weren't you?"

"I wish you would finally accept that my stories are true," I replied. "The only thing I exaggerate is how devastatingly hand-some I am…and I don't have to exaggerate that much."

Eskaminzim didn't seem as impressed with my roping, though.

"You didn't have to do this," he said. "Another minute, and I'd have had a clear shot at his horse."

"Yeah, well…I guess his horse is grateful for our help even if you're not."

Said horse had finally figured out no one was atop it anymore and had stopped a hundred yards away to catch its breath.

"Cherry okay?" Old Red asked.

Diehl nodded. "Just shook up. Our friend here drove the spare horses straight through camp. It got torn up pretty good, but fortunately, she wasn't trampled. Just scared half to death."

Joe finally stopped his squirming and used words other than curses.

"How was I to know you let your women sleep all day? She should've been out cooking or washing where I could see her."

"Oh, I see," said Diehl. "You didn't mean any harm, huh?"

Joe gave him a sneering smile. "Of course I did! I wanted to wreck your camp, and I did a good job of it. I just didn't know about the woman, that's all."

"Was runnin' the horses through something you was told to do when you could, or did you come up with that on the fly?" Old Red asked.

Joe told him what he could do with this new question. It sounded even less pleasant than his first suggestion.

None of us was surprised by his defiance. Eskaminzim, in fact, looked positively delighted by it.

"Such foul words, Shoshone. Nasty white man's words. You should be ashamed," he said, shaking his head yet grinning at the same time. "I'm glad to hear them from you, though."

In one smooth motion, he slid from his saddle and drew his knife from the sheath at his waist. The blade glinted in the sun as he moved quickly toward Joe.

"I was hoping we'd have to do this the hard way," he said.

THIRTEEN
THE HARD WAY

OR, OLD RED TRIES TO CONVINCE JOE TO SPEAK HIS PIECE BEFORE HE ENDS UP IN PIECES

"NOW HOLD ON THERE!" I said, sitting up straight in my saddle.

"Whoa whoa whoa!" cried Old Red, practically throwing himself from his horse and hurrying over to put himself between Eskaminzim—and his knife—and Joe.

Joe did his best to stay stoic, but I could see his own "Now hold on there!" slash "Whoa whoa whoa!" in his wide, frightened eyes. He was still sitting on the soppy ground, my rope around his waist, and he scooched back a foot away from the Apache. He had a knife as big as Eskaminzim's in an embroidered sheath at his waist, but his arms were pinned too tight to his sides for him to get it.

"Don't be stupid. You have questions. I will get answers," Eskaminzim said to my brother. "This fool doesn't need ten fingers anyway. Nine will be plenty for him. Or eight. Or seven. Or six. Depending on how quick he talks."

Joe scooched back another foot.

Eskaminzim started to step around Old Red.

Old Red stepped right back into his path.

"Ain't nobody loppin' off fingers while I'm here."

"Or me," I said.

To show I meant it, I sent my horse a few steps away from the others, dragging Joe with me. He didn't complain this time.

"Otto, Gustav—you need to let Eskaminzim handle this," said Diehl. He was still atop his dun mare, and he swiveled his head left and right, quickly scanning the ridges around us. "Those gunshots brought you, right? Well, it's a safe bet Vollmer and his boys heard them, too. They could be here any second."

"Doesn't leave much time for your questions," said Eskaminzim. "Maybe I'd better start with an ear, just to speed things up."

He began to step around Old Red again. And again, Old Red blocked him.

"Ears are off limits, too," he said.

"Oh, so you want me to take his nose? I was trying to leave him some spares, but all right. If that's what you want."

Once more, Eskaminzim began to move around Old Red. This time when my brother sidestepped to stay in front of him, the Apache crooked a leg behind his ankles and gave him a shove.

Old Red went flying backward and hit the ground hard.

Eskaminzim kept closing in on Joe.

I moved my horse away a few more steps, dragging Joe with me.

"Stay back, you crazy son of a bitch!" I spat.

"Yeah!" added Joe, sending a useless kick in Eskaminzim's direction. "Leave me alone!"

"*Otto*," Diehl snapped. "Are you going to make me ride over there and take that rope?"

"I'm not making you do anything, Diehl. Are you dumb enough to try it?"

Eskaminzim had stopped again about ten yards from Joe, and I swung my furious glare from Diehl to him.

"Or you?" I said. "Don't think you can take me so easy this time. I'm ready for you."

"You think so?" Eskaminzim said. He moved his knife from his right hand to his left and back again. "'Crazy son of a bitch,' huh? That's hurtful."

He crouched as if preparing for a leap.

"Keep him away from me!" Joe cried with another feeble kick.

"We can't do it all day, Joe," Old Red said. He pushed himself to his feet and wiped mud off the back of his coat. "Even if my brother drags you from one end of this valley to the other, you're gonna start losin' bits eventually. Be easier on ya if ya just talked."

"Someone ask me a damn question then!"

I sagged with relief. Finally we were getting somewhere—before I found out if Eskaminzim was about to jump Joe or me. I was still mad at him, but I wasn't *really* ready to take him on. I'd probably never be.

"I already asked you a question before all the fuss," Old Red reminded Joe. "Was stampedin' them horses through our camp your idea or something you was told to do when you could?"

"My idea," Joe said sourly.

"It just popped into your head all of a sudden? You're watchin' us down there talkin' to Loveland and Vollmer, and you think, 'Hey, here's a chance to mess with 'em.' And off you go?"

"Yeah. It was exactly like that. All Glaze and the fat man want is for us to 'mess with' Durgin. So I headed to your camp to see what I could do, and it just came to me. I thought it might be fun." Joe tried to smile, but it didn't stick. "And it was."

My brother had started walking slowly toward him, still cleaning off his slicker, but for just a moment, he froze. Something the man said had surprised him.

Both Diehl and Eskaminzim, meanwhile, were watching him dubiously, clearly wondering why it mattered whose idea running off the horses was.

"Speakin' of Glaze," Old Red said, "where was he last night? Before the storm blew in?"

Joe shrugged. "I don't know. He goes off on his own sometimes. Late. Ed asked what he was doing once, but Glaze told him to mind his own business."

"Ed?"

"Vollmer. With the scar on his face." Joe threw a little sneer first at Diehl, then Eskaminzim. "You've met him."

"Charming fellow," Diehl said.

"Very handsome," added Eskaminzim.

"Oh, yes. Interestin' gent, him," Old Red agreed as if there'd been no sarcasm to the others' words at all. "So when Glaze goes off alone—those the same nights he tells you and Vollmer or whoever to sneak around to the east of Durgin's camp? Maybe sneak around not too sneaky-like? Make a little noise, draw a little attention?"

Joe looked surprised now, jerking his head up and furrowing his brow. "How do you know that?"

My brother held up his dirty fingers and gave them a waggle. "No one's tryin' to take any of these, Joe. I don't gotta answer any questions. But you—why don't you tell me how Glaze and Loveland get along? They friendly, they fight, what?"

Joe's confusion deepened.

"How do they get along?" he said. "I don't know. I've never seen 'em shoot at each other and I've never seen 'em kiss, so I guess it's somewhere in the middle."

"Do you mind if I get in a question or two?" Diehl said to Old Red. He pulled his Winchester from its scabbard and gave the hills around us another once-over. "We won't have time for many more, and yours aren't exactly—"

"Tell me, Joe," Old Red cut in, turning his back on Diehl. "What have Glaze and Loveland been doin' at that camp of theirs?"

Diehl clamped his mouth shut and shot a glare at my brother.

Eskaminzim looked like he was about to burst out laughing.

"Digging. Like Durgin," Joe told Old Red. "It doesn't seem like they're in a big hurry about it, though. It feels more like they've been waiting to take over Durgin's spot. They're pretty sure they're gonna get it, too."

"*Amlingmeyer*," Diehl grated out.

My brother kept his back to him.

"They *really* want that big lizard Durgin's workin' on, don't they?" he said to Joe.

Joe gave him another shrug. "Sure. That's why they're here."

"I see," said Old Red. "Makes me wonder how many of them bones they want so bad were in Durgin's camp, waitin' to go back to town. How many might have been trampled to splinters by the horses you sent gallopin' through the tents? Glaze didn't have much to say when y'all paid your little call yesterday, but he didn't strike me as a particularly forgivin' fella. I don't think he or Loveland are gonna be very happy with you when they find out what you done."

I'd seen fear on Joe's long, lean face already, but when it returned now it was of a different kind. It wasn't the barely suppressed terror of Eskaminzim and his knife. It was of the "Oh, shit…what have I done?" variety. The look of a man realizing he's made a big mistake—and there might be a price he didn't want to pay. Which didn't make a lick of sense if he knew that the man supposedly collecting the debt—Glaze—was dead.

Old Red looked up at me, then back at Diehl.

Diehl nodded silently, seeing now at least part of what my brother had been sniffing around after.

Joe must've ridden off before we took off the tarp and unloaded the wagon. All he'd seen was our little party coming in to parlay with Loveland.

He *didn't* know Glaze was dead. So there was one person *we* knew hadn't killed him.

One down, the rest of Wyoming to go.

Old Red turned back to Joe.

"Now Mr. Glaze—he wasn't in camp this mornin', was he? Still off doin' who-knows-what somewhere, right? How'd Loveland take that? Glaze bein' missin' after that big squall and all?"

Joe had taken to staring down mournfully at his boots. They were pretty things to stare at, too, as boots go: beaded with patterns that suggested twirling vines and blossoms. His sheath and the deerskin vest under his sack coat were fancied up the same way, seemingly by the same skillful hand.

I hadn't found much to like in the man, but somewhere, his clothes told me, was a mother or sister or wife who loved him.

"He was nervous. In a bad mood," he said. "I mean, he's always nervous and in a bad mood when I've been around. But more so this morning. He wanted us out looking for Glaze, so we went, but we didn't look hard. Ed says…"

Joe lifted his head and scanned the distant ridges, his words trailing off.

"Who you lookin' for, Joe?" Old Red asked him. "Is there somebody else out here? More Shoshone, say?"

Joe gave that a bitter snort. "More Shoshone? Here? These days? I wish."

"He's looking for his white friends," Eskaminzim said. He lifted his knife and ran his thumb along the flat of the blade. "Don't bother. Talk."

Joe snorted again. "Friends? Ed and them? They're not my friends. They're just something to do. Some whites to blend in with. A way to stay off the reservation without getting shot for it." His gaze slid over to Eskaminzim, and for the first time that day, he looked at the Apache without fear—just bitterness. "You should understand that."

Eskaminzim aimed the tip of his knife at him and circled it in the air.

"Next question," he said, looking over at Old Red.

My brother rubbed his bushy red mustache, eyes narrowing, wheels turning.

"Just who the hell is Vollmer, anyway?" he said. "Where's he come from? What's he usually do? And how'd he and the rest of you come to work for Glaze and Loveland?"

I'd let the rope get a little slack as the conversation carried on, and rather than answer Joe squirmed both his arms free. He could go for his knife now, but instead he started brushing mud off his boots.

Maybe he was getting comfortable with the fact that he wasn't going to lose any body parts. Maybe he'd finally been asked a question he had a good reason not to answer. Maybe it was both.

"Joe…" Eskaminzim began, brandishing his knife again.

"I am not 'Joe'! I am Doyadukubichi'!" the Shoshone snapped at him. "I only let Vollmer call me 'Joe' because his white tongue is too clumsy to say a real name!"

Eskaminzim nodded calmly. "Fine. Doyadukubichi'. If you don't use *your* lips to answer questions I will assume you don't need them anymore."

He took a step toward Doyadukubichi'. This time the Shoshone didn't flinch, and his hand shot down to the hilt of his knife.

"Never mind," Diehl said. "Time's up."

The rest of us followed his gaze. He was looking to the Northwest. Three figures had appeared on a hilltop there. Men on horseback—one in a gray hat.

"What do we do with him?" Eskaminzim asked with a jerk of the chin at our prisoner.

There was a *pop* in the distance, followed almost instantly by a *ploop* into the wet sod about twenty yards to my right.

Gray smoke drifted from the hilltop.

There was another *pop* and another *ploop*, this one not far from Old Red's horse. It whinnied and trotted off.

"Dammit!" my brother said, scampering after it.

"With the Shoshone, they have four guns out here, two in town," Eskaminzim said to Diehl. There was no fear, no urgency in his voice at all. He might as well have been remarking that there was a cloud overhead that looked like a puppy. "That's one more gun than we have. We should even the numbers."

"We leave him," I said firmly.

I'm not used to speaking firmly. I prefer speaking softly. But until the shooting stopped and Eskaminzim's knife got resheathed, I wasn't taking anything easy.

"Yes. We leave him," said Eskaminzim. "That's exactly what I'm saying."

"Alive!" Old Red said.

He'd caught his horse by the reins now and was dragging it to a halt.

Eskaminzim shook his head in a way I remember our dear old *Mutter* doing when she thought us kids were being foolish.

"'Alive.'" He chuckled.

There were two more shots followed by two more *ploops* into the sod. One landed ten yards from Old Red as he hauled himself atop his horse, the other twenty yards to my right.

"I don't think they're trying to hit us," Eskaminzim said, still utterly placid. "Or they're terrible shots."

"Well, we're giving 'em plenty of time to practice, ain't we?" I said, hunching low in the saddle. (Being "Big Red" can come in handy from time to time. Not so much when it makes me "Biggest Target.") "Let's just leave him—alive—and get outta here!"

To show I meant it, I dropped the rope I'd been holding and moved my horse a few steps off. I didn't go too far, though, lest Eskaminzim take the opportunity to lunge toward Doyadukubichi' and perform some quick surgery.

More shots came whistling in, just five yards to each side of us now.

Rather than fire back, Diehl slid his Winchester into its scabbard.

"Wave to your not-friends," he told Doyadukubichi'. "Tell them to stop shooting."

Despite the rifle fire coming at us, the Shoshone had been keeping his eyes on Eskaminzim. He looked away reluctantly.

"They can't hear me up there. And they probably wouldn't listen if they could."

Diehl thumbed back the hammer thong holding his Colt in place at his hip. He drew the gun and pointed it at Doyadukubichi'.

"Wave. Tell them to stop shooting."

Slowly, glowering, Doyadukubichi' lifted both arms and moved them back and forth over his head.

"Hey!" he shouted at the men in the distance. "Stop—!"

Diehl squeezed off a shot that tore through the palm of the Shoshone's right hand.

Doyadukubichi' screamed and jerked his arms down and curled into a ball.

"What the hell—?" Old Red snarled, sending his horse toward Diehl.

"Now they've literally lost a gunhand," Diehl said, reholstering his forty-five. "Our odds are better, and he's still alive. If you want to complain, do it out of range of those rifles."

He dug in his heels and bolted past my brother, his mare kicking up clumps of earth as they went.

Eskaminzim grunted, then ran to his horse and leaped up onto it.

"Go back to the reservation, Doyadukubichi'," he said. Then he was following Diehl out of the valley at a gallop.

My brother and I looked at each other, but what was there to say?

Just in case we were inclined to stick around and try to think of something, two more shots rang out. One plunked into the ground behind Old Red's horse. The other went screaming past half a foot over the crown of my hat.

Even if Vollmer and his buddies on the ridge *were* trying to miss us, they might not be good enough shots to keep succeeding.

Old Red sent his horse charging off after Eskaminzim and Diehl.

As I did the same, I threw one last look back at Doyaduku-bichi'. He'd managed to sit up again, his damaged hand pressed hard into his stomach, the other hand atop it. The expression on his face wasn't at all what I expected. He was grimacing with pain, yes, and angry, too. But I thought I saw something in his eyes that looked strangely like regret. Almost as if, despite everything that had just happened, he'd rather have gone with us.

There was no time to look closely. Three more shots chased me out of the valley. Even after we were safely around the hills at the far end, Diehl, Eskaminzim and Old Red didn't stop pushing their mounts fast to the south—back toward Durgin's camp.

FOURTEEN
HOUSE OF BONES (PART TWO)
OR, WE SET OUT TO ROUND UP HORSES AND END UP CORRALLING NEW CLUES

DIEHL ANGLED us to the west as we continued riding southward, and soon I saw why: We were intersecting with Professor Durgin and Miss Hayes, who'd carried on toward camp in the wagon.

"I'm relieved to see you all here," Miss Hayes said as we pulled up beside them. "What was all the shooting about?"

"One of Loveland's men——" Diehl began.

"One of *Vollmer's* men," Old Red cut in.

Diehl threw a quick, irritated glance at him before beginning again.

"One of the men from Loveland's group stampeded the spare horses through Camp Cashew. Cherry's all right, but there was a lot of damage. We managed to detain him for a time and ask a few questions, but this Vollmer—he's sort of the chief of the thugs Loveland employs—showed up with two of his men and… encouraged us to keep the conversation brief."

"They shot at you," said Miss Hayes.

"Not well," Eskaminzim assured her.

"Or not sincerely," added Old Red.

The lady looked utterly befuddled by the notion of insincere gunfire.

Durgin, meanwhile, had been listening with a stiff back and an alarmed expression.

"You say there was damage to our camp?" he said to Diehl. "What kind of damage?"

"The kind stampeding horses cause," Diehl replied. "Knocked over tents, trampled equipment—"

"I had a near-perfect fibula in my tent waiting to go back to town with the next field jackets!"

"I'm sorry, Professor," Diehl said. "I don't know how near to perfect it is anymore."

"Damn! What are we dawdling here for then?"

Diehl could've told Durgin, "Talking to *you*," of course. But the professor was already giving the reins a vigorous snap. The poor, tired nag pulling the buckboard did her best to go from plodding to trotting, and a few minutes later, we were cresting the hill where Camp Cashew once stood.

It was still there. It just wasn't exactly "standing" now, being mostly flattened canvas. Cherry was sitting atop what had been her tent, cross-legged and hunchbacked. She had her fists against her cheeks and tears in her eyes.

"If you want anything to eat other than mud pies, you'll send me into town in that wagon right now," she told Durgin. "Those damn animals destroyed everything I need. All my supplies. All my secret ingredients."

To look at her, you'd have thought the "damn animals" hadn't destroyed her stores so much as pelted her with them. Her hands and the front of her calico dress were covered with flour, and there was more strewn about over the remains of her tent and the ground nearby. An empty sack lay in the mud before her, limp as a busted brown balloon.

Durgin ignored her. The second he had the brake on the buckboard set, he hopped down and scurried to his own tent, lifted the canvas, and began rooting around in the scattered debris underneath.

I tied my horse to the back of the wagon, stepped around to help Miss Hayes down, then started toward Cherry.

"Where are you going?" she snapped at me.

I stopped. "Well, I was gonna help *you*."

"Help me what?"

"Help you clean up."

Cherry swiped a hand at me. It sent a waft of what I took to be her "secret ingredients" at me, though it didn't smell like anything you'd find in Mulligan stew or Dutch oven bread. It was sweet and floral, like evening honeysuckle or a big splash of fifty-cent perfume.

"I'll do my own cleaning up," Cherry said. "You catch the horses."

"That's a good idea, actually," Diehl said to me. "You and Gustav *were* cowboys." He gave me a small, tight smile. "I have no doubts about that now."

I returned the smile—though mine was even smaller and tighter. "I'll need more rope. I left mine on that steer you and Eskaminzim wanted to butcher."

Both Cherry and Miss Hayes—who'd moved off to sort through her own scattered, trampled things—shot me puzzled looks, but neither had time to ask for an explanation.

"Take mine," Diehl said, unfastening the rope secured to his saddle and tossing it down to me.

"I'll go with the cowboys," Eskaminzim said. "In case Vollmer wants to get in more target practice."

Diehl jerked his chin at the busted-up camp before him. "You just don't want to help with the mess."

"Of course not," Eskaminzim said. "These messes you find for us are never mine."

While all this had been going on, Old Red had been riding slowly around the campsite, eyeing the wreckage. He lingered particularly long by what had been the main storage tent. The guys' ropes and pegs had been pulled out, but the tent itself was lumpy, not leveled, like a big canvas blanket over two snoozing buffalo. He dismounted just long enough to root around underneath for more ropes and halters.

"Shall we?" I asked when we were both back in the saddle.

He nodded, then turned to Diehl. "You get the rope corral back up. We'll have it filled again shortly."

Diehl gave him a silent salute, and off we went.

Unlike whatever tracks there might have been from the night before—tracks leading to and from Glaze's body, say—the ones made that morning hadn't been washed away by rain. They were so plain to see in the waterlogged sod, in fact, we could follow them at a gallop, and before long, we had the first couple strays in sight. They were making the most of their freedom by grazing on some nice, tall, succulent wheatgrass they'd come across a mile from camp. They looked so placid and pleased I hated to break up the party, but such is a horse's lot in life. Just when you're feeling free and easy, some fool throws a rope around your neck and drags you off to toil and trouble. I could sympathize.

Old Red and I gave Eskaminzim another quick demonstration of our drovering abilities, but he didn't look impressed even when we were handing the horses over to him and heading off after the last two. Just as we spotted them—one drinking from a trickle of a stream to the north, the other watching us from further west, tail swishing warily—a dull, distant *crack* of gunfire drifted to us on the breeze. We both turned to look back at Eskaminzim, but he didn't have his rifle out. He was staring sternly toward the north.

The gunfire hadn't come from Camp Cashew behind us or from Durgin's dig now directly to our east. Whatever it was—a signal of some kind or Vollmer's boys getting in some target practice, as Eskaminzim had suggested—no more shots followed, and there was nothing to do but carry on with the task at hand.

Soon enough, we were trotting south with all four runaways behind us. By happenstance, the search for them had taken us near the trench in which we'd found Glaze, and I noticed my brother drifting off on a course that would take us to it again. I expected him to seize the opportunity to return to the hole for one more going-over Holmes-style, on hands and knees sniffing around for clues like a bloodhound. Instead he stopped us before we got there, at his true destination: the macabre little house of bones nestled against a lonely hillside a couple hundred yards from the pit.

Eskaminzim groaned when he saw that Old Red was stopping. "This place? Really? It shouldn't exist at all, and you bring us here?"

"What would you rather be doin'?" my brother said as he swung down from the saddle. "Cleanin' up the camp or sittin' here holdin' horses?"

Old Red offered Eskaminzim his reins and the leads for the two horses behind him.

The Apache took them.

"I'll take holding horses," he said. "But I'd rather be doing it somewhere else."

Old Red started toward the hut.

"Are all whites obsessed with the dead?" Eskaminzim asked me.

"Pretty much. My brother does take it to extremes, though."

"I ain't just here to sightsee," Old Red growled. "I got reasons."

He stepped through the crude doorway and disappeared into the darkness inside the fossil hut.

"He's got reasons," I said. "God forbid he should tell us what they are."

"It doesn't matter," Eskaminzim said. "Whatever they are, they aren't good enough to go in there."

Out of the corner of my eye, I thought I saw him shiver. If so, it was the first time I'd seen him display anything that came within a mile of fear.

"Tell me," I said. "A little while ago, when we were trying to get Duyadub...Duba...*Joe* to talk. Were you really gonna torture him?"

Eskaminzim shrugged. "What is torture?"

"Well, I don't have my Webster's on me, but I'd think that was plain enough. Hurting a person on purpose. Inflicting pain on 'em. A lot of pain."

Eskaminzim shrugged again. "What is a 'Webster's'?"

"All right. Dodge it if you like. But—"

"Hel-lo," I heard my brother say.

I knew what that meant. Old Red's "reasons" had been justi-fied. He'd found something.

I held out the leads for the two horses behind me.

"You want some more ponies?" I asked Eskaminzim.

"Sure," he said, taking the ropes. "If I were to go back to the Mescalero reservation with all these, I'd be a rich man."

"Try to resist the urge."

I got down from my mount and then handed over the reins for him, too. Then I headed for that stack of big bones.

They weren't all fossils, I saw as I got closer. Yes, there were large, long, broken bones that must have come from giant lizards or giant rats or giant who-knew-whats from a thousand eons past. But I saw cow and horse and sheep skulls, too, and dried mud was packed in around it all to hold the bones together. Me, I'd prefer bricks.

The gruesome adobe did a good job, though. Aside from one spot where there was a gap about the size of a two-by-four, the walls were sealed tight. The long, narrow hole let in a solitary beam of sun that shot across the hut from one side to the other— perhaps eighteen feet across—but other than that and the door-way, light wasn't getting in anywhere. As soon as I stepped inside, it was hard to see where I was going.

"What did you—?" I began.

Something crunched underfoot.

"—find?"

"Back up!" Old Red snapped at me from the gloom. "You're steppin' on my clues!"

I moved back toward the doorway.

"Sorry," I said.

I looked down. Not surprisingly, whoever had built the hut hadn't bothered with bone floorboards. It was just plain dirt—

albeit covered with something that sparkled dully in the light that reached it from the doorway.

"What sort of clues are they, anyway? Someone lose their marbles?"

"That down there's broken glass," said Old Red.

My eyes were adjusting to the all-around murkiness now, and I could see him moving along one wall pushing and pulling at the fossils and skulls. None of them budged.

"Glass?" I said. "Didn't notice any windows on this place." I looked up toward the bone ceiling a foot above my head. I couldn't see it. "Could use a chandelier, though."

"Ain't ya noticed the smell?" my brother said, still groping bones.

"No. Walking into a house made of dead things, I wasn't in a rush to take a whiff."

"Well, do it now if you wanna know where that glass came from."

I bent forward and took a big sniff—and instantly regretted it. I straightened back up fast.

The smell was sulfurous and rancid. And very familiar.

Cheap lamp oil.

"Someone had a lantern in here," I said. "And it got busted."

"That's the way it looks."

"Say…after we pulled Glaze out this morning, you said something smelled funny. Was that the lamp oil?"

"Yup."

"So that's why you brought us here."

"Nope. I had no idea there'd be oil spilled in here. Didn't even recognize the smell till a minute ago."

"Well, why'd you wanna come in here then?"

"Cuz of them pebbles in Glaze's wounds."

"Pebbles?"

"Yeah. Pebbles. Little bits of rock. Or what looked like rock. Made me think he'd been brained with the very thing he spent his life chasin'."

"What? You mean a—?"

I turned to my left, toward the solitary gap in the wall letting in light.

The gap roughly the size of a baseball bat. Or a club.

"Ohhhhhhhhh," I said.

"'Oh,' indeed," said Old Red, still feeling his way along the wall to my right.

"So if that spot's where the murder weapon was—a fossil the killer pried out cuz it was just the right size for bashing a man— what are you looking for? I don't think there's going to be a hidden staircase in this thing."

"'In solving a problem of this sort, the grand thing is to be able to reason backward.'"

"Thank you, Mr. Holmes," I said (for of course that's who my brother was quoting). "Only reason backward from what? The 'pebbles'? The hole in the wall?"

Old Red shook his head. "I already did that. I'm talking about the lamp oil."

"Well, *I* already did *that*. Lamp oil equals lantern. They're known to come in handy when you're walking around in the dark."

"Sure they are. But what if you're bein' sneaky? What if you don't want to be spotted a mile away? What if you don't want Eskaminzim catchin' you in the dark with no one else around?"

"Ohhhhhhhhh," I said again.

"'Oh,' indeed."

If Glaze had brought the lantern, he wouldn't have dared use it out in the open in the middle of the night. Not with Eskaminzim and Diehl, and later me and my brother making our rounds.

No, he'd have brought the lantern to use someplace that wouldn't give him away when he fired it up. Like in a hut nestled in on the far side of a hill.

He needed light to see something inside.

Isn't reasoning backward fun?

"There ain't nothin' on the floor I can see," Old Red said. "So I'm thinkin' maybe...hel-lo."

Part of the wall he'd been pushing against was shifting. Something small-ish and white slid to the side, one edge jutting outward. Old Red took hold of it and pulled it out into the light.

It was the sun-bleached skull of a coyote. It was in perfect condition—no cracks, jaw attached, every tooth in place—but hardly the sort of thing a professional fossil hunter like Walter Glaze would've found valuable.

Old Red opened the mouth and looked inside.

"Hm," he grunted unhappily.

"Nothing?"

"Nothin'. Not now, anyway."

"Any something that could've fit in there wouldn't be very big."

"Nope."

"So if that's what Glaze was looking for…what do you hope to find in a coyote's head other than a coyote's brains?"

My brother shrugged. "Maybe he wasn't lookin' for somethin' at all. Maybe he was leavin' somethin'."

"Something that's gone now? Maybe taken by whoever killed him?"

"Maybe maybe maybe." My brother turned away glumly and put the skull back into the wall. "If so, whatever Glaze *was* here for ain't the only thing that's gone. There's the busted lantern and the bone that killed him, too. Probably splintered and smeared up with blood, that bone. Which is why the killer couldn't just stick it back in the wall like this little fella's skull. Nah—I bet it and the lantern both went into the pit with the body."

"I didn't feel anything like that when I was rooting around."

"They'd be easy enough to miss under all that mud. Only so much rootin' you could do." Old Red turned away from the wall, eyes unfocused, fingertips running slowly back and forth over his mustache. "The killer was mighty lucky that storm come along."

"And mighty unlucky you came along. If you hadn't been so fired up to learn how to dig up old bodies, we wouldn't have found the new one."

"Yeah," Old Red mused, still giving his whiskers a dreamy, lost-in-thought massage. "I been ponderin' on that 'luck'…"

"Hey!" Eskaminzim called out. "I'm happy to sit here all day, but the horses say they want to leave! They don't like this place!"

"Them and me both!" I called back. "We'll be out a second!"

Yet my brother hadn't stopped his pondering.

"You keep rubbing your mustache like that, it's gonna fall off," I told him. "Then what will you have to hide your face behind?"

Old Red lowered his hand and glowered at me.

"Just one thing bothers me about all this," he grumbled.

"Just one?"

"All right, there's lots to be bothered by. But knowin' what we know now—about the where and the how—one thing stands out to trouble me most."

I tried rubbing my upper lip for a moment. It didn't help me come up with an answer.

"And that is?" I asked.

"We still only got one why. And that only points one way."

Even without any help from my lip, I saw right off what he meant.

"Ohhhhhhhh," I said yet again.

"'Oh,' indeed."

Despite all we'd learned the last couple hours, we still only knew of one person with enough bad blood with Glaze to spill some.

The man we were being paid to protect.

FIFTEEN
AWKWARD QUESTIONS
OR, OLD RED STARTS SHOOTING QUESTIONS AT FOLKS, AND ONE RICOCHETS BACK

IT WAS about noon when we led the horses back into camp. To my surprise, everyone was there—not just Durgin, Miss Hayes, and Cherry, repitching the tents with help from Diehl. Wentworth and Mead were on hand, as well.

"You left the dig unguarded?" I asked the college boys when Old Red, Eskaminzim, and I returned from putting away the horses.

"We were alone out there for hours! Hearing gunfire!" Wentworth snarled. "For all we knew, the rest of you were being massacred! We had to come back and check!"

The way the others rolled their eyes or gritted their teeth told me they'd sat through this little tirade once already.

"We're going back shortly," said Mead (who'd both rolled his eyes *and* gritted his teeth). "We were waiting for *you* to return so we'd have an escort."

"Well, long as everyone's here, it's a good time for an awkward question," said Old Red.

I didn't grit my teeth, but I did steel myself. If my brother actually acknowledges a question's awkward, you can bet things are about to get mighty uncomfortable.

"Any of you leave camp in the middle of the night?" he said. "Or notice someone else leavin'?"

"Awkward?" Wentworth said. "That's outright insulting!"

"It's got to be asked," said Diehl. He looked like he'd been steeling himself, as well. "Of everyone."

His gaze flicked, for just a second, over to Durgin.

"Why not be plain about it, then?" Wentworth said. "Did any of us sneak off to kill Walter Glaze—that's what he's asking."

"Did you?" said Eskaminzim.

He seemed to be hoping for a "Yes." Not to wrap up the mystery and get our employer off the hook. More because he'd find it amusing.

"Of course I didn't!" Wentworth said. He'd been repounding pegs for the tent he shared with Mead, but now he threw down his mallet and stood up with his hands on his hips. "I didn't even know Glaze personally. And no—I didn't leave camp in the night. I…left to take care of my personal business before dinner, as you yourselves saw. After dinner, I retired and slept soundly until morning. Mead can confirm that."

All eyes turned to Mead.

"Well," the burlier of the college boys said, "I don't know if I'd say 'soundly.'"

He'd been on his knees to help his bunkie get their tent back up, and Wentworth spun to scowl down at him.

"What do you mean?" Wentworth said.

"You snore."

"No, I don't!"

"Yes, you do. All night, every night."

"Ridiculous!"

"How about *you*?" Old Red asked Mead. "You up and about between dinner and dawn?"

"No. Which *he* can confirm."

Mead gave Wentworth a sideways nod.

"Well, he didn't wake me up, anyway," Wentworth huffed. "But who knows? Maybe I was snoring so loudly I couldn't hear him."

Mead rose to his feet, glaring at Wentworth.

"All right, all right," Wentworth said. "No, I didn't notice him leave the tent. And despite how I may or may not sleep, I *would* have noticed him leaving."

"How about anyone else movin' through camp in the night?" Old Red asked. "Maybe goin' from one tent to another? You made a crack about that yesterday. Anything to it?"

"What do you...?" Wentworth began. Then his face simultaneously went red and stony still. "Oh."

"A crack is all that was," Mead said. "He's never really noticed anything like that, last night or any other." He gave Wentworth another glower. "Have you?"

"No," Wentworth muttered, looking down at his mud-covered shoes.

Miss Hayes stared at him steadily, unblinking, unwilling to acknowledge that she knew whose nighttime activities the college boy's "crack" had been about.

Durgin, on the other hand, was fuming.

"Are you certain this is really necessary?" he said.

He directed the question at Diehl rather than my brother.

"It's not just necessary, Professor. It's unavoidable," Diehl told him. "The law might be a long, long way from here, but it's going to show up sooner or later—with these very questions. We need to know now what our answers should be."

He might have been backing Old Red up, in his way, but my brother gave him a sharp look all the same.

Diehl wasn't saying we needed to know the truth. He was saying we needed to know what to say.

There might be a big difference. One Old Red wouldn't care for.

"Well, you don't have to twist *my* arm for an answer," Cherry said. "I'll give it to you quick with no fuss so we can get on to more important things. I didn't leave my tent all night, and I didn't hear anything either. I didn't even hear Wentworth snoring, though I have no doubt he does it no matter what he says. Hell, I barely even noticed the storm. I sleep heavy."

"You sleep the sleep of the dead," Wentworth grumbled. "Half the time, we don't even have coffee waiting for us when we wake up."

Cherry didn't tell him to shut up, but from the look she gave him, it was clear she was tempted. Or maybe she was thinking about chucking a coffee pot at his head. Either way, the rest of us wouldn't have blamed her.

"And you, Miss?" Old Red said to Miss Hayes.

"I suppose I'm a heavy sleeper, as well," she said. "I *did* wake up during the storm. I was worried about what it meant for the dig and the equipment and specimens here in camp. But I didn't notice any comings and goings."

"Yes, yes—it's the same for me," Durgin declared. "I stayed in my tent and noticed nothing till the rains came." He focused on Diehl again. "*Now* can we be done with this?"

"They haven't answered the question," Wentworth said petulantly.

He waggled a pointed finger from side to side. It was aimed, in a general way, at four of us: me and Old Red and Diehl and Eskaminzim.

Eskaminzim, for one, seemed thrilled to be included. He quickly showed us why.

"I wasn't here most of the night, but when I got back, before falling asleep, I did hear someone move away from camp. Only not far enough." He turned on Diehl. "*You.* You got up to make water…and you broke wind while you did it!"

Diehl gave him a hangdog, long-suffering, "Lord, give me strength" look.

"An Apache would go a mile from camp before doing such things," Eskaminzim went on. He shook his head reproachfully. "But you—you barely went past the horses!"

"And then I came right back to the tent, didn't I?" Diehl said through clenched teeth. "So you can confirm: I didn't really leave camp at all once we finished our rounds. And I can say the same of you."

I knew Diehl was glossing over something he'd admitted to me and my brother earlier: that he and Eskaminzim hadn't been together the whole time they were nighthawking. They'd both had plenty of time alone—time they might've run into Glaze on his mysterious errand and decided to whittle down Loveland's forces by one. They'd shown with the Shoshone that "evening the odds" was something they were happy to do given the chance…and that they weren't squeamish about how they did it.

Hard men, these new colleagues of ours. I'd say I was glad they were on our side if I could totally trust that they *were* on our side.

Still—now wasn't the time to get into all that, and if Diehl was going to gloss over things in front of the others, I was glad to gloss with him.

"It's the same for me and Gustav," I said. "We were both asleep in our tent till it was our turn on watch. Sleeping heavy while we could, knowing the second half of our night would be spent on our feet. So I guess that's that. No one saw anything, and most everyone's accounted for."

"What I still don't understand," Wentworth said, "is why you two would have gone to that pit. We all heard the Indian warn you away from it during dinner last night. Yet then you take Miss Hayes's tools and start digging around in it in the middle of the night?"

"That is peculiar," Mead agreed reluctantly.

I was surprised—and irritated—to find the college boys stopping my glossing cold. And my expression probably showed it.

"Just trying to ask the questions 'the law' will," Wentworth said smugly.

"Yeah, well…'peculiar' is totally normal when you're my brother and me," I said.

No one looked convinced. Which was fair enough, since—though utterly true—it didn't come close to explaining anything.

"Like I said earlier," Old Red said, "I wanted to try my hand at diggin' for fossils like y'all do. I knew not to do it where you're workin' now, so I went where the work is through. That Glaze had been dumped there was just…"

His face pinched up, lips puckering under his mustache. It looked like he was either going to spit or cough up a hairball.

"…coincidence," he said.

"Well, that's all the explaining *I* need to hear today," Cherry said. "Can I leave now? I gotta get going to town if I'm gonna stock up again and be back before nightfall."

"You shouldn't go off in the wagon all by yourself," I said. "Not with everything that's been going on."

Cherry swiped a hand at me. "Oh, I don't need a military escort. I just need to get a move on."

"I'll go with her," Miss Hayes announced.

Durgin turned to her, about to start sputtering to judge by the look on his face. But the lady carried on before he could object.

"We have specimens that'll be safer in our storage house in Wamsutter than out here. Plus it's been a few days since anyone's checked in with the postmaster. There might be important correspondence waiting for us, John."

"But…well…young Amlingmajor is right," Durgin said. "You shouldn't go in without protection."

Diehl started to say something, but Old Red jumped in first— and not to correct Durgin again on the pronunciation of our name.

"My brother and me'll go with 'em." He looked over at Diehl, anticipating an objection. "We need to go in anyway. It was us who found the body. We should get our side of it in front of the nearest lawman so no one flies off half-cocked after hearin' Loveland's tellin' of it."

Diehl took that in silently, then gave my brother a curt nod. He wasn't going to argue.

"Hold on," Wentworth whined. "Just like that, we're going to go back down to two guards out here? With men dying and horses stampeding and gun battles and who-knows-what next?"

"Yes!" Eskaminzim enthused. "But don't worry. I'll stay close by if you like. I can be right behind you every second. Never letting you out of my sight…or out of my reach…"

The Apache smiled.

Wentworth's eyes widened. "Oh…uhh…that won't be necessary. I suppose everything will be fine."

He didn't look sure, though.

Other than Eskaminzim, nobody did.

SIXTEEN
THE ROAD TO WAMSUTTER
OR, "LITTLE RED" WHEEDLES WHAT HE
CAN FROM CHERRY BEFORE THE
CONVERSATION TURNS TOTALLY NUTTY

WE HITCHED a fresh horse to the wagon, then off we
went: Cherry with the reins, Miss Hayes beside her, me and
Old Red riding along on either side. Cherry was in no mood to
dawdle, sending the buckboard down the hill from camp at a
clip that rattled both the cargo—the big femur Durgin had
been worried about plus two field jackets far smaller than the
big boulders we'd seen in Wamsutter—as well as Miss Hayes's
teeth.

"Please—not so fast!" the lady cried. "We don't want to shake
our samples to pieces!"

Cherry slowed the horses but didn't look happy about it. In
fact, she remained sour and fidgety long after we'd reached the
bottom of the hill and began winding our way around the next on
our way to the thin ribbon of road leading to town. Despite her
grumbling, there was only so fast the wagon could've gone anyway
with two passengers, freight in the bed and soppy-moist ground
under the wheels.

"Say—there's a curious sight," Old Red said after we'd been
creeping along for twenty minutes or so. He pointed to our right
at the scattered pile of bones south of Camp Cashew. "Seen a few

of those around here and ain't heard a good explanation for 'em yet."

He was trying for an easy, casual tone as if making conversation to keep the women entertained while we inched our way toward Wamsutter. "An easy, casual tone" isn't his specialty, though—it's mine—and entertaining anybody is usually the last thing on his mind. So I knew he was angling for something. But Cherry seemed glad enough for the distraction not to question it.

"Oh, those ain't nothin', Little Red," she said. "Just Shoshone junk piles or markers put up by the sheepmen who used to watch flocks around here. There was a bunch of Basques in Sweetwater County till the cattlemen pushed them out. Most of 'em run off to Idaho and Nevada about ten years back."

"Interestin'," Old Red said. "How you pick all that up? You live here a long time?"

Cherry did turn cagey now, the sulky frown returning to her thin, pinched face.

"I been around a while, doin' this and that. Learned a thing or two, I guess."

"Oh? What kinda this and that? And how'd you come to work for Professor Durgin?"

Cherry quickly went from sulking to seething. Prying into people's past is considered bad manners out here in the West—because so many folks are only in the West to escape their past in the East. Diehl told us Cherry had mentioned a runaway husband and dead kids. Whatever "this and that" she'd had to do since then, and how they'd brought her where she was, was clearly something she didn't care to share.

Old Red tried to give her a reassuring smile. It came off pretty halfhearted, though. All you could really make out of it was a slight deepening of the dimples on either side of his mustache.

Miss Hayes jumped in to smooth things over.

"The cook the professor used last year wasn't available, so he tried a new man. Mr. Verardo."

Cherry snorted and shook her head. "Lou."

"That's right," Miss Hayes said. "Luigi Verardo. Despite the reputation the Italians have for their cuisine, his cooking was…inadequate."

"It was swill from what I've heard!" Cherry declared. Bad-mouthing a rival cook seemed to be putting her in a better mood pretty quick.

"Well, I don't know about 'swill,' but it wasn't good," Miss Hayes said. "It's hard to keep your strength and spirits up on burned flapjacks and raw bacon. We didn't want to let him go without a replacement lined up, though, and Wamsutter isn't exactly overflowing with cooks. But then Mr. Verardo forced the issue. Or perhaps I should say Professor Loveland did."

"Lou got himself run off by those lowlifes working for Loveland!"

We'd heard this part from Diehl the day before, yet Old Red raised his eyebrows as if it was quite the surprise. "Oh, really? When did this happen?"

"A little over a week ago. Not long after the man you call 'Vollmer' first showed up," Miss Hayes said. "Mr. Verardo went into town for supplies with Peter and Andrew, much as we're doing, and apparently he had a run-in with Vollmer and his friends at the local tavern."

"'Tavern,'" Cherry scoffed. "That's a nice way to put it. You're too fine a lady to have set foot inside, so let me describe Dirty Dan's Water Trough to the boys." She leaned toward Old Red riding close on her left and dropped her voice to a stage whisper. "It's a shithole."

Miss Hayes pursed her lips and pretended not to hear.

Cherry straightened up cackling, her usual bubbly mood almost entirely restored now that she'd managed to get some cussing in.

"Gosh," I said. "With a name like Dirty Dan's Water Trough I'd have expected something classy."

Cherry cackled again. "Nope! Shithole!"

Pretending not to hear *that* seemed a little pointless, but Miss Hayes carried on doing it all the same.

"The professor don't allow booze in camp, you know, so I

guess ol' Lou was trying to get himself good and soaked while he could," Cherry went on. "But then Vollmer and that bunch come striding in, and he goes skedaddling out—and he never stops skedaddling till he reaches the Canadian border, I reckon."

"He left town?" Old Red said.

Cherry nodded. "Last folks saw of him, he was running for the train station like a grizzly was after him for breakfast."

"So Professor Durgin suddenly needed himself a new cook, and by happenstance, you were available."

Cherry kept nodding, in a good enough mood now not to notice the shrewd edge to the look my brother was giving her.

"I found myself at leisure and was willing to entertain an offer of employment," she said with a mock-haughty air. Then she burst out laughing again.

"I guess I actually owe Vollmer a thank you then," I said. "I'm sorry to hear what happened to ol' Lou, but I'm not particularly partial to burned flapjacks and raw bacon. Your bread, on the other hand…"

I patted my stomach and sighed contentedly.

Cherry took a little bow.

While she was turned my way, gaze angled downward, I glanced over her at Old Red and waggled my eyebrows.

Dr. Watson never mentioned buttering up suspects for Mr. Holmes. So I figured I was one up on him as sidekick to a detective.

My brother gave me no sign he appreciated this, of course. He just refocused on Cherry, endeavoring to maintain an air of affable nonchalance. (For him, that takes work.)

"That Vollmer…he is an interestin' one. There's somethin' about him…" he said. "Do you know him? From before this hulla-balloo between the professors, I mean."

Cherry shook her head. "No. He and his bunch are new here. Never saw 'em before until a couple weeks ago. Nobody had. Got a reputation real fast, though. Lou wasn't the only local they pushed around. Real SOBs, if you'll pardon my saying."

Miss Hayes smiled primly. "I appreciate the abbreviation."

Cherry gave that one of her snorts, then took the opportunity to change the subject.

"How about you, Miss? How'd you come to be out here in the middle of all this?" She flapped a withered hand at the vast, grassy expanse we were moving across so slowly. "I know Professor Durgin says you're a dinosaur 'en-thoo-zee-ast,' but I assume there are plenty of them who don't leave their libraries to spend a summer digging ditches and fighting over bones."

"Oh. Well," said Miss Hayes, a little taken aback to suddenly find herself on the receiving end of the prying. "I've been a supporter of Gulf Coast University, where John...Professor Durgin came to teach. I was thrilled when he joined the faculty. I really am quite an admirer."

The lady paused for breath, then quickly added, "Of his work."

"Such an admirer you wanted to help dig his ditches?" Old Red said.

Miss Hayes's expression soured. "I should think you'd understand, Mr. Amlingmeyer. After all, you were so fascinated by those 'ditches' you went digging in one in the middle of the night. With *my* tools."

I think the appropriate response from a gentleman would have been "Touché," but Old Red just conceded the point with a silent nod.

"Anyway," Miss Hayes went on, trying to smile again. "Professor Durgin has a truly inspiring vision for the future of paleontology. A great optimism for where it's headed. It's one of the most important, intriguing new sciences, and it's developing so rapidly right here in America. Just one more major discovery—the kind that could capture the imagination of the nation, if presented the right way—could push it to new places, galvanize public support for all the sciences. It's a tremendously exciting prospect. So when the professor began organizing this expedition...well, I guess I invited myself along, and he was gracious enough not to try to dissuade me. I knew it would involve hardship and difficult work, yet still I envisioned it as a sort of holiday for me. A little adventure…"

"Didn't stay little, did it, Miss?" I said. "Or much of a holiday."

"No. I suppose not."

"I wouldn't have thought it was just Professor Durgin you had to convince to let you tag along," said Old Red. "Professor Pertwee's footin' the bill for everything, ain't he? What did he think?"

"The expedition he's funding got a free worker with some expertise and a willingness to cover her own expenses. He had no complaints."

Cherry suddenly jabbed Miss Hayes in the ribs with a bony elbow.

The lady sat up so straight, so fast for a second, I thought she was going to shoot out of the wagon like a stray kernel of popcorn flying out of the pot.

"Speaking of Professor. Pertwee," Cherry said to her, "I been meaning to tell you something."

"Yes?"

Cherry nodded gravely. "Peanuts."

Miss Hayes blinked at her. "Peanuts?"

Cherry kept nodding. "Peanuts. You pass that long to Pertwee."

Miss Hayes blinked again, then smiled. "Ah. For his nut butter."

"That's right. He thinks folks like that glop of his now, wait till he tries making it with peanuts instead of cashews. Better smell, better taste, better nut butter. You take that to him, and I guarantee it'll be the biggest discovery to come outta this trip. Probably help him earn back every cent he put into it."

"Thank you, Cherry. But I believe the professor is a step ahead of you. He's experimented with all kinds of nuts—almonds, hazelnuts, pistachios—and from what I've heard peanuts are something he's giving a lot of thought."

"Well, they should be. Cashews?" Cherry shivered, then grinned. "But peanuts? I love 'em!"

Once again, I looked over the top of the women to give my brother a look—this time of commiseration. Here he was trying to dig up something useful for his deducing—clay to make bricks, as he'd put it—and Cherry and Miss Hayes were talking nuts.

To my surprise, he didn't seem irritated in the slightest. Quite the opposite. He was wearing that familiar look—intense and intent yet somehow dreamy and distant at the same time—that told me the wheels in his head were turning a lot faster than those on the buckboard.

Cherry hating cashews didn't strike me as a revelation that would break the mystery open like the unshelling of a nut, but then again, I'm not the Holmes of the Range. I'm just the Watson of the West...which means I'm completely in the dark ninety-five percent of the time.

Old Red was so lost in thought a miracle occurred: I noticed something before he did. The horses caught it the same time as me, pricking up their ears and lifting their heads to look to our left.

A rumbling was rising up that way. Hoofbeats and perhaps something more.

Someone was coming.

The trail to town was in sight now, cutting through a flat stretch of grass and scrub about three hundred yards ahead. Along it from the north, appearing over a low ridge there, came our mirror image: a wagon with two escorts on horseback.

One of the riders was wearing a gray hat.

It was Vollmer and his two friends, the tubby one and the skinny one, taking Loveland's buckboard to town. I couldn't see into the bed, but it didn't take much guesswork to know what it held. Walter Glaze was on his way to Wamsutter, too.

I put a hand to my Peacemaker, ready to draw it fast if either of the riders swerved our way.

"Don't worry," Old Red said (though I noticed his free hand

drifting down toward his own gun belt). "They ain't slowin' to say hello."

Indeed, without any cargo they had to worry about jostling—Glaze wasn't going to make any complaints—they were moving south a lot faster than we could manage. They'd be in town long before us.

Old Red and I already knew who the law was in Wamsutter. My brother had asked Cherry before we'd set out. The little town had one part-time constable and a telegraph wire to the county seat (and the sheriff there) eighty-three miles away. But now I found myself more curious than ever who this constable was—and how he was going to greet us after hearing whatever tales Vollmer told him. Apparently Old Red felt the same way.

"Cherry," he said, "what's this constable in Wamsutter like? Hellyer, you said his name was?"

Cherry snorted again. Add them up and her snorts per mile doubled those of the horses.

"Yeah. Larry Hellyer. He's fine enough…as a blacksmith. That's his real job. As a constable, he's about as much use as a minister in a whorehouse. Harder to find than one of those, too, when there's trouble. But that's what you get for twenty dollars a month."

"Hopefully he's intelligent enough to take what Vollmer tells him with a grain of salt," Miss Hayes said.

You can probably guess how Cherry responded to that.

"'Intelligent' and 'Larry' are oil and water," she said (post-snort). "Just don't go together."

"At least he's smart enough to hide at the right times," I said. "Maybe he'll dodge Vollmer, too."

"Already got plenty of practice at it," Cherry said.

"And what he thinks is moot anyway, ain't it?" I said to Old Red. "Glaze didn't die in town. It's a county matter. For the sheriff to deal with."

My brother was watching the wagon and riders move swiftly past. As he'd predicted, they didn't slow in the slightest—though Vollmer did turn and tip his gray hat to us.

"What'll the sheriff be told about what's happened—that's what I'd like to know. And how long will it take him to get here?" Old Red said. "And with him miles away and Hellyer the only one around with a badge, who's to stop Vollmer and his boys from doin' whatever they please?"

"Oh," I said. "Good questions."

They were so good, in fact, none of us could do anything but brood on them the rest of the way to town.

SEVENTEEN
THE GULF COAST UNIVERSITY DEPARTMENT OF PALEONTOLOGY SPECIMEN STORAGE FACILITY, WYOMING BRANCH

OR, SOMEONE TAKES A PAGE FROM MISS HAYES'S BOOK (LITERALLY)

WAMSUTTER'S EASY TO OVERLOOK—JUST a cluster of little buildings spread thin and low across the broad Wyoming horizon. Yet we were able to spot the town two miles off, thanks to our timing. A long, black finger pointed down at it from the sky.

Smoke. A train was at the station, the engine idling.

"That'll be the Afternoon Special on its way to Point of Rocks," Cherry said. She ran the back of her hand over her thin lips as if the thought of it made her thirsty. "Doesn't even stop most days. Not many folks coming and going from Wamsutter. Probably taking on water."

Whatever the train had stopped for, the business was finished quick. After a couple minutes, the black finger began to slant as the Afternoon Special moved westward along the Union Pacific tracks. By the time we reached the outskirts of town, it had long since dissipated, though there were a few thinner, wispier columns of smoke to be seen now—the gray fumes from fireplaces, stoves, and forges.

"This is the first time I've been back in town in a week," Miss Hayes said as we crossed the tracks. "I'll have to soak up civilization while I can." Her gaze moved to our left, and her expression hardened. "Such as it is."

Nearby was a reminder of just how uncivilized things could be around there.

Loveland's buckboard was parked on the other side of the train depot, outside the storage building we'd seen two gunhands guarding the day before. There was only one man out front now, lingering beside the horses tied near the wagon. It was the tubby, grubby man Vollmer had called "Benji." He gave us his best threatening glower as we moved past, and this much I'll give him: He wouldn't win many points for his physique or grooming, but when it came to threatening glowers he was a champ.

"You think Vollmer's off talking to the constable," I said, voice low, "or inside there getting his pals ready for whatever's to come after?"

"Let's ask *him*," Old Red said.

He nodded at Hoop, who was watching us impassively from the next building—the dilapidated old barn Durgin had rented to store his finds in. I gave him a little wave, but he didn't return it. Waving was neither his style nor particularly practicable at the moment. Not with his big Sharps rifle cradled in his arms.

"Glad to see you," he said in his dry, unsmiling way as we came to a stop before him. "Five against one ain't good odds."

"Well, now it's even!" Cherry declared as she set the wagon's brake.

Hoop was too polite to point out that a couple unarmed women didn't exactly balance out evenly against any two of Loveland's gunmen.

"We got a name for Gray Hat now," Old Red told him. "Ed Vollmer. He inside back there with his bunch?"

Hoop nodded. "I expected 'em to unload some bones, but no. They just went right inside and left the big slob—"

"Benji," I said.

"Right. Left *Benji* outside on watch. Any other introductions you got to make?"

"Just one," I said. "Their Shoshone. They call him Joe, but his real name is…long."

"Doyadukubichi'," said Old Red.

The rest of us gave him an impressed look. Even writing the Shoshone's name down now, I'd be hard-pressed to pronounce it, but my brother just popped it out like it was "Fred."

"Well, I didn't see Doyadukubichi' with 'em," Hoop said.

The impressed looks swiveled his way. He'd shot the name back like it was "Ned."

Hoop had been a soldier on the frontier—one of the "Buffalo soldiers" of the 10th Cavalry—when I was still learning to keep my diapers clean. I guess you pick up a way with Indian names if you've had enough years of practice at it.

"He still out with Loveland?" he went on.

"Must be," said Old Red.

"We had a little run-in with him," I told Hoop. "He came out the worse for wear. Maybe they're being nice and letting him take the rest of the afternoon off."

"Yeah. Right. Any idea why they'd send the rest into town all at once?"

My brother took a deep breath. "Yes…unfortunately."

From our first meeting, Hoop had struck me as a cool and collected character, and he stayed true to that as Old Red laid out what had happened: Glaze and Loveland's confrontation with Durgin the day before, our discovery of Glaze's murder as the storm blew in, and Loveland's perhaps understandably skeptical response when we'd brought him the body with assurances we weren't the culprits. Hoop's only reaction was the occasional grunted "Hm" until my brother was done. Then he allowed himself a doleful rub on the jaw—about as demonstrative as he got—before asking, "What now?"

"You boys work that out," said Cherry. She'd been antsy as Old Red spoke, climbing down from the wagon and shifting from foot to foot clearly itching to scurry off. "I got shopping to do."

"You don't need to take the wagon with you?" Miss Hayes asked her.

I was wondering the same thing. It didn't seem likely a spindly little thing like Cherry would want to come back from the general store with her arms full of beans and bacon and a barrel of flour strapped to her back. But she waved the question off as she began backing away.

"Oh. No. I'll be fine. You've still got unloading to do anyway."

And she turned and went striding off into town.

"Well?" Hoop said, bringing us back to his "What now?" of a moment before.

"Otto and me'll go talk to Hellyer, the town constable," Old Red said. "Hopefully he'll help us get our side of things in front of the sheriff. But first…like Cherry said."

He jerked his head at the wagon bed and the fossil and field jackets there.

The unloading didn't take long. The only thing that was a two-man job was the larger of the two jackets, which Hoop and I lifted and carried in using long canvas straps. We laid it on the dirt floor near its big, plaster-wrapped brethren. Durgin had said they'd send them all back east when they had enough to fill a train car, and it looked to me like they were getting close.

Miss Hayes oversaw the work then did some unloading of her own: She'd brought her tool bag along for the ride, and she fetched it inside and started rooting around in it.

"I don't think you're gonna find much digging in town, Miss," I told her. "The only fossil here you haven't already collected and labeled is Hoop."

I threw Hoop a little "Just kidding" smile.

He did not smile back.

"I'm not planning on doing any digging," Miss Hayes said. "I'm looking for this."

She pulled a notebook from her knapsack and waggled it in the air.

"Your autograph book?" I said, reaching for it. "Well, of course, I'd be happy to sign it."

I tried out my "Just kidding" smile again. It met with more success with the lady.

"My record book," she said, returning the smile. "I need to note that these specimens are now at the university's storage facility in Wamsutter."

A pencil was secured to the notebook with a rubber band. She slipped it out, pulled off the band, and opened the book.

"'The university's storage facility'?" I said, looking around at the rickety, rotted planks along the walls. "And here I thought it was a barn."

I focused on Miss Hayes again hoping to see her smile growing wider. Instead I found it gone altogether.

"Mr. Amlingmeyer," she said with what sounded like barely contained rage. "When you borrowed my tools last night, did you go through my field notes?"

Old Red had been sauntering slowly down the nearest row of field jackets like he was taking in the pictures at an exhibition. He turned toward the lady with a look that was both confused and embarrassed.

"I did not," he said.

Why would he have? He can barely read at all beyond "The dog chased the cat," and he was still working on that with the help of the primer we'd received for Christmas. "McGuffey's First Eclectic Reader" is great for teaching you "boy," "girl," "ball" and "doll," but there's nary a "diplodocus" in sight.

"Is something wrong?" I asked Miss Hayes.

She had the notebook spread wide, and she lifted it to show me a little ridge of ripped paper running down the middle.

"One of the pages has been torn out," she said.

"Oh?" said Old Red.

He headed back toward the front of the barn.

"I know this might sound dumb," I said. "But could it have been damaged when those horses stampeded through Camp Cashew?"

Hoop cocked an eyebrow at me. "Horses stampeded through camp?"

"A lot's happened," I told him with an apologetic shrug. "We haven't had time to tell you everything yet."

"The notebook was sealed, as you saw, and it appears undamaged from the outside," said Miss Hayes. "So no—there's no way a horse's hoof could have ripped out a single interior page and carried it away."

I nodded. Like I'd said, I'd figured it was a dumb question. But sometimes a dumb question's got to be asked, and I'm just the kind of selfless, dedicated detective to ask it. Plus I usually can't think of the smart questions—I leave that to my brother.

"What was on the missin' page?" he said, stepping up close to peer at the notebook.

"My notes on some of our finds. Catalog numbers and a field drawing or two."

"From the diplodocus?" said Old Red.

He sounded eager, almost pleased, and not because he'd said "diplodocus" right. He was expecting a particular answer—one that would point in a particular direction.

Clearly, the expected answer was "yes."

Which was clear because of the way my brother's face fell when Miss Hayes said "No."

"No?" he said, just in case his big ears were playing tricks on him.

Miss Hayes shook her head. "This page was from earlier. Covering some of our initial, minor discoveries our first few days out. Before the professor discovered the diplodocus."

Old Red stepped back, brow furrowed.

"*Before* the professor discovered the diplodocus," he repeated slowly. "The missin' page...is it a big problem for you and Professor Durgin? The notes and whatnot you lost?"

Miss Hayes shook her head again. "Just a big disappointment. I've tried to be meticulous. But losing a single page on some relatively minor fossils...no, it's no disaster. Most of the information can be pieced together again when the preparators demold the specimens back at the university."

"So the notes ain't worth nothin' on their own?"

"No. They'd be of little use to anyone without the fossils themselves."

"Which Loveland intends to have, one way or another," I pointed out. I turned to Old Red. "Maybe that page is what Glaze was looking for."

"In the bone hut…?" my brother mused. "Could be…"

He left unspoken—as did I—the not-so-dumb question that raised.

If the missing page had been left in the bone hut for Glaze, who left it? And where did it go after he was killed?

"'Bone hut'?" Hoop said.

I gave him a reassuring pat on his broad shoulder. "Don't worry. You'll catch up eventually."

He gave my hand a look that made me snatch it away fast.

"It's the big boy Loveland wants. The diplodocus," Old Red went on in his dreamy, distracted, wheels-are-turning voice—the one he uses when deducifying's getting done. "That's what this is all about. So why would he…or anyone…care what Durgin was diggin' up right *before* he found it?"

"I got no idea," Hoop said.

I shook my head. "You don't have to answer, Hoop. He's not talking to us."

Indeed, my brother made no indication that he'd heard either of us. He just kept staring glassy-eyed at the side of the barn for a moment before suddenly straightening up and slapping his hands together.

"*Well*," he said in that clipped way that announces a conversation is over, "Otto and me need to find this Larry Hellyer fella. Want to come with us, Miss?"

Miss Hayes nodded down at her notebook. "No, I'd like to look this over some more. See if there's anything else that's been tampered with."

"Right."

Old Red started for the door, and I did the same.

"So no one's gonna spell me?" said Hoop. "I get to keep standin' around an old barn?"

"Oh, don't complain," I told him. "At least you'll have nicer company than me."

My brother threw me a sidelong scowl as we carried on outside. He slowed just a moment to eye Loveland's larger, tidier specimen storage facility—and large, untidy Benji still standing guard outside—before we rounded the barn and headed south into town.

EIGHTEEN
BAD MEDICINE
OR, OLD RED TAKES US OUT OF OUR WAY FOR A DOSE OF USELESS DATA, AND I ACT LIKE A PILL

AS HAS BEEN NOTED, New York City Wamsutter is not. It's not even Peabody, Kansas. It's one of those little Western settlements you've never heard of—because what is there to say? The railroad passes through and a water tank goes up and a few buildings appear around it like barnacles clinging to the side of a dinghy. That's Wamsutter.

Teeny as it was, though, I quickly realized that we'd made a foolish mistake before walking off into it: We had neglected to ask for directions.

There might only be three streets—the main drag from the train depot and two more cutting crossways east to west up ahead —but we had no idea on which we would find Larry Hellyer. Little burgs where the one constable earns twenty bucks a month don't have fancy offices for them. Or even a jail. Usually that's just an old smokehouse the town council rents out for a few bits when someone's been rowdy enough to need locking up.

Yet my brother was hustling up the street without the slightest hesitation. He seemed to know exactly where he was going.

Then I remembered that we did have directions of a sort. Or at least an idea of what to look for.

"I have made a deduction," I announced.

"Oh?" my brother muttered warily.

I pointed up at the smoke drifting skyward here and there from town.

"You are taking us to those," I said. "Because we know Larry Hellyer is a blacksmith, and where you've got a blacksmith, you'll have a fire."

"Not bad," Old Red allowed. "For a guess."

He veered off toward a row of buildings to our left—none of which were smoking.

"That say what I think it says?" he asked, pointing at a crude sign hanging over one of the doors.

I squinted at the one word painted none-too-neatly on it in blue paint.

"'Druggist'?"

Old Red perked up and smiled in a very un-Old Red way. "That's what I thought it said."

He kept steering us toward the door.

"Cherry's cooking give you a sour stomach?" I asked him. "Or are you finally gonna do something about your breath?"

"Don't need no medicine," Old Red growled, his smile already fading. "Though the more you talk, the more I feel a headache comin' on."

He pushed through the door, and into the pharmacy we went. Though calling it a "pharmacy" is doing it quite the favor. A mud puddle may contain water, but that doesn't make it a lake. "Drug store" would be literally correct, as there were drugs apparently for sale: a potpourri of patent medicines lining one shelf, tooth-pastes and foot powders and muscle liniments upon another. Every bottle was spaced half a foot from the next, presumably to disguise (poorly) the thinness of the inventory. The one thing the place truly got right pharmacy-wise was the smell, for it had the sharp, spicy, alcohol-and-cloves aroma of medicine. There was some extra element to the scent—an undertone that tickled at my memory—but I couldn't put a name to it.

The real stock in trade thereabouts seemed to be out-of-date newspapers and magazines, for dozens were spread out upon the countertops to slowly fade in the dim light of the one dingy window. I did a quick scan for our own faces—or at least our own faces as the illustrators in New York choose to imagine them—but there were no copies of *Smythe's Frontier Detective* on display. I can only assume because anyone in possession of one of my stories would never dream of parting with it.

That "Magazines" hadn't been added beneath "Druggist" on the sign out front I attributed to either a lack of ambition or of paint on the part of the druggist himself. Or more likely both. He certainly didn't look like a man with a lot of get-up-and-go. Sit-down-and-snooze seemed to be more his line. He was seated behind one of the counters on a chair leaning back against the wall, an old *Ladies' Home Journal* draped across his face. As we approached, he slowly reached up a big paw to pull the magazine away, revealing a face that was puffy, pale, and unshaven. The prospect of a sale gave him just enough energy for a smile but not enough to pull him to his feet.

"Can I help you, gentlemen?" he asked, his voice soft yet rasping.

"I bet you can," said Old Red. "We're wonderin' where we might find Larry Hellyer."

The druggist's smile waned, and for a second, I thought he was going to put his *Ladies' Home Journal* back over his face and just wait for us to leave.

"Been some unpleasantness outside of town," my brother went on. "Need his help clearin' it up."

The druggist's eyes brightened. Which isn't saying much. They'd been as dull as two old corroded pennies before.

"Trouble, huh?"

Old Red shrugged. "A bit."

His tight smile made it plain nothing more was forthcoming.

"Well, good luck getting any help from Larry," the druggist said. "He's about the laziest man I know—and that's when he's *not* hung over. Which he probably is. He's got a smithy around the corner. Go out, turn left, turn left again at the first street, and you can't miss it."

That this fellow—torpid as a turtle in the sun—was calling Hellyer the laziest man he knew did not bode well for the assistance we'd be getting from the constable. You know—like convincing the sheriff we weren't murderers or keeping Vollmer and his boys from shooting us in the back. That kind of thing. It sounded like we'd be on our own.

Yet my brother just tugged politely at the brim of his Stetson and turned to go.

"Thank you, sir. You have a good…oh." Old Red froze. "One other thing. We're supposed to be catchin' up to a friend of ours somewhere around here, too. Cherry Dixon. You seen her?"

The druggist dredged up the energy to widen his eyes in surprise. "Not only have I seen her, she was standing exactly where you are not five minutes ago."

"I suppose she popped in for that foot cream she's been sayin' she needed?"

The druggist settled back against his chair, eyelids drooping again in a way that seemed as sly as it was sleepy.

"That's right," he said. "Corns…quite a malady for the working woman."

"I'm glad you could help her out," Old Red said. "She say where she was headed next?"

The druggist spread his hands in his lap in lieu of a shrug. (Shrugs take effort.)

"Nope. Probably in a hurry to find some privacy and apply her foot cream."

"I'm sure. Well, thank you."

Old Red turned to go again.

"Don't you need anything for yourself?" the druggist asked. "You look a little peaked, friend. Some Biemann's Gargling Oil would fix you right up. Or maybe a bottle of Mrs. McFarlane's Soothing Syrup? Or how about Dr. Goggins' Magic Nerve Drops? Loaded with coca. Gives a man pep."

"I got pep," my brother grumbled.

"You could always use more," I told him. I leaned from side to side, giving him a long once-over. "You *do* look a little peaked. Friend."

Old Red gave me a glare and continued on his way.

"How about you?" the druggist asked me hopefully.

"Sorry, mister." I thumped my chest. "Fit as a fiddle."

The druggist sank even further into his chair, though that had hardly seemed possible. If anyone needed a big dose of coca, it was him. The man was pep-less.

"There aren't enough sick people around here," he muttered.

"Now, now—don't lose hope. A town like this? You could get a nice outbreak of cholera any day now."

The druggist snorted listlessly and settled his *Ladies' Home Journal* back over his face.

Oh, well—I'd tried. Some folks just don't want cheering up.

I followed Old Red outside.

"How'd you know Cherry was gonna stop in here?" I asked him. "She never said anything about corns that I heard."

"'You see, but you do not observe,'" Old Red said, quoting Guess Who.

"I didn't *see* her damn corns either," I replied. "Thank god."

My brother began to roll his eyes—then locked them on something to our left.

"Hel-lo," he said.

Miss Hayes was stepping from a store across the street, an envelope in her hands.

"Didn't take long for her to 'check her notes,' did it?" Old Red said.

"Well, how long does it take to flip through a notebook looking for pages ripped out?"

"About ten seconds…which is why it seemed like a pretty thin excuse to stay behind at the barn in the first place."

Miss Hayes hadn't noticed us watching her—she was too busy opening the letter in her hands, a concerned frown on her face.

Old Red pivoted and started toward the next intersection.

"You think she just wanted to peel off on her own?" I said as I followed along.

"*Quieter*," my brother shot back. "And yes."

"Now why would she want to go and deprive herself of our company?"

"Dammit, Otto," Old Red said, head pointed straight forward, eyes angling to the side to watch the lady. "Don't you think that's exactly what I intend to find out?"

NINETEEN
ROGUE MAIL

OR, WE HAVE A SURPRISE IN STORE, THEN AN EVEN BIGGER ONE ROLLS IN ON FOUR WHEELS

"SO," I said to Old Red. Quietly. "We're pretending we don't see her."

In a moment, Miss Hayes and we were going to pass each other on opposite sides of Main Street (or whatever Wamsutterites call the broad swath of mud and manure that runs through the middle of their town). All it would take was one quick glance up for the lady to spot us heading south as she headed north.

"That's the idea," my brother said. "And we gotta make it look good in case she catches sight of us. Act like you're distractin' me with a bunch of fool blather. You know—like usual."

"But quietly."

"Yes. But quietly."

"Right." I pointed at nothing in particular up ahead. "Blah blah blah, you go to hell. Blah blah blah blah blah, you horse's ass."

"Just stick to 'blah blah blah,' would you?"

"You said to make it look good. And it wouldn't seem natural if you didn't look annoyed."

"You got a point there."

"You bet I do. Blah blah blah. You crabby little goat."

My brother heaved a sigh. By the time it was done Miss Hayes was past us.

"Don't look back," Old Red said.

He looked back.

"You just told me not to do that," I said.

My brother faced forward again. "I'm better at it than you."

He threw another glance over his shoulder.

"I don't see anything special about how you do it," I said.

"That's why I'm better at it than you. Come on."

He darted into the street.

I looked back—and did it just fine, thank you very much—and saw that Miss Hayes was still absorbed in her letter as she continued on toward the north end of town. We'd gotten by her unnoticed.

I hustled after Old Red. My strides being half-again longer than his, I caught up quick.

"Where are you going? Shouldn't we try to beat Vollmer to the constable?"

"This'll just take a second. There's something I'd like to know about that woman, and this might be my chance to know it."

We both peeked over at the lady again. She had her shoulders hunched and head down, still reading. Not only had she not noticed us, she wouldn't have noticed a herd of buffalo stampeding up the street. A young couple walking toward her arm-in-arm had to split up and hop around her to avoid being trampled.

"Must be one hell of a letter," I said.

"Yup," said Old Red. "And I wonder who it's from."

We stamped the mud off our boots—or as much as we could stamp off, anyway—and entered the store Miss Hayes had stepped from a minute before. The sign over the door said "Flory's General Supplies," and it was immediately obvious that this Flory was an altogether peppier person than the druggist across the street. The shelves were fully and neatly stocked, the floor was well-swept (with the broom leaned beside the door for easy and frequent access), and the clerk—presumably Flory himself—stood at attention behind a new, polished cash register.

"Can I help you?" he said.

He was a tall, genial-looking, gray-haired man with a pencil mustache and garters on the sleeves of his spotless, ironed shirt. If he wasn't already the mayor, he soon would be.

"I hope you can," Old Red said. "I'm lookin' for the local postmaster."

"Your hope is not in vain," the man replied. "You are looking *at* the local postmaster. W.D. Flory, at your service."

"Oh, well, that's just perfect," my brother said as though pleasantly surprised.

Of course, I knew him to be neither. (Surprised nor pleasant, that is.) He'd just seen Miss Hayes walk out with a new letter. It didn't take much deduction to figure Flory had given it to her.

"Do you need to mail a letter, or are you hoping there's something here for you, general delivery?" Flory asked.

"Oh, it ain't that," said Old Red. "I'm lookin' for a lady."

W.D. Flory suddenly looked a little less genial.

"Friend of a friend," my brother added quickly. "We was supposed to be on the lookout for her. Got something important to tell her."

Flory's expression turned downright skeptical.

"Heard she might be lookin' to collect some mail, so thought we'd see if the postmaster could help us out," Old Red said. "Don't recollect the lady's full name, though. Miss O'Something? Or maybe it was Haines or Hayes or Hale? Handsome woman? About forty?"

Flory shook his head but said nothing. For just a moment he moved his gaze to me, still shaking his head, as if saying, "You should *both* be ashamed of yourselves."

"Is that a 'No, she hasn't been here' or a 'No, I've never heard of her'?" my brother asked.

"It's a 'Nice try, cowboy, but I'm not falling for it,'" Flory said.

"Not fallin' for what?"

Flory stopped shaking his head and cocked it to one side instead.

"The one where you wrangle a pretty lady's name out of me,"

he said. "I'm supposed to say, 'Golly—what a coincidence! Your friend-of-a-friend Miss Hmm-hmm was just in to collect her mail!' Please. You want to get to know her, fine. I understand. Good luck. But this kind of monkeyshine isn't the way to go about it. Just wait for your chance to help her over a puddle or carry a bag for her or something, then take off your hat and introduce yourself. That's the way a gentleman would handle it, son."

"I tried to tell him that, sir, but he just wouldn't listen," I said. I gave Old Red a tsk-tsk. "What would mother say?"

"Thanks for the advice," my brother told Flory (with the same sort of grumble one would usually use for "Thanks for nothing"). "We got another friend who should be comin' by. *Really*. Not for mail but for supplies. Cherry Dixon. Have you seen *her*?"

Flory smiled, our sins apparently forgiven.

"Oh, Cherry? Well, that's different," he said. "But no—I haven't seen Cherry in a while. I understand she's working for some of those university people out in the hills. Is that how you know her?"

He looked us over again, some of his skepticism returning. I guess my brother and I don't look much like "university people," especially when we've just spent a day crawling through, riding over and stepping in mud.

"That's confidential," Old Red said.

"Yes," I told Flory at the same time.

I guess my brother wanted to tit-for-tat the man for refusing to talk about Miss Hayes, but I'd upended that. He gave me a little sideways glare before stiffly wishing Flory a good day and heading for the door.

"You wanna tell me what that was all about?" I said when we were outside again. "Cuz it sure seemed like a lot of fancy finagling to try to learn a name we already know."

"*Do* we already know it?"

"Uh, yeah. I guess you missed it, but folks have been calling her 'Miss Hayes,' not 'Hey You.'"

Old Red jerked a thumb at the door behind us—and Flory beyond it. "*He* didn't show any sign he knew any 'Miss Hayes.'"

I furrowed my brow, running the conversation we'd just had through my head again.

My brother was right. He'd slipped in the lady's name, but Flory hadn't reacted to it at all.

"Well, you confused things, didn't you?" I said. "Throwing out those other names like you did. I mean, why would you start off with 'Miss O'Something'?"

"Because last night, when I brought out one of the hammers from her tool bag, I noticed it had initials engraved at the base of the handle." Old Red drew himself up a little straighter and waggled his bushy red eyebrows. "Neither letter was an 'h.' I didn't give it much thought at the time, but when we got to town, it sure seemed like 'Miss Hayes's didn't want to collect her mail with any of us around. So I grabbed the chance to check. And lo and behold—the man who just handed her a letter didn't think 'Hayes's was her name."

My brother looked uncommonly pleased by this little bit of detecting, and I couldn't blame him. Just a few months before— when every letter remained a mystery to him other than the "X" he signed his name with—it would have been utterly beyond him.

Not for the first time, I wondered what need he'd have for me once he mastered reading. I was handy to have around for heavy lifting and providing a nice, big, distracting target people could shoot at that wasn't him. But other than that, I wasn't sure what I brought to the A.A. Western Detective Agency beyond the free advertising my stories provide. Charm? Wit? Good looks? These I have in ample supply, but it's not like they catch murderers.

"So what *were* the letters on the hammer?" I asked. "The second one an 'o,' I assume? Hence 'Miss O'Something'?"

"Exactly. It was damn dark out in that hole, but I'd've sworn the first letter was a 'd.' I was thinkin' there might be a dumb explanation. Something simple, like it's a borrowed hammer or the initials were put there by whoever made it. But that"—Old Red waggled his thumb back at Flory again—"that tells us our 'Miss Hayes's ain't who she says she is."

"She's really Dolores O'Shaughnessy. Or Dorothy O'Neil. Or

Deborah O'Hara. Or Dagmar Ortmann or Diana Orwell or Daniella Lucia Maria Ortiz-Perez-Domingo."

"Well...maybe not that last one."

"Yeah, probably not. But tell me this, brother: What difference does it make? It's not like Miss O'Blahblah snuck away from camp, brained Glaze with a fossil, then dragged him up a hill and buried him in a pit all by herself. So maybe she's lying about her name. What does that matter?"

Old Red rubbed his chin and gazed off over the ramshackle buildings on the other side of the street, at the sun lowering itself toward the hills far beyond.

"We won't know till we know...if we ever know..."

I nodded thoughtfully as that sank in.

"You know," I said, "you've come a long way as a detective. But when it comes to pithy sayings, you're still not a patch on Mr. Holmes."

"Oh, shut up. I wasn't tryin' to be pithy," Old Red said. "Come on."

He headed into the gloopy, wet street again, angling toward the next intersection. Left around the corner, the druggist had told us, and we'd have Larry Hellyer's blacksmith shop in plain view. We were finally about to reach the man we'd supposedly set out to see half an hour before: the town constable. The only law within eighty miles.

When we reached the corner, my brother stopped cold.

"Shit," he spat.

He stretched an arm out to pull me over with him a step, going tight to the side of the nearest building.

"What the hell...?" he went on in a stunned mutter.

Up ahead, as expected, was a grimy, barn-like structure with two wide open doors out front—your typical blacksmith's shop. It was set apart a bit from the neighboring buildings on both sides, no one wanting to crowd a business known for smoke and sweat and the incessant banging of hammers on metal.

Parked near the doors was Professor Loveland's buckboard. Ed Vollmer and a burly man in a blacksmith's heavy leather apron were beside it, looking down into the bed. A couple feet behind them was the gangly gunman we didn't yet have a name for. He was peering over the others' shoulders with a smirk I could make out even from fifty yards away.

"I don't know why you're surprised," I said to Old Red, voice low. "So Vollmer beat us to Hellyer. You had to know there was a chance that'd happen while you took us around to chat with half the town."

"That ain't what surprised me. Don't you see it?"

"I see Vollmer showing Glaze's body to a blacksmith. What else is there to see?"

"*Look at the skinny fella.*"

I looked…and saw a skinny fella. He wasn't doing anything but looming behind the other two men with a smug expression on his long, lean face.

Old Red must've spotted *something*, though, so I looked the man over again from head to toe. It was closing in on the toes that I finally noticed it.

I couldn't remember what the man had on his feet before. I usually don't make a habit of noting such things, especially if it's just a pair of cheap boots of the sort you might pull off the shelf in W.D. Flory's store. The boots he was wearing now, though, were most definitely not from any shop.

For one thing, they were the yellow gold of deerskin, not your standard black or brown leather. Playing over the amber were swirls of other colors—green and red and white—that, if viewed close, took the shape of entwined vines and blooming flowers.

I knew about those shapes because I *had* viewed them up close just a few hours before. On another man's feet.

"He's wearing Shoshone Joe's moccasins," I said.

"He sure is," said Old Red.

"Doesn't seem like Joe had time to lose 'em in a poker game since the last time we saw him."

"Nope. There was time for him to lose a lot more than his shoes, though."

"Well, I'll be damned."

My brother and I just watched the three men a moment. Vollmer was doing all the talking, his words indistinct, while his skinny friend lingered behind him silently. The blacksmith nodded from time to time, eyes wide, face somber.

Vollmer pointed down at something in the wagon bed, then moved his hand to point at something else beside it.

I'd assumed before that he was showing the constable a body, but now I knew better.

He was showing him two.

TWENTY
STUFF AND NONSENSE
OR, CONSTABLE HELLYER SHOWS US WHAT HE'S MADE OF (AND NONE OF IT COMES CLOSE TO CURIOSITY OR COMPETENCE)

SINCE BECOMING PROFESSIONAL DETECTIVES, my brother and I have gotten in plenty of practice following folks and lurking around unseen and such. But there's a lot of me to keep unseen—my friends don't call me "Big Red" because they love irony—and even a third of me leaning out around a corner is a lot of man to lean. So when Vollmer's skinny friend finally remembered to do his job and keep a lookout by glancing up and down the street, he spotted me and Old Red (but mostly me) quick.

He reached out a long arm, tapped Vollmer on the shoulder, then pointed our way.

Vollmer looked up at us…and smiled.

"Now what the hell do you think *that* means?" Old Red said.

It wasn't the sort of smile a man like Vollmer seemed apt to give. There was no smirk to it. No implied threat. No cocky "We'll deal with you later" sneer.

"I think he's actually trying to look…friendly?" I said. "Like…nice?"

Vollmer said something to Hellyer, the constable/blacksmith, still smiling.

When Hellyer glanced over at us, Vollmer gave us a wave.

I smiled and waved back. What can I say? It's the way I was raised.

My brother was raised the same way, of course, but it didn't stick. He neither smiled nor waved.

"Well, that changes everything," he said.

"Vollmer acting friendly?"

"Yup."

"'Changes everything' for the better?"

"Nope."

I lowered my hand. "I was afraid of that."

Vollmer spoke to Hellyer again, fiddled with something in the wagon bed—probably drawing the tarp back over Glaze and Shoshone Joe's bodies—then climbed up into the driver's seat. Before he turned around and picked up the reins, I caught a flash of color at his side.

He was wearing a beaded sheath for a big Bowie knife. Like the moccasin boots on the bony fellow's feet, it had once belonged to Shoshone Joe.

The skinny man gave us a smile of his own before joining Vollmer in the wagon, but he wasn't as good an actor. He looked like a rattlesnake trying to smile at a prairie dog—a plump one the snake wasn't sure it could get down its gullet, though it meant to try.

As the two men started off in their buckboard, Hellyer raised a hand and waved us over. We didn't head his way straight off, though. We stood watching Vollmer and his friend depart, making sure they were indeed leaving and not just waiting for us to step out into the open and make larger targets of ourselves.

Neither man looked back as the wagon rolled slowly eastward.

"Come here!" Hellyer called to us. "I need to talk to you!"

My brother went on watching the wagon.

Vollmer and his pal were keeping their eyes on the end of the street eighty yards ahead. At that point Wamsutter turned back into rough grassland, and they could swing north and head back to Loveland's storehouse by the depot.

"Doesn't seem to be a trap," I said.

"Not the kind where they shoot us anyway," Old Red muttered.

Ever the optimist.

"*Come here!*" Hellyer called out again, pinwheeling his hand now.

"We supposedly came here to talk to the man," I said. "So…?"

Old Red nodded. "Let's go talk to him…and hope he ain't about to arrest us."

"That does get old, doesn't it?"

My brother and I have only been thrown in the hoosegow three times, but that's three times too many as far as I'm concerned.

It was some comfort to confirm, as we approached Hellyer, that he wasn't wearing a gun or bandying handcuffs. And he didn't look stern or grim, as a small-town lawman might when about to say, "Howdy, boys. I hear you been murderin' folks." If anything, he seemed cautiously hopeful, like he had a gift for us he wasn't sure we'd accept.

"Welcome to Wamsutter," he said as we joined him in front of his shop. "I might not look it, but I'm the town constable. Larry Hellyer. I'd offer to shake, but…"

He held up a big, calloused, grime-covered paw.

"Pleased to meet you, Constable," I said. "I'm Otto Amling-meyer, and this is my brother Gustav."

"Jesus, Larry—more chitchat?" a woman croaked from inside the dark, smoky smithy. "I've been waiting for these horseshoes for an hour."

"You've been waiting ten minutes, Daisy, and you can wait five more," Hellyer replied. He gave us an embarrassed, apologetic shrug. "Sorry."

Old Red jerked his head to our left, at the wagon about to reach the end of the street. "What was he tellin' you?"

"Vollmer? That there was bad blood between your two groups. That there've been some run-ins."

"I'd call 'em more than run-ins at this point."

"Yeah. About that. Vollmer says you two found a man dead this morning? One of the bone hunters from his party?"

"The man wasn't just dead," said Old Red. "He was murdered."

"Right. And they thought you'd done the murdering."

I was surprised by the casual way Hellyer put it. Even if he didn't mean to drag us inside and clap us in irons, I'd have thought he'd at least act suspicious. But he had a different air about him—like a teacher about to tell two brawling schoolboys to shake and be friends.

"Fortunately, they caught the real killer and dealt with him," he said. "So Vollmer wants things squared between you, and that's what I want, too. There's no need for any trouble in town or anywhere around it."

"Wait," I said. "'Caught the real killer'? You mean the Shoshone? Joe? Vollmer says *he* killed Glaze?"

Hellyer nodded, either too thick or too disinterested to puzzle over how I'd leaped to Shoshone Joe as the killer.

"They found some of Glaze's things on him and confronted him about it, and he pulled a knife. So they shot him," he said matter-of-factly.

"What 'things' did he have?" my brother asked.

Hellyer gave us another shrug. "Vollmer didn't say. Some of his stuff, I guess."

"Ohhhh, I see. Stuff," Old Red said, voice dripping with sarcasm Hellyer didn't seem to notice. "You guess."

"Yeah, you know how Indians are. They'll steal anything that's not nailed down. And so superstitious. Those college folks digging up old bones—?" Hellyer waggled both hands in the air like a fellow telling a spooky story by the campfire. "Stirs up evvvvvvvil spirits, this 'Joe' probably thought. That's why he killed one of 'em over it, most likely...though an Indian doesn't need much reason to kill a white man, am I right?"

I wasn't sure if he was right or not when it came to Joe. But I could tell what Old Red thought. The way he puckered his lips and narrowed his eyes told me that.

I spoke up before he could spit out a "No."

"So Vollmer comes and tells you all this so you can report it to the sheriff…while also making sure *we* know everything's been wrapped up tidy and neat and there's no need for any more fuss between us. Am I getting that right?"

Hellyer nodded eagerly, a relieved smile creasing his broad, soot-smeared face. "That's it! Vollmer wants peace around here, and so do I."

"Sounds like that's that, Larry!" gravelly-voiced "Daisy" called out from inside. "Now how about getting back to your real job and finishing these horseshoes?"

"Still conducting official constable business here, Daisy!" Hellyer shouted back. He shook his head and lowered his voice. "God, I can't wait to get a drink."

"I hear Vollmer and his pals are new in Wamsutter," Old Red said. "How well you know 'em?"

Hellyer gave my brother a disappointed "Do we really need to keep talking about this?" look. Despite what he'd told Daisy, it was obvious he didn't really care about conducting official constable business. He just didn't want to go back to conducting official blacksmith business.

"Like you say—they're new," he said. "I don't really know them at all."

"Didn't you have any run-ins with 'em yourself?" Old Red asked. "We heard they did some bullyin' when they first showed up. Ran at least one fella outta town."

Hellyer fidgeted uncomfortably. It suddenly looked like he would've preferred dealing with Daisy.

"Yeah, there were some complaints. Nothing ever got out of hand, though. I mean…there was nothing *I* could do about it. So Vollmer's been a bit of a son of a bitch. He's not the first around here, and he won't be the last."

"That doesn't sound like law business to me," Daisy said. "Sounds like gossip."

Hellyer waggled a thumb at the smithy behind him. "Look, she's right. I should get back to work."

"This *is* your—" my brother began.

But Hellyer was already nodding a quick goodbye and retreating into his shop.

"Finally!" said Daisy.

"Typical," grumbled Old Red.

Yes, we've encountered enough lawmen to have opinions about them. Most aren't drawn to the crime-busting business because they're intrigued by the puzzles it presents, like my brother. Easy answers are their preferred stock-in-trade. And Hellyer had his.

Fortunately, Daisy was gracious in her victory.

"You want to hear people bad-mouth Ed Vollmer?" she said from wherever she was in the underlit smithy. "Go to Dirty Dan's Water Trough. Right around the corner on Main Street. Buy a round there, bring up Vollmer, and just sit back. The chin wagging won't stop for an hour."

"Thank you, ma'am!" I called into the darkness. (She sounded more like a "ma'am" than a "miss," though who knows? There are misses out there who smoke corn cob pipes and gargle turpentine, I suppose.) I turned to Old Red. "Well?"

He was looking down at his boots and rubbing a hand over the back of his neck.

"This changes everything," he said. "I thought it was all about the diplodocus. But this business with Vollmer and the Shoshone? It just don't fit. Or more like it fits altogether too neat to be believed."

"So you don't think Joe killed Glaze?"

Old Red looked up to scowl an "*Of course not*" at me.

"Right," I said. "Cuz Joe didn't even know Glaze was dead. And last we saw him he had a brand new hole in his favored hand, so would he really 'pull a knife' on Vollmer and his boys? And why would they have suddenly been going through Joe's things to find 'stuff' from—?"

"Yeah yeah yeah. It all adds up to one thing."

"Vollmer's story is horseshit. Gosh, if only there were some way to learn more about the man. Oh, wait! There is!"

Old Red nodded. "We buy a round at Dirty Dan's Water Trough."

I clapped him on the back and pulled him toward the corner.

"Brother," I said, "that is the best idea you've had in quite a while."

He came along slowly, though, despite the promise of a drink at the end of a long, strange day. When we turned at the corner, he looked back up the street we were leaving. At the far end, Vollmer and the skinny gunman were turning, too, their wagon heading north toward the train station. Both men were eyeing us again—and they weren't bothering to smile this time.

TWENTY-ONE
THE TROUGH

OR, WE ROOT AROUND FOR DIRT ON VOLLMER BUT OLD RED ENDS UP FEELING PIG-IGNORANT

MY BROTHER and I have been in seedier dives than Dirty Dan's Water Trough—places where we were taking our lives in our hands just walking in and asking for a beer. But this much I have to give the place: It was the first saloon we've visited that one could call fit for pigs. Literally.

There were two of them, and being a former farm boy, I recognized the breed right off. Hampshires, with their telltale round, black bodies and pink-white stripe around the shoulders. I've always liked Hampshires—the ones I tended as a boy were as smart and good-natured as dogs—but I'd never considered drinking with any before. Then again, they'd probably make better company than some of the men I've raised a glass with. So I decided not to be picky and make a fuss.

I wasn't alone in that either, for the pigs had company. There were three customers scattered around the place, each seated (and in one case slumped over snoring) at his own rickety-looking table. The pigs seemed to prefer one in particular, grubbing around happily at his feet, and it didn't take long to figure out why: He was going through a bag of peanuts in one-for-me, two-for-you fashion.

"Whoa," he said, looking up at me and Old Red. "Is it Friday already?"

I had no idea what that meant, but—as my brother would surely tell you—lack of understanding won't stop me from talking.

"It's still Wednesday, by my count," I replied. "But if we all wanna agree it's Friday, that's fine by me. Or better yet, let's call it Saturday night and *really* enjoy ourselves."

"Works for me," the man said. "Long as it's not Monday morning." He shivered. "Lord, I hate Monday morning."

The pigs, momentarily peanut-less, craned their thick necks to watch me and Old Red step up to the bar.

"And a good afternoon to you, ladies," I said to them, tipping my hat. "I do hope you're not here as part of the free lunch."

The bearded barman laughed.

"Naw. They're in here, so nobody steals 'em," he said. "Used to keep 'em in a pen out back, but too many got borrowed for bacon. What can I get for you, fellas?"

"Four whiskeys," I said.

The barman looked impressed. "You two aren't wasting any time."

"Oh, they're not all for us," I said. "One's for me, one's for my brother, one's for you, and the last one's for whoever wants to talk to us about Ed Vollmer."

The barman had started lining up glasses in front of us, but now he froze.

Old Red threw me an incredulous look.

"You *aren't* wastin' any time, are you?" he said.

If we were about to get thrown out or shot at, it would indeed be in record time. Never before had I managed to say the wrong thing before the first drink was even poured.

"Daisy made it sound so easy," I said, as much to the barman and his customers as my brother. "Like everyone here had something to say about Vollmer."

"Maybe we do," the man with the peanuts said. "But that doesn't mean we'd say it to just anybody."

"Who the hell are you, anyway?" asked the man at the next

table over.

He had no peanuts, but he did have something his neighbor didn't: a gun belt. Which held, as is so often the case, a gun. A Smith & Wesson forty-four, to be specific. A long-barreled and clunky weapon, in my humble opinion, but the holes it would make in one's middle were the perfect size, if killing you is the idea.

All the same, I smiled.

"We are Otto and Gustav Amlingmeyer. Big Red and Old Red to our friends—of which we have many, being so agreeable and generous with drinks."

"How about Vollmer?" the man with the Smith & Wesson said. "He one of your friends?"

Here's where I *really* put my faith in Daisy. If she'd been trying to trick us into sticking our necks through a noose for some reason, we were about to find out fast.

"Friends with Vollmer? Hell no," I said. "Up till ten minutes ago, he was acting like he wanted to kill us. We still can't figure out why he changed his mind."

The fellow with the gun pushed back his chair and rose to his feet—and proceeded to make a beeline for the bar with a smile on his face.

"In that case, I'm claiming that fourth whiskey," he said.

"Aw," whined the man with the peanuts.

"Don't worry," I told him. "We'll set you up, too, if you wanna talk."

"Sure, I'll talk! I'm thirsty!"

The man hopped up and joined us at the bar. His friends, the pigs, did, too, even though he'd left his peanuts at the table.

The sleeping man, meanwhile, went right on sleeping.

Old Red nodded at him. "Should we wake him up so he can join the party?"

The fellow with the Smith & Wesson swiped a hand at the napper. "Nah. We know everything he does."

"He's already too drunk to tell it to you right anyhow," the pig man added.

The barman had our whiskeys nicely lined up on the counter-top, and each of us took one and lifted it in a toast to the others.

Up close now, I could see that the two men who'd just joined us had scrapes and bruises on their faces. Not fresh and wet, but new enough not to have faded away entirely.

"Cheers," I said.

We drank.

Four of us threw our whiskeys back in one gulp. One of us took a prim little sip then put his glass down again. I'll let you work out which.

"Another round," I said to the barman.

Old Red cleared his throat and gave me a significant look.

"...for you and our new friends here," I added with a stifled sigh.

There we were with a murderer running around and a whole gang of gunmen in town meaning us no good, and my brother wanted me to stay sober. Damn him.

"So tell me, gents," I said after round two had been quickly disposed of down-the-hatch style. "Who do we have the pleasure of inebriating today?"

The barman, not surprisingly, turned out to be Dirty Dan himself, while the peanut eater was one Michael Patrick Dulaney and the Smith & Wesson man simply introduced himself as "Jones." The pigs were Sally and Sunshine, though of course they didn't tell us this themselves.

"Why do you wanna talk about Vollmer?" Jones asked.

"Cuz he's the competition," I said. "We're guards for one of the fossil hunters out in the hills, and he and his boys are guards for another. There's been...friction."

Dulaney barked out a laugh. "I bet there has! Sparks do fly when Vollmer's around."

"How is it you all know him?" Old Red asked.

"He rode into town and made himself known, that's how," said Dirty Dan. "About two weeks ago, he and his man showed up. Spent a couple days just loafing around, then they picked out jobs for themselves and took 'em."

"From us," Jones added bitterly.

My brother swung toward him so suddenly he startled Sally and Sunshine. They squealed and skittered behind Dulaney.

"Hel-lo," Old Red said.

"Um...hello," said Jones. "We've been introduced."

"My brother has a habit of helloing things he finds interesting," I explained. "Such as you two being Professor Loveland's guards before Vollmer and his boys came along? Is that what you're saying?"

Jones nodded.

Dulaney tapped the biggest and darkest of his fading bruises —the shadow of a shiner under his left eye.

"They convinced us to quit," he said.

Jones patted the big, ungainly gun at this side. "Those bastards aren't gonna convince *me* of anything that way again. Let 'em just try it..."

Dirty Dan busied himself wiping a non-existent spill off the bar to conceal the rolling of his eyes.

"Oh, it was a boring job anyway," Dulaney said. "And the pay was shit. We shouldn't have fought as hard as we did."

"That ain't the point," Jones growled.

My brother impatiently flapped a hand at the two men, waving away their back-and-forth like it was the smell of the pigs rooting around at their feet.

"Let me get this straight," he said. "Professor Durgin comes to town with his party, and he hires some locals to work for him. Then Professor Loveland comes to town with Walter Glaze, and they hire *you*."

"So far, so good," said Dulaney.

He let out a little cough and eyed the empty glasses lined up before us.

I held up three fingers and gave Dirty Dan a nod.

"Then Vollmer's bunch rides in," Old Red went on as Dirty Dan poured out three more shots, "and they kick the crap out of you cuz they want your jobs? The borin' ones with the shit pay maybe split six ways now instead of two?"

Jones snatched up his glass and tossed back his whiskey without waiting for the others. This was obviously his least-favorite part of the story.

Dulaney shrugged. "I guess they were hard-up for work."

He toasted Dirty Dan, and they drained their glasses together.

"Then they did the same thing to Durgin's guards?" Old Red continued. "And his cook—Luigi Verardo? Thrashed 'em so they'd quit?"

Dulaney lifted a finger. "Ah. Now there, you don't quite have it. Most folks *think* they thrashed poor little Lou, but who knows? They might've done more than that."

He gave Old Red a wink.

Jones wasn't in the mood for such subtlety.

"Vollmer killed him," he said. "Didn't have to lay a finger on Chalky and Lopez after that. They quit as soon as Lou went missing."

"Chalky and Lopez were Durgin's original guards?" I asked.

"That's right," said Dulaney.

He jerked a thumb at the snoozing man still slumped over his table. Despite all the gabbing going on mere feet away, he hadn't so much as lifted his head once.

"Chalky," Dulaney said. "Lopez was able to get a new job over at the livery."

"This talk of Vollmer doin' something to Verardo—is it more than talk?" said Old Red. "Did anyone actually *see* anything?"

Dirty Dan perked up and grinned.

"Sure. I did!" he said, pleased to finally earn the whiskeys he'd poured himself. "Happened right in front of me. Right where you're standing, in fact. Plain as day."

"*What* happened?" Old Red said.

"Well, I was alone in the place. Just me and the girls." Dirty Dan nodded down at Sally and Sunshine on our side of the bar. "It was early in the day, before the boys here had come in. Just a little past noon."

"The crack of dawn," I said.

My brother shot me a glare that told me what I could do with my asides.

"And Lou Verardo comes hurrying in," Dirty Dan went on. "Says he's in town with some of the folks he's been cooking for and he's supposed to be stocking up on supplies but he wants to stock himself up first, if you know what I mean, cuz the fella he works for don't allow booze in camp."

I looked over at Old Red and nodded with my lips sealed tight, keeping my "Sounds familiar" to myself.

"So Lou's standing right there across from me sucking down a beer," Dirty Dan said, "and who should happen to walk in?"

He stopped his story and gave us an expectant look.

I held out a hand to my brother, my mouth still resolutely closed.

"Ed Vollmer," Old Red said.

"Not just Ed Vollmer but Ed Vollmer and Benji Boulden and Bones Lono and Billy Kochuk and Uwe Walfenburger."

"Uhh...those are Vollmer's men?"

"The whole bunch, except for Joe the Shoshone. They spent a fair amount of time here in the Trough getting the lay of the land before they...uh..." Dirty Dan gave Jones a sympathetic look. "...wrangled themselves the jobs they have now."

Jones turned away and spat.

"Hey now!" Dirty Dan said. "Not so close to the gals!"

I guess he didn't mind spitting in his place as long as you missed the pigs.

"Sorry," Jones muttered.

Old Red took a deep breath. "So they come in, and...?"

"And they're in a good mood for once," Dirty Dan said. "They're together in town for the first time in a few days—the only one stuck out at the camp was the Indian—and what's more, this 'Glaze' fella they work with? Who's usually such a tight-ass SOB, they're saying? He just rode in, too...and *told them* to go get a drink. Sent everyone they had in Wamsutter to the Water Trough! They're so happy they forget to be nasty for a minute. They're getting their drinks, giving treats to the girls, joking, laughing. And the whole time poor Lou's standing here with his mug stuck to his mouth, trembling like a leaf. Wondering when they're gonna notice who he is and remember who he works for."

"And when they do…?" said Old Red.

I could tell he was thinking, "My god—could you just get to the end of the damn story without me having to push you every ten seconds?" He managed to keep the irritation out of his voice, though. For the most part. (There's always *some* irritation in his voice.)

"They play it sneaky," said Dirty Dan. "Don't let on that they're paying any attention to Lou at all. And he takes one last sip of his beer, sets it down, and hightails it outta here. And do you know what Vollmer says when that happens?"

Old Red's face was starting to flush.

I patted one of the hands he had on the counter.

"Please, brother," I said. "Allow me."

I turned to Dirty Dan.

"No," I said. "What does Vollmer say?"

Sometimes there's not much I can do to help with the actual detecting, so it's nice when I can step in and provide some little service. Like preserving my brother's sanity.

"'Be right back, boys,'" Dirty Dan intoned ominously. "'I gotta take a dump.'"

Old Red and I stared at the man, waiting for him to walk away and do as he'd just announced.

"Oh!" I said after a moment came and went, but Dirty Dan stayed. "That's what *Vollmer* said! I thought you were speaking for yourself."

"So Vollmer goes outside, *and*…?" my brother grumbled.

"And he doesn't come back for five, ten, fifteen minutes," Dirty Dan said. "And poor Luigi Verardo is never…seen…again."

The barman waggled his eyebrows.

"Some story, huh?" enthused Dulaney, looking like he wanted to call for an encore.

"It's…something, all right," I said—thinking that the "something" was akin to what Sally and Sunshine might deposit on the barroom floor from time to time. If folks we don't like were guilty of murder every time they went to the outhouse, it wouldn't be long before there's no one left alive on Earth.

Yet now that Dirty Dan's "story" (it seemed to me it was barely an anecdote) was over, Old Red had set his annoyance aside and was mulling what he'd heard over with that familiar, faraway look in his eyes.

"Any of the other fellas leave the Water Trough around the same time?" he said slowly.

"No," said Dirty Dan.

"How'd Vollmer seem when he come back in?"

"Oh, normal. Still chipper, for him. I didn't give it a second thought until later when I heard Lou'd disappeared."

"Vollmer's a cool and crafty one. You gotta give him that," Dulaney said.

"I got something to give him," Jones muttered, caressing the dark grip of his forty-four.

My brother had gone back to ruminating silently, so for a moment the only talk in the place was whatever sunshine was saying to Sally. (It was probably "Why'd the peanuts stop coming?" but all I could make of it was "Snort snort oink.")

"So…is Vollmer giving you trouble out there?" Dulaney asked us, fiddling with his shot glass in a way that emphasized its unwelcome emptiness.

I shrugged—and chose not to take the hint. (It seemed like Old Red's questions were winding down. And you can call me petty, but there are only so many rounds I'm going to buy when I'm not allowed to join in myself.)

"Well, I wouldn't exactly call Vollmer neighborly," I said. "But I can't say for sure who's to thank for the trouble we've—"

"All right. That's enough of that," my brother cut in. "Just one more question."

He reached over to his glass, which was still half full. Instead of lifting it to his mouth, he slid it down the counter to Dulaney.

"When me and my brother walked in here, you said, 'Is it Friday already?'" Old Red said. "What did that mean?"

Dulaney opened his mouth to speak. He should've used it to

drink.

In a flash, Jones snatched up the glass, threw back the whiskey in it, and smacked his lips.

"Hey!" Dulaney cried.

Jones ignored him.

"You two look like mine guards," he said to Old Red. "And there's mine guards in here every Friday from 1:35 to 1:44."

"Why would there be mine guards in here for even nine minutes?" Old Red asked. "Wamsutter ain't got no mine."

Dirty Dan grinned. "But it does have ice-cold beer."

Jones waggled a hand. "Ice-cold?"

Dirty Dan's grin wilted a bit.

"Cool beer," he said.

"That tells me what the guards are comin' *for*," said Old Red. "It still don't tell me where they're comin' *from*."

"The Union Pacific Afternoon Special," said Dulaney, still pouting over his lost shot. "Friday is payday for the Big Butte Coal Company, so they got payroll going to the mines at Hanna, Rawlins, Point of Rocks, Green River—east to west across the state. They don't drop off anything here, but the Special does stop and take on water."

"Ah," I said. "And some of the guards run off and take on beer."

Dirty Dan nodded happily. "Two men. Two rounds. Like clockwork."

"And today is Wednesday," Old Red mused. He pointed his eyes toward the floor, gaze reglazing. "Today...is...*Wednesday*."

"Uhh...yeah. That was the joke?" said Dulaney.

My brother was frozen now, stare fixed downward on the Water Trough's warped and filthy pinewood floor.

Dulaney caught my eye and jerked his head toward my brother, silently asking, "He all right?"

"Don't worry," I said. "These little spells come over him from time to time. If he's still like that after an hour, I just pick him up and carry him home."

Dulaney and Jones, and Dirty Dan all turned to stare quizzically at Old Red, unsure if I was joking or not.

Dulaney tentatively reached out a hand and waved it in front of my brother's eyes.

"Oh, stop that," Old Red snapped.

Dulaney jerked his hand away.

"Pay the man, and let's go," my brother told me. "Hoop and the others are gonna be wonderin' what we been doin'."

"I couldn't blame 'em," I said. "I've been with us the whole time, and I'm not sure *I* know."

I pulled out some coins, plunked them down before Dirty Dan, and bade everyone (pigs and a softly snoring Chalky included) a good evening. The looks the (awake) men gave me and my brother as we left made it plain what they'd be talking about the rest of the night. Us.

I like to think that being naturally fascinating and providing fodder for gossip is a little public service Old Red and I provide as our new line of work takes us to podunk towns across the West.

Pioneers—you're welcome.

When we stepped outside, my brother paused to give the street a long, careful looking over from one end to the other. There was no sign of Vollmer or any of his men.

"They ain't got nobody watchin' us," said Old Red.

He almost sounded disappointed.

"Would you prefer it if they were shooting at us?" I asked him.

"Part of me would. At least that I'd understand."

Old Red pivoted and headed north, back toward the depot and the storage buildings there.

"They didn't kill one of their own bunch just 'cuz they wanted his knife and boots," he said. "They're tryin' to hide something... and it ain't got nothing to do with dinosaurs. And when they're ready to *stop* hidin' it..."

My brother threw a quick glance over his shoulder, hoping to catch some furtive figure stepping out to follow us.

None did.

"That," he said as he faced forward again, "is when the shooting's gonna start."

TWENTY-TWO
SOMETHING STUPID
OR, MY BROTHER FILLS HOOP IN THEN PROMPTLY HUSTLES HIM OFF

MY BROTHER and I found Hoop, Miss Hayes, and Cherry waiting for us impatiently by the wagon when we returned to Professor Durgin's rented barn.

"There they are!" Cherry said as we approached. "About damn time! What took you so long?"

Despite her words, she didn't seem angry with us. In fact, there was a little lopsided grin on her sunken face.

"Was there a problem with the constable?" Miss Hayes asked.

"No," I told her. "Actually, our talk with him went a lot smoother than we expected."

Old Red and I both looked past the lady at the other storage building nearer to the station. There was nothing and no one out front—no men, no buckboard, no horses.

Hoop noticed us checking.

"Vollmer and the skinny one came back in the wagon about twenty minutes ago," he said. "They brought Glaze's body inside —got a cheap-looking coffin for it while they was in town—then they headed out again with the one called Benji."

Old Red nodded. "Loveland's gonna ship Glaze off to wherever his people are, probably. Can't do that with just some canvas thrown over it. Is it just the one corpse they unloaded?"

The woman's eyes widened in surprise. I guess Hoop's too used to talk of corpses (and the making of them) to be taken off guard, though.

"Just the one," he said coolly. "Any reason there'd be more?"

"The best reason," I told him. "There *were* more. We think Joe the Shoshone was keeping Glaze company as he got carted around town."

"You mean that redskin SOB who tried to trample me this morning?" Cherry said. "You boys kill him?"

I shook my head. "Vollmer's boys did. He told the constable Joe murdered Glaze, and when they figured it out, there was a fight."

"And Doyadukubichi' lost," said Hoop.

His face was still expressionless, his tone flat, yet his skepticism came through.

"That's their story," my brother said.

He gazed northward again, past the other storage building and the train station and water tower and tracks. Far off in that direction, not even a speck in the distance now, was the buckboard headed back to Professor Loveland's camp with half its cargo still in the bed so far as we knew.

"Guess they're not shipping Joe home to his folks," I said.

"Nope. They'll probably just dump him somewhere out there for the wolves and coyotes," said Old Red. "He served his purpose."

"What do you mean?" Miss Hayes asked.

"Vollmer wanted to assure the constable everything's all wrapped up. That there's no more trouble to worry about. No need for the sheriff to rush out this way."

"Good," said Cherry, entirely missing the ominous insinuation in my brother's words—that these assurances had nothing to do with the truth. "Let's get going, then!"

She climbed up into the driver's seat, and I noticed now that there were fresh supplies behind her in the wagon bed. Not much, though—just a few sacks and a single crate of vegetables that looked as shriveled-up as her, packed in alongside Miss Hayes's tool bag.

"If we don't get a move-on now, we won't make it back before sunset," Cherry said, snatching up the reins. "And if there're wolves and coyotes out in the dark fighting over an Indian, I wanna be beside a fire with my twenty-two when they're doing it!"

She cut loose with a cackle.

None of us joined in.

"How many fellas they leave over there?" Old Red asked Hoop, nodding at Loveland's storage building.

"The same two as always."

My brother nodded. "That'd be Uwe Walfenburger and Billy Kochuk, if we was told the names right. 'Bones Lono' is probably the beanpole."

"We managed to squeeze in a little reconnaissance while we were gone," I explained.

Hoop leaned in close to me and took a sniff. "A little whiskey, too."

"All in the line of duty," I said.

"Ha! Dirty Dan's! I shoulda known!" Cherry crowed. "Now, can we wrap up this sewing bee and *go*?"

"Cherry's right," Miss Hayes said. "We really should get back before nightfall."

She had a strangely somber, downcast air about her as if the letter she'd picked up at the store—tucked away somewhere out of sight now—had informed her of the passing of her favorite dog.

"Absolutely," said Old Red. He stepped toward the lady while sweeping an arm out toward the wagon. "Allow me to help you up, ma'am."

But once he had her deposited on the seat beside Cherry, he didn't head for our horses tied up nearby. Instead he looked over at something propped against the side of the barn—Hoop's big Sharps rifle.

"Oh...don't go snappin' the reins quite yet, Cherry," he said.

"There's one more thing me and Otto need to talk over with Hoop."

"Oh, for Christ's sake..." Cherry muttered as my brother started toward the rifle.

Hoop and I exchanged a quick look—we both knew Old Red was bullshitting, but neither of us knew why—before walking over to join him.

When my brother reached the Sharps, he picked it up and carried it off a few more paces into the empty lot between Durgin's barn and Loveland's.

He lifted the rifle with an "Oof" and sighted down the barrel.

"I was thinkin' of borrowin' this, but now I ain't so sure," he said. "Feels like tryin' to shoot with a telegraph poll."

"It ain't for everyone, that's for sure," said Hoop. "The recoil would probably send a little fella like you halfway to Texas."

He and I stopped beside Old Red, and Hoop pretended to correct the way my brother held the Sharps.

"What'd you wanna talk about?" he said, voice low so the women in the wagon would only catch a murmur.

Old Red squinted at the gunsight again.

"The men Vollmer likes to leave in town, Uwe and Billy...how are they as guards?" he whispered.

"Disgraceful," Hoop replied. He moved a pointed finger up and down the barrel as if explaining how bullets work. "Just hang around watching the trains during the day and sneak off for fun at night."

"Ah. You know where they go for their fun?"

"Not for certain. *I* take my guarding seriously, and there hasn't been anyone here to take over my watch while I follow them two. But we scouted around when we first showed up, so I know there's a hog ranch just south of town. Odds are that's where they go. They come back drunk and happy enough."

"Ah," my brother said again.

The "hog ranch"—slang for a bawdy house of the seedier kind, where the "house" is probably a shotgun shack—was on the opposite end of Wamsutter. I could see the wheels that set in motion in Old Red's head.

He handed the Sharps to Hoop.

"Yeah, you're right. I'll stick with a Winchester," he said loudly, for the women's benefit. "You might want this while you're on your way to Camp Cashew. If you spot any of them wolves and coyotes, I mean."

"Right," said Hoop.

He dropped his voice again.

"So you're telling me I'm the ladies' escort out of town?"

"Let's say I'm strongly suggestin' it. So me and Otto can get in a little more 'reconnaissance' here tonight. Surely you must be tired of sittin' around by yourself polishin' your rifle."

Hoop cocked an eyebrow at Old Red.

"You're not planning on doing something stupid, are you?" he said.

"Stupid? Course not."

Hoop grunted, then walked off toward the horses.

"You can roll out, Miss Dixon," he said. "I'll catch up in a second."

Miss Hayes shot Old Red and me a perturbed sort of look, but before she could say anything Cherry hyahed their horse, and the wagon jerked forward toward the north.

My brother gave the ladies a wave and a smile as they rolled away, so I did the same.

Cherry didn't even notice, so fixed was she on the horizon. Miss Hayes waved back half-heartedly, the smile conspicuously absent.

A moment later, Hoop trotted after them, and Old Red and I watched as he crossed the railroad tracks with the wagon, leaving us the lone A.A. Western Detective Agency operatives in Wamsutter, Wyoming.

"Well…you gonna tell me what you're thinking, or do I have to guess?" I said.

"I'm thinkin' Vollmer wants us unworried. Feelin' like the

worst has come and gone," my brother said. "And I want him believin' it worked."

Old Red stopped there, though clearly he was thinking much more that he chose not to share.

"You *are* planning something stupid, aren't you?" I said.

"I don't do 'stupid.'"

"How about 'dangerous and ill-advised' then? You definitely do that…and expect me to do it with you."

"Feh," Old Red said, and he turned and headed into the barn.

I knew what that meant for my night.

Dangerous and ill-advised it would be.

TWENTY-THREE
THE WAREHOUSE

OR, WE FIND THAT BOTH THE MYSTERY
AND OUR LIVES HINGE ON A
SURPRISING DISCOVERY

I SOAKED up a moment of sunshine (and the oh-so-fleeting feeling of peace that came with it) before following my brother inside.

It was gloomy in the old barn—and getting gloomier by the second as the sun sank low in the west. Old Red was over by a crate that appeared to have been Hoop's makeshift office: There was a stool beside it and a lantern, matchbox, and deck of cards on top. He pointed at a spot to my right, near the door, where one of the side planks had been angled down a bit on one end.

"Looks like Hoop made him a peephole for watchin' them fellas across the way," he said.

Stepping up to the plank, I saw that he was right. The resulting crack in the wall was at perfect eye height (providing your eyes are as high as Hoop's and mine), and it looked out directly onto Loveland's warehouse.

"I don't expect 'em to get up to anything till nightfall," Old Red said. He took out a match and fired it up with a scrape against the crate. "All the same, keep an eye out while I look around in here."

He lit the lantern and blew out the match.

"What are you looking for?" I asked.

"You know the answer to that."

He started toward the nearest corner of the barn.

Data—that's what he was hunting for. Clues, you could also say. Information.

You could also call it "Whatever the hell he could find." Because he didn't really know *what* he was looking for. He'd just know if he saw it. Hopefully.

Equipment was piled up in the corner—pulleys and coils of rope and cans of paint and such—and Old Red moved closer to investigate. He seemed particularly drawn to twin stacks of heavy-looking sacks and boxes: He held the lantern up close and kept it there. There was printing on the sides, and though he wasn't sounding the letters out loud, I could tell he was trying to decipher it. If he couldn't do it, he'd ask for help—grumpy about it, but he'd ask—so I went back to squinting through the peephole and left him to it.

"'Plaster of Paris,'" he announced after a moment.

I gave him a neutral "Mm-hmm." (If I sounded too pleased or complimentary, he'd tell me he didn't need a pat on the head.)

Half a minute of silence followed.

"'Burlap,'" he said.

"Mm-hmm."

I heard a little rattle, and when I glanced back, I saw that my brother had squatted down beside a bucket near the bags and boxes. He was jiggling a wooden handle that jutted up from it. Gloopy white stripes ran down the sides of the bucket, like streaks of thick, dried paint.

"The field jackets probably get a little dinged up on the way in," I said. "Looks like they give 'em another coat before they ship 'em out."

"Yeah. Probably," Old Red said, sounding unenthused.

Whatever "data" he hoped to find, this wasn't it.

He stood and moved off toward the gray shapes that filled the back half of the barn. The field jackets were lined up in rows, and

I couldn't help thinking they could have been the headstones and monuments in a nighttime cemetery.

My brother stopped beside the first one he came to and spent a full minute staring down at the writing across the top—a jumble of letters and numbers in thick, black paint. He furrowed his brow and cocked his head, and finally, I had to risk his wrath by telling him what "JDX–WY–3B–5/24/94" meant.

"They're not words," I said. "They're serial numbers and dates. I assume they match up with the notes in Miss Hayes's journal."

"Oh. Of course."

Old Red moved on to the next field jacket, then the next, and the next, and the next. He didn't have much to say as he went about it—just the occasional grumble about people who need to tidy up their brushwork. "Now who could make head or tail of these damn smudges?" he said at one point. "Even I could've done better than whoever wrote on this one." But there was no "Hel-lo" or "A-ha!" of the sleuth discovering a clue. And I certainly didn't hear what I wanted to: "Good news—now I understand everything! We don't have to risk our lives tonight on crazy foolishness after all!"

Because I knew what Old Red had in mind. And eventually the time came for it.

My view of Loveland's warehouse grew dimmer and dimmer as my brother went up and down the rows of big plaster blobs. By the time he reached the last couple jackets, it was so dark all I could make out was a black silhouette blotting out the stars. But that was enough, especially when I saw two dark shapes moving away from it—and caught some of what they had to say to each other.

"…got dibs on Bonnie."

"Keep your voice down, dammit."

"I just want it known now. Bonnie is mine."

"All right, all right. She's yours—if that asshole Norwegian ain't around. He's as stuck on her as you are. Now shut up till we're…"

And the voices faded away.

"Uwe and Billy are off to the hog ranch," I told my brother, managing to keep my voice lower than they had. "And one of them is in love. No idea which."

"Good," Old Red said. "Now we just gotta hope they ain't broke."

"Cuz you want 'em gone for a nice long time so we can go over there. Go over and go *in*. Right?"

"Yup. That's where the answers are. I think."

I sighed.

Crazy foolishness, here we come.

We gave Uwe and Billy another few minutes to make their way to Bonnie, then out we crept. I looked this way and that as we made our way toward Loveland's storehouse, my Peacemaker drawn and ready should someone come hustling back for the twenty dollar bill he'd accidentally left tucked under his bunk—or should this be a trap. But I saw nothing save darkness to our left, darkness to our right, the flickering lights of town behind us, and the looming shape of the storage building ahead.

When we reached the door, we found it locked. (Uwe and Billy might have been crappy guards, but even they had their standards.) Old Red had brought the lantern along tucked under his slicker, the burner turned low, and now he brought it out and held it close to the keyhole.

"Hold this steady," he told me.

"Great," I said as I stepped around him and took the lantern with my left hand. "Now *I* can be the one it's easy to shoot even in the dark."

"If you don't want to be the one holdin' the lantern," Old Red said, "learn to be the one pickin' the lock."

And he pulled two straight pins from his coat pocket and got to work.

We'd first read of this method of lockpicking in non-Watson magazine stories, so for a time, we'd been skeptical. Then my brother discovered, after a little experimentation and practice, that it not only worked (most of the time) but that he was good at it (that aforementioned most of the time).

Which now left me leaning in over him, holding a light that may as well have been a bull's eye.

"Come on, come on, come on," I said helpfully.

"Gabbin' at me ain't gonna help me go faster."

"No, but it'll help me feel better. Come on, come on, come on."

My brother went on fiddling with his pins.

"Calm down," he said. "We saw them two leave. They got a routine, and they'll stick to it. We got time."

"Yeah, well...Hoop had a routine, too, didn't he? Watch over Durgin's barn all by himself. And we broke it. Sent Hoop riding out of town for all to see while we stayed here. Don't you think Vollmer could put two and two together if he found out about that?"

Old Red paused to look up at me. He said nothing at first. But when he got back to working on the lock, he did speak to *it*.

"Come on, come on, come on," he said.

At last there was a *click*, and Old Red reached out, took hold of the knob, and turned it.

The door opened.

Old Red held a hand out toward it, palm up.

"Viola," he said.

"*Voilà*," I corrected, pronouncing it the proper French way. (Our friend Diana had corrected *me* some months before.)

My brother tucked away his pins and stood up with an incredulous look on his face.

"Wah-lah?" he said. "That don't make a lick of sense with them letters."

"Can we debate it inside? With the door closed behind us?"

"Right."

In we went. The second the door was closed, I turned the flame up higher and lifted the lantern to spread its light throughout the building. There was more room than in Durgin's barn but less to fill it. Loveland had only collected four field jackets, it seemed, none of them as large as the biggest of Durgin's. There were ropes and sacks and crates in a corner, just like in Durgin's place, as well as a table and chairs and, pushed against the far wall, two cots. There were scattered leftovers from the building's days as a railroad warehouse, as well—a sledgehammer here, a couple shovels there, a rusty pickax.

And there was the coffin, of course. Hoop had been right: It was a cheap one. Narrow, knotty, unvarnished. It was on the floor not far from the door, which made sense seeing as it would probably be going right back out again the next day—off to the depot for its journey to Glaze's final resting place, wherever that might be.

Old Red walked past it, headed for the field jackets.

"Where'd you run across 'voilà'?" I asked him. "I doubt that pops up in a *McGuffey's Reader*."

"I read other things," my brother mumbled. "Or been tryin' to…"

His voice trailed off as he reached the first of the field jackets. Like Durgin's, they had black writing across the top: letters and numbers indicating where the fossils within had been found and when and by whom.

"Not much to show for the time Loveland's been out here," Old Red said.

"Durgin was his prize bloodhound when it came to sniffin' out and diggin' up bones," I said. "I guess Loveland and Glaze just didn't have the same knack."

"Yeah. And maybe they was just bidin' their time, too. Lettin' Durgin go on doin' the diggin' for 'em at first…cuz they'd get the bones later." Old Red shook his head and stamped a foot. "But dammit…what's it got to do with Vollmer? And the Shoshone? How's it all fit together?"

I had no answers, of course, so I just holstered my gun and switched the lantern from my left hand—and the now-aching arm attached to it—to my right.

Old Red circled the other field jackets, but it was quickly

apparent there was nothing to learn from them. They were just more plaster blobs with gobbledygook painted across the top.

My brother sighed and looked around in frustration. Here we were risking our lives for a peek inside Loveland's warehouse, and what was there to see? So far almost exactly what we could've seen where we'd come from.

Old Red's gaze lingered here and there on the things that were different. The coffin. The windows, covered over with newspaper. The cots. The sledgehammer and shovels and pickax propped against the wall.

Old Red jerked around to face the cots again. Unsurprisingly, the ratty linens on them were heaped in disarray. Vollmer's men weren't going to be the tidy types who make their beds every morning.

But something was visible among the jumble of dingy sheets and frayed blankets. Something that *did* look tidy. New and clean and neatly folded.

Old Red walked to the cots for a closer look. And at last I heard the word I'd been waiting for.

"Hel-lo."

"What is it?" I said.

My brother looked back and forth from one cot to the other. "Two brand new suits."

"Suits?"

Old Red nodded. "Both black." He reached down and carefully sorted through the little pile of clothes on the nearest cot. "With white shirts and cellophane collars and neckties. From that general store we was in today, I bet. Didn't see no haberdashery in Wamsutter."

"Store-bought suits," I said again. "For Uwe and Billy."

"That they didn't put on for their call on Bonnie at the hog ranch," Old Red pointed out. "So they ain't just for makin' a good impression. Well...ain't least not on Bonnie."

"Who then? I don't think those two are planning on going to church Sunday morning and trying out for the choir."

At first, it looked like Old Red was going to treat my little joke as he did most others. Meaning he'd ignore it. But after scratching at his chin whiskers a moment, puzzling over the new suits, he froze.

"No, they ain't goin' to church," he said slowly. "But maybe they do wanna look ready for a service."

"What do you mean?"

Rather than answer, Old Red turned to face the coffin.

"Oh," I said.

My brother started walking *toward* the coffin.

"Oh, no," I said.

He knelt down *beside* the coffin.

"Oh, lord," I said.

He put a hand *on* the coffin.

I went back to "Oh, no."

I'd already had enough of Glaze's cadaver earlier that day. I didn't care to see what condition it was in after a long wagon ride in the afternoon sunshine.

Old Red felt different.

"Did you notice? This here lid's on hinges," he said. "Now why would Vollmer spring for that on this cheap pinewood thing? You'd want a coffin nailed tight before it goes on a train."

"I know what you're gonna do." I put my free hand over my eyes—but cracked the fingers apart wide enough for me to peek through. "Just go on and do it, would ya?"

Old Red took a deep breath, steeling himself. He might be willing to do all kinds of stomach-turning things if they'll crack open a puzzle, but that doesn't mean he has no stomach to turn.

"Right," he said.

He flipped up the lid.

Walter Glaze stared back up at us.

I let out another "Oh, lord." Mucking around with corpses really wreaks havoc on my vocabulary.

Glaze's eyes were half-open, as was his mouth. He hadn't begun to stink yet, thank god, but it was impossible to tell if he was discoloring: No one had cleaned off the mud caking him from head to toe. The muck had long since dried, leaving the crust-covered body looking like it had been battered and fried like a chicken.

It was a disquieting sight but one I could handle.

I lowered the hand that had been not quite over my eyes.

"Kinda shameful to send a man back to his family looking like that," I said.

"You coulda cleaned him off before we took him to Loveland, but you didn't," Old Red reminded me.

"Yeah, well...I wasn't the one packing him up for shipment, was I? What are you doing?"

The answer to my question was actually quite obvious.

My brother was reaching into the coffin.

"There's a reason for them hinges," he said. "And it ain't so Glaze can play Jack in the Box."

He began rooting around beneath the body. Almost instantly, his eyes widened.

"Hel-lo?" I said.

Old Red nodded. "Hel-lo."

He pulled what looked like a thick, folded flap of burlap out from under the small of Glaze's back. When he unfurled the cloth, a Colt Lightning revolver dropped down into his hands.

My brother grunted, set the gun and burlap on the floor, and reached under Glaze again.

A moment later, he brought out another length of burlap, this one from beneath Glaze's thighs. When he unwound it, he found himself holding another Colt.

"Why in god's name would they hide guns under Glaze's body?" I said.

"Cuz they're gonna need 'em," said Old Red. And he did something that would turn out to be a deadly mistake—though we couldn't have known it until five seconds later.

He put the second Colt down by the first one and slid his hands beneath the corpse again.

That was when the door opened.

"Goddamn—I knew it!" someone behind me snarled.

I whipped around to find Ed Vollmer a step inside the warehouse. I still had the lantern in my hand, so a quick-draw was out of the question for me. Not that the attempt would've done anything but get me killed fast, for Vollmer was already halfway through *his* draw.

All that remained to be seen then was whether he was going to go ahead and shoot us now or bother closing the door first.

TWENTY-FOUR
DAMMMMMMMMMMMMN

OR, WE TRY TO CONVINCE OUR CAPTORS THE JIG IS UP WHILE VOLLMER GETS SET TO DANCE ON OUR GRAVES

VOLLMER CHOSE NOT to shoot us right away. But he didn't immediately close the door either. Instead he barked out, "Hold it right there!" and stalked toward us a few steps to give his friends Benji (the chubby one) and Bones (the skinny one) room to come in with him.

I put up my hands without even being asked. Old Red did the same. (We've had some practice at this kind of thing.)

"Bones—get their guns," Vollmer said. "The ones on the floor, too."

Bones started toward us.

"Benji—close the door."

"Right, Ed."

Benji pulled the door shut as Bones yanked my Peacemaker from its holster. I was still holding the lantern aloft, and as Bones moved on toward Old Red, I realized what I should have done: thrown the lantern (the only source of light in the place) at Vollmer, dived to the side, drawn my gun and blazed away.

Maybe it would've gotten me and my brother killed, maybe not. But at least we'd have had some kind of chance instead of being at Vollmer's mercy. Assuming he had any. Which I didn't.

There were still a few seconds left before Bones had a hold of Old Red's gun and the Colts beside him. Perhaps it wasn't too late. I could still hurl the lantern, leap aside in the dark, and leave the shooting to my brother.

Vollmer seemed to read my mind.

"Don't move a muscle," he warned me, his own gun now aimed squarely at my broad chest.

I gave up on the lantern idea. I tried to console myself with the thought that it was a pretty bad one anyway. We'd have just ended up dead a few minutes sooner.

"Get the lantern," Vollmer told Benji. In case I had any second thoughts about it, I guess.

"Right, Ed."

Benji hustled over, snatched the lantern from my hand, and quickly backed off again.

"What are we gonna do, Ed?" he said.

"Shut up. I'm thinking."

Bones finished his errand behind me and rejoined Vollmer and Benji with an armful of guns.

"What do you want me to do with all these?" he asked Vollmer.

"Pick one," Vollmer grated out, "and point it at *them*."

He jerked his chin at me and Old Red.

"Got it."

Bones created a little pile of guns by his feet, then turned my own Peacemaker on me. Oh, the indignity. I was about to meet my maker courtesy of a bullet I'd loaded myself.

"Benji," Vollmer said. "Go down to the whorehouse and see if Uwe and Billy are there. They need to get back here and help clean up the mess they made."

Benji nodded vigorously, looking relieved to be sent out of the warehouse before whatever was going to happen next.

"Right, Ed."

Benji handed the lantern to Bones and started toward the door.

"And, Benji," Vollmer said.

Benji stopped and looked back.

"Don't dawdle," Vollmer told him.

"Right, Ed," Benji said—mumbling it this time. Clearly he'd had dawdling in mind.

"What brought you back to town tonight, Vollmer?" Old Red said. "Y'all don't need to be here till Friday afternoon."

Benji slammed to a stop again.

"What the hell, Ed?" he said, the color draining from his round, jowly face. "How could he—?"

"*Go*," Vollmer snapped. "*Now*."

"Right, Ed."

Benji stumbled off, looking shaken. A couple seconds later, the door was closing again behind him.

"Ed—" Bones began.

"Shut up, Bones," Vollmer said. "The only one I want to hear talking right now is him."

He shifted his gun from me to my brother.

"You answer my question first, and maybe I'll answer some of yours," Old Red said.

Vollmer snorted. "You're pretty cocky, considering the circumstances."

"That's just it. I *am* considerin' the circumstances," Old Red said. "Which is how I know you don't want any gunplay tonight. Can't go drawin' attention to this storehouse and the depot and what you boys are gettin' set to do the day after tomorrow."

"And just what *are* we getting set to do?" Vollmer asked.

"Grab the mine payroll off the Afternoon Special. That's the whole reason you've been hangin' around Wamsutter these last couple weeks."

I don't know how Vollmer would have reacted to that—if he'd have bothered with a "My oh my, what a crazy thing to suggest." If so, he didn't get a chance to say it. Bones made sure of that.

"Damn, Ed! They *do* know!" the skinny man blurted out. "What are we gonna *do*?"

"Shut…up…Bones," Vollmer said through gritted teeth.

I took the opportunity to glance back at my brother.

"Did you work it all out right this second, or have you been sitting on it a while?"

"It was the suits and the hinges and the guns in the coffin that pulled it together for me," Old Red said. "But I been thinkin' about that payroll train ever since we left Dirty Dan's."

"You two," Vollmer snarled at us. "Don't talk to each other, or the conversation's gonna be over quick. You talk to *me*."

He focused his attention on my brother and relaxed a bit. Almost even smiled.

"So...you just figured it out, huh?"

Oops.

We couldn't play the "We already told everyone what you're up to, so you'd best let us go" card.

I told you we'd had some practice at this kind of thing, but that doesn't mean I couldn't use more. Unfortunately, now I was pretty sure I'd never get it.

"It's all there to see, ain't it?" Old Red said. "And it will be seen if we go missin'. Those men we work with—they are hard, shrewd characters. And they're gonna know exactly who to come after."

"Ed...?" Bones said, a panicky warble in his reedy voice.

Vollmer gave my brother's words some thought, then shook his head.

"They're used to leaving the Black fella in town alone for days at a time," he told Bones. "Went half a week without checking on him once. And now they've got fresh supplies from the store—we all saw that. No. There's no reason to think they'd come back in before Friday."

"Is that what brought *you* in tonight?" Old Red asked. "You stopped to watch our wagon and saw we'd switched with Hoop? 'The Black fella'? So you knew we'd changed up our routine and figured we was plannin' something?"

Vollmer did smile now. It didn't make his hard, scarred face any more pleasant. Quite the opposite, in fact. It was that kind of smile. The ugly kind.

"Well, our friends can notice the same thing," my brother

went on. "'Cuz they're always watchin' for *you*, of course. And when they see you've brought the whole gang into town—"

"We weren't seen," Vollmer cut in. "We made sure of that."

"You think you did," Old Red said. "But those men you're so sure you slipped past—they're professionals. Seein' and not bein' seen is their bread and butter. Why, the Apache's so good at creepin' up on a man he could be behind you this very second, and you wouldn't know it...not till the knife went slidin' across your throat."

A metallic rattling rose up as my brother spoke. It was the lantern in Bones' left hand. Shaking. The man was actually trembling.

He set the lantern down on the floor and wiped his palm on his trousers. The gun in his other hand—my gun—dipped and quivered, but soon enough, it was pointed my way again.

Vollmer, on the other hand, went right on smiling, seemingly amused both by Old Red's attempt to talk us out of death's door and the attack of nerves it was giving Bones.

"So the only thing for us to do," he said, "is let you go with our sincere apologies and light out while we can. Right?"

My brother nodded firmly. "That'd be the smart thing."

Vollmer burst out laughing.

The sudden, explosive noise of it gave Bones a start. But that just made Vollmer laugh harder.

"You really are something, mister," he said to Old Red. He sighed happily, apparently grateful for the entertainment my brother and Bones were providing. "So...you said something about Dirty Dan's a minute ago. What are they saying about us over there?"

"If you're wonderin' if they're suspicious, the answer is 'you bet,'" Old Red said. "You made some enemies there, Ed. Roughin' men up so you could take their jobs and keep an eye on the trains. Even doin' away with one 'em. Now there, I'd say you overplayed your hand."

Vollmer's expression turned confused—though he remained amused.

"Who'd we supposedly do away with?"

"Luigi Verardo. Durgin's cook."

Vollmer scoffed. "Why in the world would we kill Durgin's cook?"

"Maybe you had someone else in mind for his job. Someone who'd help you keep an eye on Durgin's camp."

Vollmer swatted the idea aside with a flick of his gun. "We don't give a shit about Durgin's camp. I'd have thought you had that figured out, smart man."

"But Verardo did disappear after you all came into the Water Trough one day," Old Red persisted. "You was seen steppin' outside right after he did. Some folks don't think that's a coincidence."

"It's probably not. The cook got spooked by us and ran off. If people want to say I *killed him* cuz of that..." Vollmer shrugged, grinning. "I don't mind another notch on my gun, whether I earned it or not."

"How about Doyadukubichi'? You earn that one?"

"Oh, Joe? Sure. Him I killed."

"Ed," Bones protested, voice still warbly with nerves.

"So I killed an Indian," Vollmer said dismissively. "Some people would give me a medal for it."

"Killed him because you needed a story for the constable. One that would head off questions about what happened to *him*." Old Red nodded at the body he was still kneeling next to. "And there was Doyadukubichi', shot through the hand, useless to you as a gun. He'd just complicated things by runnin' off on his own to mess with Durgin's horses. Could've stirred up more trouble you didn't want—more attention—if anyone had been hurt. So you was mad at him, and he was a problem for you...and you found another use for him."

Vollmer's eyes steadily widened the more he heard.

When Old Red was done, he barked out another laugh.

"Mister," he said with what looked like genuine admiration, "you are the best guesser I ever come across."

"They ain't guesses," my brother grumbled. "They're deductions."

"*Ed...*" Bones whined again. He lowered his voice, but not so much that Old Red and I couldn't hear it. Which made it kind of a pointless thing to do. But I suppose folks feel a trifle uncomfortable when they're about to suggest it's time for other folks to die. "Do we really need to keep talking to these two? Shouldn't we... you know...?"

"Shut up, Bones," Vollmer said yet again. It came out mildly this time, though. Like he was so confident he had the situation in hand, he could go on being tickled by it. "And keep 'em covered."

He holstered his gun and started toward us.

"Don't mind him," he said, jerking his head back at Bones. "You got any more 'deductions' you want to tell me about?"

"Well..." Old Red said warily, watching the man approach.

Vollmer's fists weren't clenched, nor did he have a knife in his hand (for now). So what was he up to?

He drew even with us—then carried on past, headed for the wall beyond, and the old tools leaned up there near the papered-over window.

"Go on," Vollmer said. He stepped up to one of the tools: the sledgehammer. It was the big, heavy, long-handled kind for busting up rocks and driving in spikes. "Show me how hopeless it is for us. How it's so obvious what we're here to do. Why we should leave you be and get while the getting's good."

He wrapped his hands around the handle and lifted it up with a grunt.

He immediately let go again, and the sledgehammer thudded back to the floor.

He reached for a pickax instead.

"On Friday, the Union Pacific Afternoon Special will stop in Wamsutter," my brother said. The words came out quick as Vollmer hefted the pickax and tested its weight. "As usual, two of the guards for the Big Butte Coal Company will hop off and run up the street to Dirty Dan's Water Trough for a couple beers. While they're gone, your friends Uwe and Billy, unarmed and dressed in new suits, will start loading a coffin onto the baggage car. When the time is right—this part I ain't sure about—there'll be some kinda signal, and they'll pull guns from the coffin and maybe take the baggageman hostage. Some of your other boys'll make sure them guards at Dirty Dan's never make it back, while the rest of ya…well, I don't know. I haven't been watchin' that train up close like y'all have. But whoever's still in your way gets dealt with, and your gang heads back to the Hole-in-the-Wall or wherever you came from with the payrolls for five or six mines. That's the plan."

"Dammmmmmmmmmmn," Bones said.

It came out like a groan, low and miserable.

Vollmer nodded, looking impressed, and gave the pickax a test swing.

"And if we could figure out that much," I said to him (including myself in the deducing for strategic reasons), "the other detectives here with us will work it out as well. They don't even need to get the whole picture to mess your plans up good. Just an inkling's all it'll take."

Vollmer started toward us—still holding the pickax.

"Now hold on!" I said. "You gotta keep things quiet for another—"

Despite my panic as Vollmer drew closer, I managed to do some quick figuring.

"—forty-one hours! That ain't gonna hold! Especially if something happens to us!"

Vollmer was just half a dozen steps away now. I got set to jump him, even if it meant a bullet in my back. I wasn't going to just stand there while my skull got busted open. I need it to keep my brains in.

"Shhhhhh," Vollmer said.

He stepped wide of us and carried on toward Bones.

"Ed," Bones said.

Vollmer shushed him, too.

When he reached Bones's side, he pivoted to face me and my brother again.

"Yeah...you know just about everything," he said casually, perfectly relaxed. "The part with the guns in the coffin—that wasn't even part of the original plan. I'm just making the most of an opportunity there. For which I thank you. You and your friends handed that to me on a silver platter."

"What do you—?" Old Red began.

The door opened, and Uwe and Billy came tramping in with sheepish, fearful looks on their faces. Benji followed, closing the door as soon as he was inside.

"Finally," Vollmer said. "I'd just about run out of things to talk about. I was gonna have to start asking these two what they thought of the weather next."

He nodded at me and Old Red.

Uwe and Billy glanced over at us, neither looking us in the eye. They'd stopped a few paces into the storehouse, but Vollmer waved them closer.

"Come here, Billy."

Neither man moved.

"I'm sorry, Ed," one of them said. I still wasn't sure which was Uwe and which was Billy. I just knew this was the younger of the two—the one in love with Bonnie at the hog ranch. "I know we messed up real bad."

"Yeah, you sure as hell did, Billy," Vollmer said. The composed, almost friendly tone he'd taken with us was quickly fading away, replaced by anger and steel. "All you two idiots had to do was stay in this goddamn room for a couple more days, and everything would've gone smooth as silk. And instead, you go sneaking off to get some tail, and look at what we have to deal with now."

"I didn't wanna, Ed," said the older one—Uwe, I knew now. "Billy was always—"

"Shut up," Vollmer snapped. "Billy...come here. *Now*, dammit."

Billy eyed the pickax in Vollmer's hands nervously. Uwe eyed the pickax nervously. Benji and Bones eyed the pickax nervously.

And you can sure as hell bet Old Red and I were eyeing the pickax nervously.

The only one who wasn't eyeing anything nervously was Vollmer. He was just thrusting the pickax at Billy as the younger man slowly stepped toward him.

"I got big lungs," I said. "I can scream real loud."

"Louder than gunshots?" Vollmer said without looking at me. His eyes were locked on Billy. "I doubt it."

"This ain't the smart way to play it," said Old Red, speaking not to Vollmer but the cowed men around him. "Us bein' in here means it's over. You ain't gettin' away with it. If you don't hightail it outta Wamsutter now, you're gonna end up leavin' like him."

He pointed down at Glaze in his coffin.

The men ignored him.

Vollmer whispered something to Billy.

Billy shook his head.

Vollmer whispered again, shoving the handle of the pickax into Billy's chest.

Billy, still shaking his head, whispered something back.

Vollmer sighed and lowered the pickax.

Thank god. Billy seemed to be listening to reason.

"Suit yourself," Vollmer told him.

He reached down to his side, drew out the big Bowie knife he'd taken from Doyadukubichi', and held it out to Billy.

Billy took it.

"You help," Vollmer told Uwe.

Billy turned and took a step toward us.

The only reason he'd been listening to was the kind that told him a pickax wasn't the tool for the job. Why get fancy when there's a knife handy?

Uwe was following a step behind as Billy carried on toward us, the blade in his hand so long and gleaming-clean it flashed even in the dull light of the lantern.

TWENTY-FIVE
GOODBYES
OR, YOU DON'T REALLY WANT ANY HINTS ABOUT WHAT HAPPENED NEXT, DO YOU?

AS BILLY and Uwe came toward us—both of them moving slow and wary—Old Red and I shared a quick look that was half "Get ready to fight" and half "Goodbye." There was a lot I could've said to him—a lot I wanted to say, and not just "I never should've read you that first damn Sherlock Holmes story." But there was no time left to say it.

A sudden *thunk* jerked our gazes across the room, beyond the men closing in on us.

Vollmer had dropped the pickax he'd been holding so he could redraw his forty-five. Benji pulled out his gun, too.

Billy and Uwe stopped and looked back, distracted by the noise. It didn't give me and my brother enough time to work up a brilliant escape plan, though. A week probably wouldn't have been enough time, given what we were up against. As is, the pause only gave us the briefest of moments. Then they were coming at us again.

Billy was out in front, just a dozen paces away. He held the Bowie knife low, the tip pointed ahead. At me. Apparently, I was to be first. Uwe would probably make a grab for Old Red while I took a blade to the belly.

I took a step back, giving myself maybe an extra half second to prepare. An extra half second to live.

My brother was still in the position he'd been in when we were taken by surprise: kneeling by Glaze's open coffin. But now he straightened up and moved to his left so we could face what was coming shoulder to shoulder.

As the distance between us and Billy and Uwe shrank even more—eleven paces, ten, nine—Vollmer and Benji and Bones spread out to keep Old Red and me in their gunsights. Even if we managed not to get gutted, there was no escape. They'd risk the noise and shoot us down.

Billy was eight paces from me. Then seven. Then six.

I looked into his eyes, searching for mercy. I saw fear and determination instead. He was about my own age—twenty, twenty-one, around there somewhere—and killing a man up close appeared to be new to him. It didn't look like he'd enjoy it—yet he seemed hell-bent on doing it all the same.

I gave up on his eyes. He was five paces away—close enough now for a lunge. I had to watch that blade.

Billy's right hand—the one with the knife—slid out to the side. He wasn't going to go for a straight jab. He'd probably come in with his left hand, grab me, then swing in with his right. Try to bring the knife around from behind and rip me open beneath the ribs.

"Slice!" as Eskaminzim had said the first time he jumped me the day before. "There goes your liver!"

Now I was about to lose it for real.

I brought up both my hands, getting set to block Billy's right at all costs—just as Billy threw the knife sideways into his left with a quick flick of the wrist. He had more skill with a blade than I'd figured, and he'd used it to take me by surprise. Next would come a quick stab into my unprotected side.

But that little toss to the left gave Old Red an opportunity. Billy was watching me, not my brother. So he didn't see Old Red pounce until there were already hands locking onto his left wrist, yanking the hand down hard onto a swiftly rising knee.

As Billy yowled and dropped the knife, Uwe leaped forward and gave Old Red a shove that sent him staggering backward. That both broke my brother's hold on Billy and left Uwe wide open for a plain, old-fashioned haymaker, which I quickly delivered. I connected with the right side of his jaw, and he grunted and stumbled away but managed to keep on his feet.

I turned back to Billy in time to see him bending low to snatch the knife back up. I went for a kick to the head but mostly got shoulder, and though Billy went sprawling onto the floor, he did it with the knife in his hand. I was about to try a stomp next—I hadn't decided if it would be on Billy's wrist or the back of his head—when Vollmer's voice stopped me.

"Dammit," he said. "If you want something done right..."

He had his forty-five up high so he could squint down the barrel at me. He was going to risk making some noise after all. There was no telling who might hear the shot, but that wouldn't matter to me, being dead and all. It was probably too late to even get out that scream I'd warned Vollmer about. Still, I sucked in a quick, final breath to give it a try.

There was a knock at the door.

It was a civilized knock, too. A polite *rap-rap-rap*. Which made it more startling than a door-rattling pounding would've been. One second we were in the midst of a life-and-death struggle, the next it sounded like a neighbor lady was popping by to borrow a cup of sugar.

Everyone froze. Partially out of surprise, partially out of confusion. It'd been clear enough what we were doing a moment before. Trying to kill each other. But suddenly that seemed rather improper. After all, we had company.

There was another knock, just as light. *Rap-rap-rap* again.

Benji, the last to come in, was still nearest to the door.

"Should I see who it is?" he whispered.

Vollmer scowled at him.

"Just tell 'em to go away," he said. He sighted down his gun barrel at me again. "And don't you make a peep. Either of you. Or you're gonna get whoever's out there killed."

"Go away!" Benji shouted at the door. "This here's private property under armed guard! Trespassers will be shot!"

He looked over at Vollmer, proud of his improvised flourish.

Vollmer kept scowling. And pointing his gun at me.

"Mmm humm funt gruh," someone outside said. Or sounds to that effect.

It was a man, that much I could tell. But his voice was so low and muffled that I couldn't make out words or recognize the voice.

It was the same for Benji.

"What's that?" he said, tilting his head and stepping closer to the door.

"Don't—!" Vollmer barked. But it was too late.

With a roar, a hole appeared in the top half of the door. And in the top half of Benji. Square in the chest.

I could see the puzzled look frozen on his face as he flew backward, alive then dead in the span of a second.

Everyone in the barn flinched. Which is what saved my life. For the moment.

I don't know if it was surprise or spite or a simple desire to wrap up one bit of business before dealing with the next, but Vollmer squeezed off a shot at me. It went high, though—almost close enough to part my hair but not so close it could take any of me with it. Then he and Bones were both spinning to fire at the door, quickly riddling it with three or four new, though much smaller holes.

Another big blast punched through the wood from outside, lower this time, and Bones crumpled with a shriek.

Uwe still stood near Old Red and me stunned into inaction by what was happening. But Billy managed to collect his wits quicker. He scrambled to his feet and whipped around to face me, and once again, I found the tip of the knife aimed at a spot just north of my belt buckle.

"There's still time to surrender!" I told him.

It might've been a silly thing for an unarmed man to tell someone brandishing a knife the size of a dachshund, but I had to try *something* that didn't involve grappling with him, and "There's still time to surrender!" was the first thing that popped into my head. Maybe it could've even worked…though I doubt it from the hateful gaze Billy gave me and the way he tightened his grip on the knife's dark oak handle.

Before Billy could either drop the knife and put up his hands or send the blade plunging into my gut, there was an explosion of shattering glass and ripping paper behind us. We all spun around toward the sound to find Eskaminzim, freshly burst through the papered-over window, rolling to his knees with his Winchester in his hands. He brought up the rifle the second he was steady and got off three shots.

The first went through Billy's heart.

The second went through Uwe's head.

The third went through Vollmer's legs. As in between them—somewhere around the knees to judge by the hole it punched in the wall beneath the building's other window, behind him.

I'd lost track of Vollmer's shots. Did he have two rounds left? Three?

One was all he'd need for Eskaminzim, and he intended to use it, taking aim with remarkable coolness considering all the men in the room who were suddenly, bloodily dead.

Eskaminzim rolled to the right as Old Red and I scrambled to the left toward the field jackets that would provide some cover if only we could reach them. We were diving for the first we came to —a gray blob of plaster that looked like a giant wad of used chewing gum—when there was another crash of glass followed by two shots in quick succession.

Old Red and I poked our heads up to see Vollmer stumbling forward. The window behind him had been busted in, and someone in the darkness outside was aiming through it with a Colt.

Eskaminzim, off to our right, was steady on his knees again, and he brought up his Winchester and levered in another round.

"No!" Old Red shouted at him. "Don't shoot!"

Eskaminzim listened. The man outside the window did, too.

Vollmer didn't.

His gun had tilted down toward the floorboards as he staggered, at least one bullet in his back. But now he jerked the gun up again and fired it at my brother, his scarred face twisted into a hateful grimace.

The bullet slammed into the field jacket we were hiding behind, cracking it open with a puff of pulverized plaster.

Eskaminzim and the man outside fired at the same time. Both shots found their target.

Vollmer spun and hit the floor face down.

It was over.

The shooting part, anyway. The dying was going to take a bit longer for some.

Billy and Uwe were as dead as the dinosaurs, but I could hear raspy, gasping breathing from two of the three prone men near the door. Old Red and I pushed ourselves to our feet and headed toward them. Eskaminzim stood and went with us.

"Pretty good, huh? Through the window and come up shooting?" he said. He heaved a happy sigh. "It's been years since I got to do that."

"Yeah, pretty good," I told him. "Thank you."

"Thank *you*," he replied. For the opportunity to jump through a window and come up shooting, I guess.

To each his own.

A face appeared in the broken window on the other side of the storehouse—one that looked pinched and ghostly pale in the dull light of the lantern on the floor fifteen yards away.

"And thank you, too," I said to Diehl.

The face disappeared.

"He's mad that you got yourselves in trouble…and that Hoop let you," Eskaminzim said. "The second Hoop got back to camp instead of you he knew you were going to do something foolish. Or maybe it was something moronic. Or something 'damned idiotic,' I think? You whites have so many words for stupid. I guess you need them."

We walked past the coffin, and Eskaminzim took a long look down at Glaze's body.

"I don't know, though," he said. "Seems to me you had an interesting time."

Up ahead, first Diehl, then Hoop came through the door. Diehl was pointing his Colt at Vollmer's bloody back. Hoop angled his big Sharps down at Bones.

There was no reason for either to take aim at Benji as they stepped over him. And soon enough no reason to take aim at Bones.

Hoop moved his rifle over to Vollmer as he carried on inside.

Bones had stopped gasping for breath. Stopped breathing entirely.

Diehl reached Vollmer first. The man had dropped his gun before hitting the floor, and Diehl nudged it further from his outstretched hand with the toe of his boot.

There were two holes in Vollmer's back, one down low on his left side, the other higher on his right. Diehl took in the wounds, then looked up at us.

"If you've got anything you want to say to him, you'd better say it fast."

Old Red moved to Vollmer's side and went down on his knees.

"Vollmer...you got no reason to hold back now," he said softly. "There're things I still don't understand."

Vollmer just kept staring down at the floor, his every breath weaker than the last.

"Vollmer...Ed..." my brother said, leaning in even closer.

"Watch it," Hoop said.

Vollmer was stretching out his right arm. He wasn't searching for his gun, though.

Slowly, trembling with effort, he lifted his hand and folded back every finger but one. The middle one.

The hand dropped, and Vollmer let out one final, wheezing breath, then was still.

He'd died as he'd lived. Covered in blood and giving the world the finger.

Old Red sat on the floor beside him, sagged, and sighed.

Diehl looked over at Eskaminzim. "Have either of these two said, 'Thank you'?"

The Apache nodded at me. "He did."

"My thanks go for both of us," I told Diehl.

Diehl grunted, then took a look around the storehouse. Gray gun smoke swirled over the bodies and shattered glass and coffin.

Hoop cocked his head, listening to something outside.

"Folks coming," he said.

"Of course there are," said Diehl. He holstered his Colt. "Quite a show we just put on. We're gonna have a crowd running up with popcorn and soda. They'll be disappointed they missed the opening act, but that's okay. There's always the inquest to look forward to."

He turned to Eskaminzim and held out his hands.

"You know how this works," he said. "You didn't kill anybody."

"Aww," said Eskaminzim. He handed over his Winchester without arguing, though.

He probably wanted to brag some more on jumping through a window and coming up shooting. But when you're an Apache shooting white men in Wyoming, it's best not to brag.

"And I've got to take my chances?" said Hoop.

A Black man who shoots whites in Wyoming isn't always going to get a fair shake either.

Diehl jerked his head at Benji's body and the big holes in the door beyond him.

"You've been seen around town with that canon of yours all week," he said. "Plus I don't think we could get away with claiming we had *two* unarmed observers."

Hoop grunted, unhappy with the situation but accepting of it. Having to take his chances was something he seemed accustomed to.

I could hear voices outside now—men whispering to each other as they drew near.

"Vollmer's men kidnapped the Amlingmeyers and brought them here to kill them," Diehl said quietly, calmly. He fixed his gaze on me. "You didn't break in. They forced you in at gunpoint. Right?"

"Right," I said.

Diehl looked down at my brother. "Right?"

Old Red started to look up at him, but something across the storehouse caught his eye. He stared at it hard—so hard the rest of us turned to look, too. Not that looking told us why the sight seemed to mesmerize my brother.

All we saw was the field jacket Old Red and I had hunkered behind a couple minutes before. The shot Vollmer had taken at us had blown off a chunk, revealing what had been wrapped up inside.

Rock, earth and—jutting like a big, dingy-brown tongue sticking out at us—the knobby end of a giant bone.

"Uhh…is the shooting over?" someone said from the darkness beyond the doorway.

"Absolutely, Constable," Diehl said. "Please—come in, come in."

Moving slowly, reluctantly, Larry Hellyer moved into the light and stepped inside. His thinning blond hair was tousled, and he was clad only in a wrinkled shirt and trousers he had to hold up with one hand.

In his other hand, shaking, was a little twenty-two pistol. It wasn't pointed at any of us yet, but I kept thinking that was going to change as Hellyer took in the carnage around us with wide, frightened eyes.

"What…? What…? What…?" stammered the blacksmith-turned-constable (who looked like he wanted to turn back into a blacksmith *immediately*).

"I know. Awful, isn't it? But don't worry," said Diehl. He gave Hellyer a reassuring smile. "I can explain everything."

TWENTY-SIX
LOOSE PIECES
OR, DIEHL DOES HIS BEST TO SWEEP EVERYTHING UNDER THE RUG, YET MY BROTHER CAN'T HELP BUT MAKE A MESS

DIEHL COULDN'T EXPLAIN *EVERYTHING*, of course. The why—that the dead men around us were a gang out to rob the payroll train—I had to supply. But Diehl filled in the rest for Hellyer, and the eavesdropping townsmen crowded around the door.

How the outlaws kidnapped my brother and me from Professor Durgin's storehouse (supposedly). How they planned to kill us because they thought we'd stumbled upon their plot (somehow). How he and Hoop had rescued us in the nick of time (led to the scene by their trusty—and unarmed—Indian scout Eskaminzim). He even helpfully walked Hellyer through what to do next: take statements, appoint a medical examiner (Wamsutter doesn't have one), alert the local justice of the peace, organize an inquest, make sure no one from the crowd outside snuck in to pilfer souvenirs off the bodies, etc.

Diehl skipped a part some people would've included. You know—the one about him and Hoop being taken into custody until the inquest could clear them of murder? None of us was going to pipe up to remind him he'd left it out, of course, and it didn't occur to Hellyer. Either that or he simply didn't want to tell men like Diehl and Hoop—standing amid the carnage so cool they could've been gnawing on brisket at a ranch barbecue if not for the rifles in their hands—to come along quietly to jail. Which Wamsutter also doesn't have, giving Hellyer all the more reason to let that slide on by. What was he supposed to do? Stick Diehl and Hoop in his closet and ask them kindly not to come out till told to?

The crowd was on our side anyway. After all, we'd just rid the area of its biggest assholes while providing free entertainment on a quiet spring night. We were heroes. We even got pats on the back —Eskaminzim included—as we finally filed outside, headed for Durgin's barn.

"Oh...uhh...don't leave town before the inquest," Hellyer called after us weakly. "Please."

"Oh, yeah!" Diehl called back to him. "Sorry I forgot that one!"

Five minutes later, he, Hoop and Eskaminzim were leaving town.

"We need to tell Durgin what happened," Diehl said as they got set to sneak back out of the barn and mount up. "And he was furious that we were 'abandoning' them out there."

"He wasn't the only one who was furious," added Hoop.

Diehl glowered at him.

"I'm used to pulling clients' asses from the fire for stupid reasons," Diehl said. "I don't care for it when it's men I have to work with."

He shifted his glare to my brother, who'd hardly said a word since Vollmer died giving him a one-finger salute.

"You're damn lucky we came back to pull your fat out of the fire, Amlingmeyer," Diehl said.

If he was angling for another "Thanks," it didn't work.

"Just do me one more favor, Diehl. You'll be doin' yourself one, too," Old Red said. "Tomorrow morning, bring in everyone from Camp Cashew."

Diehl scoffed. "Oh, they're going to love that."

"What they love don't matter," Old Red said. "Warm spring day, bodies gettin' ripe, a constable who'd rather be poundin' out horseshoes. That inquest's gonna come together quick. And you'll want every witness you can grab on hand to testify about the threats against us Vollmer and Loveland and Glaze made. That'll help the story about Vollmer go down all the more smooth, don't you think?"

"He's right," Hoop said.

Diehl chewed it over a moment. It was clear he didn't care for the taste of it.

"Fine," he finally spat. "Try to get through the night without getting yourselves killed."

He whirled away and headed out into the darkness.

Hoop started to follow him.

"Hoop," my brother said.

Hoop paused.

"*Everyone*," said Old Red.

Hoop nodded, then was gone.

"Aren't you going, too?" I asked Eskaminzim.

"I like to give them a head start," he said. "That way they can be amazed that I got where we're going first again."

He looked for dirt (or perhaps blood) under his fingernails, brushed something invisible off a calico shirt sleeve, examined the rafters for bats and owls, then left.

"Well...that's that, right?" I said to my brother. "Getting wrapped up nice and neat."

He didn't even have to say it. His look said it loud enough.

Feh.

That was *not* that.

He drifted off toward a corner—the one with the buckets and bags of plaster powder—and I didn't press him for more as he carried on silently around the barn, walking slow and silent. I knew what I'd get if I forced him to talk about it.

It is a capital mistake to theorize before you have all the evidence.

You know my methods. Apply them.

Data! Data! Data! I can't make bricks without clay!

A dodge, in other words. Dressed up in Mr. Holmes's clothes, yet still basically "Dammit, I don't understand it" when you stripped it bare.

It was a restless night for both of us. You don't come that close to death and then drift off into sweet dreams with a smile on your face because he didn't get you. And we were only alive because he *did* get five other men, right before our eyes. That they were SOBs didn't make it any less ugly or my dreams about it in any way sweet.

I don't know if it was those dreams or our less-than-plush accommodations—we had to sleep on bedrolls laid out on the floor—but I awoke in the middle of the night to find the lantern on again and Old Red squinting at his well-worn copy of *The Adventures of Sherlock Holmes*. He was silent, but his lips were moving. Slowly. At the rate he seemed to be going, he might get through the first paragraph by dawn.

As I watched, he lowered the book and gazed off at the neat rows of gray shapes looming in the gloom like a parade of half-pint ghosts. In a way, I realized, that's exactly what the field jackets were: the dead risen from the earth and tidied up for a trip. Like Glaze in his cramped coffin…the memory of which provided more sour dreams as I drifted back to sleep.

When I awoke again, I could see dim light here and there through the cracks in the rough-hewn pine walls. Old Red was either up again or still up, fiddling now with the old tools in the corner.

"You sleep at all last night?" I asked through a yawn.

"A little, maybe," he said. Like he truly didn't know. "About time you roused yourself. We got work to do."

"Oh, yeah?"

I turned over, pulled my blanket over my head, and made snoring sounds…which were quickly actual snores.

The next time I woke up, it was with the toe of Old Red's boot digging into my back.

"Come on. Get up. I want this done before we have company."

"What are we doing?" I groaned, reaching back to swat at him groggily. "Baking a cake?"

"Something like that."

It wasn't my baking skills he was interested in, though. (Which was good, as I have none.) It was my strong back.

A couple hours later, our company arrived.

Diehl and Hoop came loping in on either side of Durgin's wagon, Eskaminzim riding drag behind. Like the day before, the professor was in the driver's seat, the reins in his hand and Miss Hayes at his side. Cherry and the college boys, Wentworth and Mead, sat behind them in the bed.

Professor Durgin and his students all wore glum, put-upon expressions, but Cherry and Miss Hayes seemed pert and alert and pleased to see us.

"Gentlemen—how are you?" Miss Hayes asked as the wagon rolled up to the barn. "It sounds like it was quite a close thing last night."

"Thank you for asking, Miss. A close thing it was," I said. "We came through it all right, though."

"With some help," said Diehl.

He, Hoop, and Eskaminzim dismounted as Durgin stopped the wagon and set the brake.

"I'm sure it was quite harrowing," Durgin said. "But was it really necessary to bring us all in like this? I don't like leaving the dig and the camp abandoned, even with Vollmer and his men...gone."

"It's important that the law hear from everybody on this," Old Red said. "All that shootin'...it leaves quite a mess to clean up."

He and I stepped up to the wagon to help the women down—my brother moving to Cherry in the back and leaving Miss Hayes to me.

Cherry waved Old Red off and jumped down to the ground on her own.

"What mess?" she said. She jerked her chin at Hoop, Eskaminzim, and Diehl as they tied up their horses nearby. "These boys saved you from a gang of outlaws, and the outlaws ended up dead. *You* might've been in a mess, Little Red, but it got cleaned up for you last night!"

The little woman was in one of her peppery moods, and Old Red winced when she trotted out her nickname for him again.

"You're forgettin' something," he said. "Or some*one*, more like. A few someones."

I had Miss Hayes firmly on the ground by then, and she turned to my brother with a quizzical look on her face.

"You're thinking of Walter Glaze? And that Shoshone man?"

"Diehl explained about all that," said Durgin, looking tempted to unset the brake and go flying back to his holes in the ground. He forced himself to start climbing down from the driver's seat as Mead and Wentworth hopped out of the bed behind him on opposite sides. "Vollmer killed them. Glaze because he must have figured out what Vollmer was up to, and the Indian to take the blame for it."

"Yeah," Old Red said. "We could probably offer it up that way at the inquest and make it stick."

"So why wouldn't we?" said Diehl.

He, Hoop, and Eskaminzim were joining us in front of the barn doors, which my brother and I had opened wide as we waited for our visitors to arrive.

"Because it ain't true," Old Red told him. "Not the part about Glaze, anyway."

Everyone was gathered before the barn now. And everyone froze.

"How do you know that?" Hoop asked.

"Vollmer told us," Old Red said. "Not in so many words, but it was clear what he was thinkin'."

Diehl locked eyes with me. It was clear what *he* was thinking.

He wanted my read on what had or hadn't been said the night before. Just in case my brother was full of shit.

I nodded. "It's true. Vollmer told us that using Glaze's coffin to get guns onto the train wasn't part of his original plan. He added that because we'd 'handed him a body on a silver platter.'"

There were furrowed brows all around as the others worked out what that meant. I saw Diehl and Hoop get to the gist quick. They looked at each other.

Damn it, the look said.

Eskaminzim laughed.

"So we thought he killed Glaze," he said, "and he thought *we* killed Glaze!"

"Exactly," said Old Red. "Vollmer and his men knew that Glaze went off pokin' around on his own some nights. Doyaduku-bichi' told us that. So they assumed that the other side—us—caught him at it and did away with him. But that's not what happened…right?"

He turned to Diehl as if offering him one last opportunity to 'fess up.

"*Right,*" Diehl said firmly.

"So if it wasn't us and it wasn't them," Old Red said. "Who was it?"

"The spirits of the dead, angry that their resting places have been disturbed…" Eskaminzim said.

Everyone from Camp Cashew stared at him wide-eyed.

"…is what the Shoshone would've said," he went on. "Me, I think it was one of you!"

He burst out laughing again.

No one joined in.

"Who knows? They might come to the same conclusion at the inquest," my brother said.

"Only if somebody contradicts the story Vollmer told Hellyer about the Shoshone," said Diehl.

Only if Old Red and I didn't keep our mouths shut about it, in other words.

Old Red glowered at him.

If Diehl thought there was a chance Gustav Amlingmeyer would be satisfied passing off an easy, expedient lie rather than digging and clawing his way to the truth…well, it was one more indication how very much he had to learn about my brother.

"Oh, that snake Vollmer was just tauntin' ya," Cherry said dismissively.

I shook my head. "He had no reason to lie at that point. He thought we were going to be dead in five minutes. So did I, in fact."

"It's awful..." Miss Hayes said quietly.

She seemed to be commenting on both the dire situation Old Red and I had faced and the one we were all in now.

"Still..." said Mead.

Both he and Wentworth were dressed in suits and ties, as if the young men were in town for an ice cream social at their Presbyterian church rather than a bunch of murder talk. "Even if we don't understand *why* Vollmer would deny it later or make some disingenuous 'silver platter' comment, Occam's Razor would indicate that what he told the constable earlier—that the Shoshone was the killer—was true."

Mead seemed perfectly earnest, yet I couldn't hold back a snort.

"What?" he said to me.

"I know Occam's Razor," I said. "And let me tell you: The simplest explanation is *never* the right one when my brother and I are around."

"That hardly refutes his point," Wentworth scoffed.

"Let's see if we can do the refutin' another way, then," said Old Red. "What we got here...it must be kinda like what you paleontologists see when you come upon a bunch of fossils. The other day Miss Hayes was sayin' they ain't just lyin' there all connected-up still. They're spread around, piece here, piece there, and you gotta figure out how one fits to the other...or if they even go together at all. Only these ain't old dead things we're looking at now. They're connected, yeah, but they're livin'. Movin'. Reactin' to each other. Not a skeleton but a...a...a..."

"Chain of events?" I suggested.

My brother snapped his fingers. "A chain of events."

Wentworth leaned toward Mead (who'd been keeping his

distance from the other student, perhaps to lessen the seemingly inevitable urge to punch him).

"It feels like we're in one of Professor Napier's philosophy lectures," Wentworth said in a stage whisper, "only given by the janitor."

Mead ignored him.

"Get to the point, Amlingmeyer," said Diehl.

"There's a missin' link in the chain," Old Red said. "One that holds all the rest together."

Mead raised a hand.

My brother blinked at him, not comprehending. How could he have? He'd spent just a few months in a classroom—a little cold one in Kansas—when he was maybe six. So I gave Mead the response he was waiting for.

"Yes, Mead?"

"This all could be true. I don't know," he said. "But what's the use of all this speculation if we don't have the 'missing link'?"

"I think we do have it," Old Red replied. "We just ain't seein' it for what it is. There's lots of loose pieces rattlin' around. One of them is the one we need."

"What loose pieces are you thinking of?" said Hoop.

Diehl gave him an exasperated look of the "Don't encourage him" kind.

Oddly enough, my brother suddenly seemed like he could use the encouragement. He sighed and rubbed the back of his neck and took a moment to work up the nerve to continue.

"Well...I suppose we could start with Miss Hayes."

He turned reluctantly toward the lady, who gaped back at him with a shocked expression on her face.

"Or whatever her real name is," he said.

TWENTY-SEVEN
THE MISSING LINK
OR, OLD RED AND I CRACK THE CASE...
LITERALLY

CHERRY AND MEAD looked as taken aback by my brother's words as Miss Hayes.

Durgin and Diehl seemed incensed.

Hoop managed to retain his usual air of impassive calm. (If the day ever comes when he's either taken aback or incensed, I don't want to be anywhere nearby, because things would have to be *bad*.)

And Eskaminzim and Wentworth—two men you wouldn't think shared anything in common beyond a fondness for getting under other men's skins—both appeared utterly delighted.

"You leave Miss Hayes out of this," Durgin snapped at Old Red.

My brother shook his head sadly. "I wish I could, Professor. But like I said: We got loose pieces to sort through. And one is why does the lady take such pains to collect her mail when the rest of us ain't around? And why does her little hammer—the one she keeps in that tool bag I borrowed—have the initials 'd.o.' on the bottom of the handle? Seems to me a Lydia Hayes would have an 'l.h.'"

"'D.O.'?" Miss Hayes said with genuine confusion.

Then, ever so slowly, realization dawned, and her confusion turned to something that looked like embarrassment.

"It's not 'D.O.,'" she said.

Old Red squinted at her.

"That's sure what it looked like to me," he said, suddenly uncertain.

He usually has an unshakable faith in his own observations and deductions, but letters and words were still unfamiliar ground.

"I can see why that might be," Miss Hayes said. "But you were looking at the monogram upside down."

My brother went right on squinting. He couldn't picture it.

I could. It wasn't d.o. he'd seen—and there wouldn't have been lowercase letters in a monogram anyhow. What he'd noticed on the hammer had been two capital letters, flipped.

"So your real initials," I said to the lady (and Old Red, since I wanted him to get the message without more dwelling on his mistake), "are O.P.?"

The woman we'd known as Miss Hayes paused, debating an evasion. It would be easy enough to say she'd borrowed the tool from a friend or that it had been forged by the world-renowned hammer maker Omar Pifflefable.

She settled on the truth.

"Yes. That's right. The hammer was a gift from Professor Durgin, actually. One I should've left at home."

"Olivia..." said Durgin.

He and Miss P. were standing near each other in the shade at the front of the barn, and he took a step closer looking like he might gather up her hands in his.

"Olivia?" Wentworth said. "Olivia *P.*?"

He'd moved into the shade, too, taking up position just inside the barn doors.

Durgin stopped and turned toward him, scowling.

Wentworth flashed him a grin in return.

"It's Olivia Pertwee, isn't it?" he said. He looked past Durgin, at the lady. "I bet you're Oliver Pertwee's daughter!"

She didn't scoff or deny it.

"Ahh. I see," said Old Red. Not in a gloating way, though. More pensive, mournful. "That's why Pertwee's usin' his nut butter money to bankroll this expedition and Professor Durgin's work at the university. His daughter is crazy for dinosaurs."

All eyes were on the lady now.

"No," she said, her own gaze locked on my brother. She chuffed out a bitter little laugh. "I would've hoped for better from you, Mr. Amlingmeyer."

Old Red went back to squinting at her, puzzled again. It didn't last long, though.

He nodded slowly, looking chagrined.

"I apologize for the assumption." He jerked his head to the side at Wentworth in the doorway. "He threw me off the trail or I might've seen it myself…Professor."

Miss *Pertwee* gave him a small, forgiving smile.

"I'm not really a professor," she said. "Women aren't exactly warmly welcomed in academia."

"More's the pity," Durgin said.

I saw the revelation dawn on the others' faces one by one— Wentworth, then Hoop, then Diehl, then Mead, then Cherry.

There was one exception.

"I have no idea what any of you are talking about," said Eskaminzim.

"She's the real Professor Pertwee," Hoop explained. "The person who's paying us to be here."

"Oh. All right," said Eskaminzim. "Why the lies?"

"Because no one wanted to back Olivia Pertwee's Health Miracle Nut Butter when I went looking for investors five years ago," the lady said. "But *Professor* Pertwee's Nut Butter—that was different. And it's been expedient to keep up the ruse, the buying public being what it is. I'm afraid plain old Olivia just wouldn't inspire confidence the way 'the professor' does. So I've carried on living with the lie…even to the point of using my mother's maiden name when my association with 'Professor Pertwee' might raise questions."

Old Red nodded along with the explanation, silent and thoughtful.

"So," Durgin snapped at him, "you ferreted out someone's secret. But it has nothing to do with Walter Glaze, does it? All you've done is embarrass a brilliant woman."

My brother blew out a long breath, still nodding. "Yeah, well…that's what happens when you try to put the pieces together sometimes. You gotta see which ones don't fit to get to the ones that do."

"Anyway…" Diehl said.

Clearly "That's enough of that" was coming next.

Before he could go on, Old Red turned to Cherry.

"I suspect it's the same with you, but I gotta ask," he said. "After that stampede through Camp Cashew, you made a big fuss about it wipin' out your cookin' supplies. Yet the flour I saw strewn about at camp was on top of your tent, not inside the supply tent…which them horses hardly touched. Then yesterday, you barely brought anything back with you from the store. Certainly not enough to make up for bein' 'wiped out' cookin'-wise."

"I needed more flour and coffee and lard," said Cherry, glaring.

My brother shrugged. "Maybe. But that's not the thing that really mattered, was it? It's why your tent smelled of flowers and spice after the stampede. The horses didn't trample your flour sacks, and I don't think they trampled your perfume either… perfume not bein' your style, if I may say so. No. They trampled your laudanum."

Cherry's mouth twisted into such a prodigious frown it looked like she was about to spit. In Old Red's face. But for the moment, she managed to hold back both the spittle and the obscenities she was ready to spew.

"I guess they flower the stuff up 'cuz the opium in it's so bitter…?" my brother continued. "Well…that's neither here nor there. The important thing is the professor runs a dry camp. You kept reminding us of that. So you had to keep your little habit to yourself. That's why you insisted on comin' to town then run off alone soon as you could. You didn't want us seein' you go to that 'druggist' and makin' use of what he sold you before headin' to the general store. Right?"

"You little something-something something-something something," Cherry said.

(That's a paraphrase. She was actually quite specific in her choice of words for Old Red. So much so that Miss Hayes—henceforth Miss Pertwee—gasped, and even Hoop raised an eyebrow.)

"It's actually better for you if you admit it," my brother replied calmly, unoffended. "Or would you rather have us think you're hidin' something else? Like the fact that you were spyin' for Glaze, and Vollmer ran off Durgin's first cook—or did worse to him—to get you into Camp Cashew?"

"That's a something-something lie!" Cherry screeched. "I had nothing to do with Vollmer or Glaze or Lou Verardo running away!" She swung her blazing gaze over to Durgin. "And even if I did break a something-something rule or two, I don't see what business it is of anyone's so long as the something-something cooking got done!"

Durgin had nothing to say to that. He just looked like he wanted to scamper back to the wagon and either dive under it or drive it out of town as fast as it would go.

Wentworth, on the other hand, was thoroughly enjoying the show.

"Do him next," he told Old Red with a jerk of the thumb at Mead. "He must have a deep, dark secret you can share with everyone."

"Shut up, Wentworth," Mead said.

Wentworth smirked back at him.

"This is accomplishing nothing," Durgin said. "Olivia...at least there's one advantage to having the truth about you out in the open. They know now that you are their employer. And you can tell this man..." He aimed a shaking finger at Old Red. "...to stop."

Miss Pertwee took in a long, deep breath, then shook her

head. "Mr. Diehl and Mr. Hoop are facing an inquest and perhaps more because they were here working for me. Trying to protect us. If it's going to clear their names, we have to see this through." She turned to my brother. "Do you have more 'loose pieces' you're trying to fit in?"

"Thank you, Miss. I sure do," Old Red said. "And the biggest is *you*."

He looked a little to the lady's left. At Durgin.

"Oh, you must be joking," the professor groaned.

"He don't joke," I said.

"All along," Old Red went on, eyes still locked on Durgin, "Loveland's acted like he had a claim to everything from your dig. He assumed he was going to get hold of it all somehow. Now why would he think that?"

"Because he's a vain, grasping, presumptuous old tyrant," Durgin said.

"One you were workin' for, with Glaze, in this very area just one year ago. Correct?"

Durgin nodded warily. "Yes."

"And then you return the followin' spring, free now from your tyrant, and what do you find almost immediately?" Old Red said. "Why, the very thing Loveland would want most in the world. A big, practically intact diplodocus."

"It was a great stroke of luck," Durgin grated out.

Old Red cocked his head and gave the professor a disbelieving look.

"'Luck,'" he said skeptically, like the professor had brought up leprechauns or Santa Claus with a straight face.

"Oh, he just went back to the middle of those piles of bones he left last year," Eskaminzim said. "The ones north, south, east, and west of his big animal in the ground."

"Wait," said Diehl. "*What?*"

"Sounds like you've known about that all along," said Hoop.

Eskaminzim shrugged. "I have. It was obvious."

"How come you never mentioned it?" Diehl asked.

Eskaminzim shrugged again. "It was so obvious I assumed you

all knew. Plus an Apache pointing out one more trick a white man's playing...who wants to hear it?"

"John, is this true?" Miss Pertwee said. "You found the diplodocus last year?"

Durgin looked down, unable to meet the lady's gaze.

"Just some caudal vertebrae and chevrons. But I knew what it was," he said. "There were already bone piles scattered around. Left over from the Shoshone or sheepherders or I don't know who. I just...relocated a few of them. By that point the season was almost over, and I knew the job you'd arranged for me with the university had been approved and I'd be free of Loveland soon. So why hand the old toad one last triumph that was really mine? And soon yours? And the university's?"

"Because if he could prove you found it while working for him, he'd get it anyway." Miss Pertwee shook her head. "Such a huge risk to take. And then lying about it..."

"So you were just play-acting when you followed the signs to those fossils," Mead said coldly. "Feeding us nonsense as part of a ruse."

Durgin finally raised his gaze from the barn floor yet found nothing to say.

"Well, this trip is turning out to be a disaster for my curriculum vitae," Wentworth said with a theatrical sigh.

My brother, meanwhile, had drifted a few steps further into the barn, his eyes going glassy.

"Ahh," he said. "Ahhhhh!"

Eskaminzim leaned toward me. "Is he about to sneeze or is this some kind of fit?"

"Something's fitting together," I said.

Old Red nodded. Not at me, though. At whatever he was seeing in his head. The shape forming as pieces locked into place.

"That's what Glaze was snoopin' around after," he said. "Proof Durgin knew about the diplodocus all along. Something more solid than a few bone piles around the dig site." He swung toward Miss Pertwee. "That page that was torn from your notebook. Was there anything in it about how the diplodocus was found?"

The lady shook her head. "No. Just specimens we collected before the diplodocus was discov—" She threw an unhappy glance at the professor. "Before John led us to the diplodocus."

"When you were still pretending not to know exactly where it was," Wentworth added, just in case the salt in the wound hadn't been rubbed in hard enough.

Durgin scowled at him, his shame giving way to disdain.

Wentworth folded his arms across his chest and smirked.

Clearly, the little toad had realized that he'd be coming out of the expedition with something he could use after all: leverage over the professor. For he now knew a secret that could destroy Durgin's career.

Mead had the same leverage, but he didn't look happy about it. In fact, he was staring at Wentworth with as much contempt as the professor.

"Those early finds were inconsequential," Miss Pertwee told Old Red, ignoring Wentworth's gloating. "I doubt the preparators or anyone else would even look at them until the diplodocus was completed. I haven't given them a second thought myself in over a week."

My brother lifted his chin and narrowed his eyes. Something he'd just heard had caught his interest.

"These 'preparators' back at the university," he said. "You told me the other day they work slow. Take months to get the fossils outta the field jackets and sort 'em out."

"That's right," Miss Pertwee said.

"Loveland still has specimens I collected years ago that haven't been examined yet," Durgin added sourly. "They're just sitting in a basement in New York."

Old Red nodded slowly, then looked over at me. Even if he hadn't nodded one more time—giving me the signal I'd been waiting for—I'd have seen it in his eyes.

All the spare pieces had been disposed of.

All the important ones had locked into place.

He knew.

"Y'all ever hear," he said, "of the blue carbuncle?"

"The what?" said Durgin.

Diehl put a hand to his forehead.

"Jesus Christ," he moaned.

"Is it a medical condition?" asked Mead.

Cherry scoffed at him. "I never heard of nobody having a touch of 'the blue carbuncle.'"

"But a carbuncle is a boil, isn't it?" Mead said.

While the others debated what a blue carbuncle might be, I went sliding sideways toward some tools leaned up against the side of the barn nearby. I passed Eskaminzim and Hoop as I went, and I met their questioning gazes and nodded back at the spot where I'd been standing—dead center in the broad open doorway.

Hoop and Eskaminzim got the message and took my place between everyone else and the wagon and horses. And escape.

"It's one of Sherlock Holmes's cases," said Diehl, too distracted (not to mention annoyed) by my brother's seeming foolishness to notice what was going on behind him. He went on in a sing-song voice, as if reciting a poem he found particularly insipid. "'The Adventure of the Blue Carbuncle.'"

"Sherlock Holmes?" said Durgin. "What's he got to do with this?"

Cherry swiped a hand and blew a raspberry. "Buncha bull. I never believed a thing I ever heard about that phony."

Old Red cleared his throat but otherwise let the sacrilege pass.

"A carbuncle is also a jewel…apparently," he said. "I'd never heard of 'em spoken of that way, but I guess in England, it's done. So this one—the blue carbuncle—got stolen a few years back. And the fella that done it knew he was about to get caught. So he hid it somewhere no one would look for it. He caught him a goose, and he forced that jewel down its throat. He figured he could come back later, get the goose, and *voilà*. He'd have the jewel again."

Little dimples appeared on either side of my brother's bushy red mustache. Under all the whiskers was a satisfied smile.

He'd remembered to pronounce "voilà" right.

"What'd I tell ya?" Cherry said. "That is the dumbest bullshit I ever heard."

Old Red's dimples disappeared.

"I never believed those stories either," Wentworth said with a snort.

Diehl's hand was back on his forehead. He suddenly seemed to be suffering from quite a migraine.

"Oh, the stories are true," my brother insisted. "Instructive, too. Helped me see the key piece we've all been missin'. The one that holds everything else together once you know it for what it is."

"And what is this oh-so-important piece?" Durgin asked.

"Luigi Verardo," Old Red said.

"Wait, wait, wait." Wentworth laughed. "The little Italian cook? The one who could barely fry an egg?"

My brother nodded serenely. "Yup."

"But he ran off over a week ago," Mead said. "He has nothing to do with what happened to Glaze."

"Oh, he has everything to do with it."

"Little Red," Cherry said, shaking her head. "You're trying to tell us that shrimpy lil' Lou Verardo got his nerve back, snuck out into the hills, and brained Glaze for some reason?"

It sounded like she was tempted to blow another raspberry.

"I didn't say he did the killin'," Old Red said. "He's the reason for it."

"So someone killed Glaze on the Italian's behalf?" Wentworth said incredulously. "And this has something to do with 'blue carbuncles' somehow?" He shot a sideways glance at Mead. "At least we're going to come out of this with an incredible story."

Of Mead's two preferred responses to Wentworth—"Shut up" and stony silence—he opted this time for the second.

"*Explain*," Diehl told my brother.

He didn't add "*Now*," but his tone got it across.

"Yesterday," Old Red began. "Otto and I had a talk with the regulars in Dirty Dan's Water Trough. The place Luigi Verardo was havin' a drink right before he disappeared. And they told us that Vollmer and his boys came in happy as larks...because Walter Glaze had just cut them loose to tie one on. So we know Glaze was in town at that same time, yet he wanted all his guards else-where, distracted. Mighty curious. Now, Verardo—naturally he got spooked havin' that bunch all around him, so he skedaddled. Well...where would he have gone?"

"Outta Wamsutter," Cherry said.

"How?" Old Red replied. "He just ran off into the hills? You yourself told us he was seen scamperin' toward the train station. Yet no one saw him buy a ticket and get on a train, did they? And no one saw him grab a horse and light out."

"So Vollmer did away with him," said Diehl.

Now it was my brother who looked like he wanted to blow a raspberry.

"'Did away with him,'" he said scornfully. "I would think that you of all of us here would know that when you kill a man, he don't just disappear in a puff of smoke. And why would Vollmer have killed Verardo anyway? We know he was ready to bend over backward to avoid legal trouble in town before the train robbery. That's why he cooked up that story about Doyadukubichi' killin' Glaze. Nah. Vollmer don't fit in at all."

"So what *does* fit, Mr. Amlingmeyer?" Miss Pertwee asked.

"The question ain't 'What?'" Old Red told her. "The question is 'Where?'"

He looked around the barn. To his right, at a downcast Professor Durgin and, standing stiffly a step further from him now, deeper in the shadows, Miss Pertwee. At an irritated Diehl to their left, Eskaminzim and Hoop behind him several paces, ready for anything in front of the wagon. At Wentworth, looking eager for more outrageous details to add to the story he planned to tell friends (assuming he had any) later. At a glowering, exasperated Cherry and—careful to keep the cook between himself and his hated tentmate—a stony-faced Mead.

And finally at me lurking by the tools leaned up against the wall.

"So there's Verardo," Old Red said. "He sees that Vollmer's bunch is in town, and he gets spooked. He wants to go someplace safe. Where he can tell somebody what's happenin'. Get him some protection. And it's obvious where that'd be."

"To the town constable? Hellyer?" Mead guessed.

"No. Hellyer's useless," Diehl told him. When he looked at Old Red again, his expression had changed. He didn't look annoyed. Or at least not *as* annoyed. Now he was intrigued. "I believe Mr. Amlingmeyer is trying to tell us, in his roundabout way, that Verardo came here."

Old Red nodded. "To his boss's storehouse near the train station…where he saw something he wasn't supposed to see."

My brother began backing deeper into the barn, the light going grayer on him with each step.

"I didn't want to do this till I was sure," he said. "But now… after hearin' what we've heard…I think it's time."

He reached the first row of field jackets and turned toward the one at his feet—the one he and I had moved from its far, dim corner that morning. We'd left a tarp over it, but now Old Red bent down and whipped it off.

Beneath was the usual lumpy white mass of plaster, this one perhaps five feet by three feet and two tall. The only thing that set it apart from its boulder-like neighbors was that the black serial numbers painted across it were runny and smeared. Illegible.

"Professor Durgin," my brother said.

"Yes?"

"Do you remember this here field jacket?"

Durgin peered at it a moment, then shook his head. "I can't remember them all by sight."

Old Red turned to Miss Pertwee.

"How about you, Miss?" he said.

She shook her head as well. "No. I'd have to consult my—"

The lady froze.

My notes, she'd been about to say.

Old Red nodded, then took two big steps to the side.

"Brother," he said.

I turned to my right and picked up the sledgehammer there—the one Old Red had me retrieve from Loveland's storehouse a couple hours before—and started toward him.

I think Diehl realized what I was going to do first, but all he could get out was an uncertain "Uhh…Amlingmeyer…?"

Then Durgin got it.

"No!" he cried out. "Don't!"

"If we're wrong about this," Old Red told him, "we apologize to science."

I lifted the sledgehammer higher, swung it over my head, and brought it down hard on the near end of the field jacket.

The plaster broke away in a big crescent chunk as if I'd cracked open a dinosaur egg to make the world's biggest omelet.

For the second time in as many days, Old Red and I found ourselves looking down at shoes where there shouldn't be any. And just like with the ones my brother had dug up in the pit, these had feet, ankles, and shins attached.

"Good lord!" Durgin said.

"Christ almighty!" said Cherry.

Miss Pertwee gasped.

Wentworth laughed.

Only Diehl moved in closer for a better look. Not that there was much more to see. The rest of the body remained plugged up in the field jacket—for which I was profoundly grateful. I wasn't sure what condition a man would be in after days shelled up in plaster like the meat in the middle of a walnut, but I'd assumed it wouldn't be pleasant.

"Luigi Verardo, I presume," said Diehl.

I rested the heavy head of the sledgehammer on the barn floor and gave Diehl a shrug. "If it's Grover Cleveland, I'll be mighty surprised."

Old Red swiveled to face the men who'd come into town with Verardo the day he disappeared: Professor Durgin's squabbling students, Peter Wentworth and Andrew Mead.

Mead glared back at him. Wentworth smirked.

Cherry slinked away from between them while Hoop and Eskaminzim remained at attention in the sunshine just outside.

Mead glanced over his shoulder at the open barn door—his only way out.

Eskaminzim smiled at him, inviting him to try it.

Mead turned back to Old Red.

"I've known for a while that Glaze and Loveland had a spy at Camp Cashew," my brother said. "Yesterday, we found where Glaze was killed—that hut made of bones out near the abandoned dig—and there was a slot in the wall where messages could be hidden." Old Red focused on Mead. "That's why you'd borrow Cherry's twenty-two to 'go huntin'' from time to time, right? Why you never actually brought back any game? You were really firin' off a signal to Glaze that you'd left a new note for him."

Mead said nothing. His handsome face could've been carved from marble, so lifeless was it.

Wentworth was staying silent, as well, though his expression said plenty. He was still leering, amused, above it all. Like a mean little boy refusing to apologize for a prank.

"Plus, whoever tore that page from Miss Pertwee's notebook had to be near it, right? It must've been someone in camp," Old Red went on. "So when Verardo came runnin' in here a week ago, I think he found Glaze gettin' a grand tour of Professor Durgin's finds courtesy of his spies. And they killed him. And someone had the bright idea of hidin' the body with the tools at hand and lettin' it get shipped off to the university…where it'd sit in storage until they could get rid of it permanently. They just had to make sure no one took too good a look at it and realized it was an extra, which is why they had to mess with Miss Pertwee's notes."

"I can't believe it," Durgin said—though the horror on his face said that he did. "Both of them? Together?"

"Oh, I've figured for some time now it was more than one person," Old Red said. "It'd be a hell of a job for somebody to kill Glaze in that hut then drag him up the hill to that hole all alone. Nah. Had to be at least two. What I ain't so sure of is *why* kill Glaze."

Wentworth and Mead finally had something to say—and they said them at the same time.

"Ask our lawyers when we sue you for slander," Wentworth sneered.

"Because Wentworth lost his nerve again," said Mead.

Wentworth jerked toward Mead, his eyes going big and round. "Andy!"

Mead ignored him.

"First he panicked and killed the little Italian when he walked in and heard us reporting to Glaze," he told Old Red. "Crushed his skull with a hammer that's in that field jacket with him now. Then he panicked about Glaze knowing it. We were already risking our futures by spying on Professor Durgin for Glaze and Loveland. Now Glaze could blackmail us for life. So Wentworth wanted us to be rid of him, too. He insisted on it."

"Andy!" Wentworth cried again. "For god's sake, what are you doing?"

"Shut up, Peter," Mead said without looking over at him.

The words—ones we'd heard so often from Mead the last few days—came out sad and resigned this time. Like he wished he'd said them even more. They could've saved him, perhaps, if he'd really meant them.

"So you signaled for Glaze to come to the hut, and later you snuck outta camp and bushwhacked him. Then you put his body where you figured no one would find it," Old Red said. "The pit Eskaminzim had warned us to stay away from that very night by the fire."

"Not realizing that my brother hears 'Keep away from that dark, dangerous hole' as 'Ooo—interesting! A dark, dangerous hole!'" I added.

"Yeah…Wentworth thought it was pretty clever hiding Glaze there. Then you went there anyway." Mead sighed. "And I've been waiting for this moment ever since."

Wentworth was still staring at him incredulously. "Andy…why?"

"Because I hate you. And I hate me," Mead said. "And I want this over with."

"But don't you see?" Wentworth managed to put a hint of his old sneer back on his face. "There's nothing they can do about it. We just heard Durgin admit that he cheated Loveland out of the biggest, most complete diplodocus yet discovered. If that comes out publicly—like at a trial—he'll have to turn it over, and his reputation will never recover. They have to let us go, or Durgin's ruined."

"Oh, I can think of another way to handle it," Cherry snapped. "We could save the state of Wyoming a buncha trouble and just take care of you two murderers right now!"

Eskaminzim let out a chuckle.

"I like the way she thinks," he said.

He looked past Wentworth and Mead, at Diehl, as if a quick lynching was actually something they should consider.

"You got me and my brother all wrong if you think we'd help hush up a thing like this," Old Red said—as much to Cherry, Eskaminzim, and Diehl as to Wentworth, I think. He looked over at the professor and Miss Pertwee. "I'm sorry."

"But...y-you can't mean it," Wentworth spluttered. Then he turned to Durgin and Miss Pertwee, as well. "You can't let them destroy everything you've worked for! Let us go!"

"Peter..." Mead said. "It's over."

Wentworth's whole body sagged. "Maybe for you..."

Then suddenly he was spinning on his heel and making a dash for the doorway. He was angling to the far left, trying to shoot past Hoop and duck around the side of the barn.

Diehl whipped out his Colt and pointed it at Wentworth's back. But Old Red was on him fast, lunging forward to lock his hands on Diehl's wrist and force the gun toward the floor.

Hoop, meanwhile, managed to snag hold of Wentworth's coat as he raced by, dragging the fleeing—and now hysterically screaming—man to a stop.

Eskaminzim drew his knife and started toward him. He was

still thinking Cherry had the right idea, and this was his chance to act on it.

"Otto!" my brother barked.

I knew what he wanted me to do. There was no time to be graceful about it or use any of the lessons on attacking from behind that I'd learned from Eskaminzim himself. No, I just did what had to be done the old, clumsy Otto Amlingmeyer way.

I charged the Apache and threw myself on top of him.

I was careful to keep my arms low around his waist so that his own arms would remain free after I tackled him. That way he could keep the blade out away from both our bodies as we hit the floor.

Which is exactly what he did. But leaving his arms free also meant he could elbow me in the face the second he got his wind back. Which is exactly what he did next. *Twice* before I could grab him by the hair and get set to smash his face into the floorboards.

I didn't have to bother. Something else came crashing down first, stopping our fight cold.

It was Wentworth—stretched out unconscious and bloody-nosed.

"Boys, boys, boys," Hoop said. "That's not necessary."

Eskaminzim and I looked up at him.

Beyond him was Mead, gazing down at Wentworth in sad disgust. He hadn't even tried to run.

Hoop shook his head at us, his blood-smeared fist still clenched.

"*Now* it's over," he said.

TWENTY-EIGHT
PAPERWORK
OR, WE TRY TO TIE UP MORE LOOSE ENDS, BUT ONE ROPES US IN FOR MORE TROUBLE

IT WASN'T REALLY OVER, of course. Not entirely. Murder's like that, I've learned. There's still plenty to work out even after someone's come jumping through a window guns ablazing.

What happened? *Why* did that happen? Are you okay? Am *I* okay?

And dear lord—the paperwork. You never read about that in *Smythe's Frontier Detective* or *Deadwood Dick, Jr.,* or even *The Adventures of Sherlock Holmes*, do you? Just one person ends up dead on you, there are reports to write and statements to sign and hearings to suffer through. You rack up eight, and you've got enough home-work for a month of school.

Still, we tried to wrap things up in Wamsutter as quickly as possible. After all, there was no paying work for us there anymore. We'd seen to that ourselves.

Professor Durgin didn't bother going back to his digging. Why should he when he knew whatever he unearthed would end up in Hiram Loveland's pudgy hands? So he just rented a room in town and did his best to avoid us (and the reporters who started showing up from Cheyenne and Denver and Billings looking for the scoop on the big shootout and the college boy killers who'd gone from hunting dead things to making them).

Hoop, Eskaminzim, and Diehl hung around through the inquests, but once those were out of the way they got set to move on. They had the bright idea of poking around the Hole-in-the-Wall country to see if "Ed Vollmer" and his pals had other names —and bounties to collect.

Old Red and I weren't invited.

We came out to Durgin's barn, where they'd been staying, to see them off anyway. Eskaminzim and I had patched things up fast after our little tussle. It was all in good fun as far as he was concerned. So he greeted us with a smile as he swung up onto his horse.

"Don't get killed before I see you again," he told me. "I still have a lot to teach you. I don't even know if you could die right before I show you how it's done."

"I guess I am pretty bad at that," I said. "I haven't managed to do it yet."

"It's not for lack of trying from what I've seen," said Hoop, hauling himself up into the saddle nearby.

He'd remained his usual cool, aloof self, and there was no smile to accompany the joke. Which, from his perspective, was probably true enough not to be a joke at all.

Diehl was already set to ride out, and he sent his mare ambling over toward us.

"Well, it's been...educational," he said.

"That it has," Old Red agreed.

"If not lucrative," Hoop added.

We still hadn't been paid for our days as Durgin's guards, and given how things had turned out, it was unclear if Miss Pertwee was going to open up her purse for us. I couldn't blame the lady if she felt we hadn't guarded the expedition from squat.

"You're still new to this professional detective thing," Diehl said to us. "So here's a chance for you to educate yourselves some more. In this business, staying alive isn't always the hardest thing.

It's collecting the bill. I'm going to tell Colonel. Crowe we've left that to you."

"Thanks," Old Red said dryly. "I always appreciate an opportunity to learn."

"Oh, I can tell you do," Diehl said. "We go about things differently, Amlingmeyer. And we might value different things."

"Like the importance of getting paid," Hoop threw in.

Diehl acknowledged that with a nod before turning his attention back to my brother.

"But the way you worked out everything that happened... what it was really all about...well..."

"Uh oh," said Eskaminzim, seeing what was coming.

Hoop rolled his eyes.

"'Like water that encrusts the rose, still hardening its core,'" Diehl recited, "'so pride encases human hearts until they feel no more. Shut up within themselves they live, and selfishly they end a life that never kindness did to kindred...or to friend.'"

"Uh-huh," said Old Red. "And that means?"

Diehl smiled wryly and leaned down toward us.

"I'm trying to be humble," he said, stretching out a hand. "No hard feelings?"

"Oh. You coulda just said that," my brother said. "Sure. No hard feelings."

He shook Diehl's hand, then I stepped up and did the same.

"No hard feelings," I said.

"Good," Diehl said. "The West is big, but it's not that big. I'm sure we'll see each other again." He straightened up and steered his horse away. "Now, for god's sake, get us our damn fee before the A.A. Western Detective Agency goes broke."

He got his horse up to trot, and Hoop and Eskaminzim headed after him doing the same.

"If there are bounties on those SOBs, me and my brother get shares!" I called after them. "You wouldn't have got 'em if we hadn't gathered 'em up in one place and distracted 'em for you!"

Diehl waved without looking back.

"Curious fella, that Diehl," Old Red said. "Terrible taste in poetry."

I couldn't disagree on either point.

We started back toward town headed, I thought, for Dirty Dan's Water Trough. (I'd gotten in the habit of bringing Sally and Sunshine a bag of peanuts each afternoon…and buying myself a couple beers as long as I was there.) But when we came to the first cross street, Old Red steered us right, toward the west end of town.

"We going where I think we're going?" I said.

"You heard Diehl," Old Red said. "We may as well get it over with."

And he heaved a heavy sigh.

He liked Miss Hayes, a.k.a. Miss Pertwee. So did I. So neither of us was looking forward to hearing what she thought of *us* now.

She was renting not just a room but a whole house out on the edge of Wamsutter. One of the nicest houses around, too. I guess that's an option when it turns out you're the cashew queen of America.

We went through the gate in the white picket fence and swept off our Stetsons as we approached the porch. Old Red let me do the knocking on the front door. I rapped three times, gently, then took four big steps back.

My brother gave me a curious look over his shoulder.

"I just remembered they had a couple shotguns out at the dig," I explained. "I want an extra step head start if Miss Pertwee decided to hold on to one of 'em."

Old Red scowled at me…then took two steps back himself.

It turned out we didn't have to worry about Miss Pertwee turning a scattergun on us. We had to worry about Cherry doing it.

It was the bony little cook who opened the door and glowered out at us, and growled, "Oh. You."

"Yes. Us," I said with what I hoped was a winning smile. "We were wondering if Miss Pertwee might be available."

"I'll see," Cherry said sourly.

She closed the door again. Firmly.

Old Red and I looked at each other. My smile had clearly *not* won her over.

We each took another step back.

A moment later, the door swung open again, and Cherry waved for us to come inside. Without a shotgun, we were relieved to see.

"Wait in there," she said, pointing at a parlor room to the left as we stepped into the foyer. "Try not to break anything."

We shuffled sheepishly into the parlor, steering wide of the end tables with their fancy lamps and the writing desk with a loudly ticking, glass-domed clock atop it.

I slowly lowered myself onto a velvet-covered sofa while Old Red perched on the edge of a wingback chair as if ready to spring off it and flee at a moment's notice.

"Cherry…" my brother said. "I am sorry about how—"

"It's coming out fine," Cherry snapped from the doorway. "I work for the lady now. She's helping me with…my bad habit. She's real nice. You oughta be nice *to* her."

"We aim to be," I said.

Cherry snorted. "I'll be in the kitchen. Chopping vegetables."

She spun around and stalked off.

I think she wanted us to know about the chopping so we'd picture her down the hall with a cleaver in her hand.

"One thing Doc Watson and Mr. Holmes never mentioned about deducifying," I said, "is all the friends you make doing it."

"Yeah, well…I don't do it to be popular," Old Red grumbled.

"Good thing, too."

My brother avoided further needling by silently studying the wallpaper as the clock counted off the seconds. When perhaps thirty had gone by, there were footsteps in the hallway, and a moment later, Miss Pertwee appeared.

She was in a gray silk tea gown, her long blonde hair—tied back in a simple ponytail in the field—pinned up neatly. She took just one step into the room before stopping.

In her right hand was a single piece of paper, lines across the back indicating it had been folded for stuffing into an envelope at one point. (My brother's not the only one who can note such things.) That she was thinking of showing it to us seemed obvious —why bring it with her otherwise?—but what it might be, I couldn't guess.

A letter from her lawyers saying not to pay us no matter how much we begged? A message from Colonel Crowe apologizing for the fiasco and letting her know he was dissolving the A.A. Western Detective Agency forthwith? Drawings of Old Red and me with buck teeth and our fingers up our noses under the words "BIG DUMB POOPHEADS"? Whatever it was, I got the feeling it wasn't good news.

"I'm sorry to have kept you waiting," Miss Pertwee said as Old Red and I rose to our feet, hats in hand. "I didn't know when to expect you."

"You knew we were coming?" I said.

"I suspected. You don't strike me as the types who'd just slip a bill under the door."

"Ah," I said. (Thinking: *Just slip a bill under the door? Damn—I should've thought of that!*)

"You're right about that, Miss," said Old Red. She hadn't taken a seat, so he and I remained standing, as well. "There's something I'd like to say. I tried sayin' it to Cherry, but…well, folks don't always understand."

Miss Pertwee said nothing. Whether she'd understand remained to be seen.

My brother took a deep breath, then continued.

"When you go diggin' for the truth, you never know which ones you're gonna turn up. I reckon with Mead and Wentworth alive to blab whatever they like before they go to the rope, you bein' Professor Pertwee ain't gonna be a secret much longer. I'm sorry about that…and about what'll happen to Professor Durgin and the paleontology department at the university. I know you put a lot of money—a lot of hope—into him and it, and now it's all for naught. I'd have preferred it if things hadn't worked out that way. Truly. That a fine person like yourself—our client, no less—

has been hurt as a consequence of our actions is something I deeply regret."

The lady blinked, a bit taken aback by Old Red's eloquence.

She looked over at me, and all I could add was, "What he said."

I was a bit taken aback, too.

"I appreciate your apology," Miss Pertwee said. "And I do understand. Two murderers are in jail thanks to you, and a violent robbery was thwarted. It's extremely unfortunate about Joh— Professor Durgin...but he was prepared to lie to me and the world to get what he wanted. He brought his disgrace upon himself. As for my being 'Professor Pertwee'...I don't think most people will care. Not now that they know how good my cashew butter is. At least that's what I'm hoping."

"We'll hope that, too," Old Red said.

"Indeed. We very much appreciate your understanding," I said. "So...uh...does that mean...?"

Miss Pertwee nodded. "Oh, I'll pay your full fee. Whatever I owe."

I smiled.

"On one condition," the lady went on.

My smile stiffened.

Uh oh.

On one condition: that the two of you go to hell?

It didn't seem like the lady's style. But you never know when it comes to hurt feelings and owed money.

She lifted the hand holding the piece of paper.

"You were partially right about the mail I was receiving here in Wamsutter," she said. "It was critically important that I not be completely incommunicado even though I'd taken great pains to hide myself away."

"Hide yourself away?" Old Red said, his prodigious curiosity piqued.

"Yes," the lady said. "I wasn't just using an alias to protect 'Professor Pertwee.' I was also protecting *me*. You see, someone's been trying to destroy me for some time now. I've just learned that they tried again…with tragic results."

She finally came further into the room, heading toward me with the paper outstretched.

"Despite the unfortunate consequences of your investigation, you two have impressed me," Miss Pertwee said. "You have intelligence and courage and integrity. So I'd like your help with this."

I took the paper from her and gave it a quick look. It was a letter written out in a wavering, unsteady hand. One word toward the top—larger than the others and underlined twice—jumped out immediately.

DEAD.

"All is forgiven," Miss Pertwee said. "If you'll come with me to Galveston and catch another killer."

A LOOK AT: DEAR MR. HOLMES

SEVEN HOLMES ON THE RANGE MYSTERIES

UNCOVER THE THRILLING MYSTERY OF BIG RED AND OLD RED AMLINGMEYER'S SHERLOCK HOLMES-INFLUENCED PAST.

Old West drifters Big Red and Old Red Amlingmeyer have starred in six *Holmes on the Range* novels—rustling up award nominations and fans aplenty while they solved mysteries using the methods of their hero, Sherlock Holmes. But the origins of their interest in the infamous consulting detective, what they were doing before their sleuthing adventures began, and how their early stabs at deduction turned out have remained a mystery—until now.

Follow along as they get the itch to turn to detective work after being targeted by a killer, plans go haywire when someone is served a side order of arsenic, deadly predators are faced, and the cowboy brothers' secret pasts are uncovered in seven adventure-filled western stories.

For the very first time, everyone's favorite Sherlock Holmes-worshiping cowpokes are venturing into the past and uncovering how their love of deduction began.

AVAILABLE NOVEMBER 2023

ABOUT THE AUTHOR

Steve Hockensmith's first novel, the western mystery hybrid *Holmes on the Range*, was a finalist for the Edgar, Shamus, Anthony and Dilys awards. He went on to write several sequels—with more on the way—as well as the tarot-themed mystery *The White Magic Five* and *Dime* and the *New York Times* bestseller *Pride and Prejudice and Zombies: Dawn of the Dreadfuls*. He also teamed up with educator "Science Bob" Pflugfelder to write the middle-grade mystery *Nick and Tesla's High-Voltage Danger Lab* and its five sequels.

A prolific writer of short stories, Hockensmith has been appearing regularly in *Alfred Hitchcock* and *Ellery Queen Mystery Magazine* for more than 20 years. You can learn more about him and his writing at stevehockensmith.com.

Printed in the USA
CPSIA information can be obtained
at www.ICGtesting.com
LVHW031125240923
758948LV00003B/6